CRITICS CHEER FOR KIMBERLY RAYE!

"[Kimberly Raye's writing is] hot, hot, hot!"
—*Romantic Times* on *Midnight Fantasies*

"*Midnight Fantasies* is . . . a very funny book, and a hot one, too."
—*All About Romance*

"Kimberly Raye has a unique and special talent that will no doubt be heard and remembered for years to come!"
—*Affaire de Coeur*

"If you're lamenting the lack of sexy, funny, character-driven romances on the bookshelves these days, you absolutely will not want to miss reading . . . *Midnight Kisses*."
—*All About Romance*

"[*A Little Bit of Magic*] is magical and charming, not to mention steamy!"
—*Under the Covers* Book Reviews

"Ms. Raye's creative plotting and vivid characterization herald a strong new voice in romantic fiction."
—*Romantic Times*

A DEVILISH KISS

"I came for *you*." Before Callie could so much as breathe, the man leaned forward and captured her mouth with his.

She didn't get a chance to think about what she was doing, much less stop herself. She couldn't. One instant, she was a disjointed fragment, alone, isolated, and the next, she became a part of this other being, fitting with him to make a perfect whole. She softened. Her lips parted. Her tongue met his, its insistent demand.

He tasted of mystery, of dark secrets and erotic dreams. Overwhelmed, she found she couldn't deny herself, couldn't think. He surrounded her—his scent, his taste, the raw strength of him—and Callie was lost and damned at the same time, for she knew better than to let a stranger get so close to her. A stranger who made her burn and ache and crave things she hadn't even let herself imagine in her wildest, most private thoughts.

KIMBERLY RAYE

A STRANGER'S KISS

LOVE SPELL NEW YORK CITY

For three of the best writers in the world;
Nina Bangs, Gerry Bartlett and Donna Maloy.
Y'all are the best!

A LOVE SPELL BOOK®

January 2002

Published by

Dorchester Publishing Co., Inc.
276 Fifth Avenue
New York, NY 10001

Cover art by John Ennis
www.ennisart.com

ISBN 0-505-52462-7

The name "Love Spell" and its logo are trademarks of Dorchester Publishing Co., Inc.

Printed in the United States of America.

Visit us on the web at www.dorchesterpub.com.

A STRANGER'S KISS

Chapter One

He wanted her.

Staring across the lobby of the elite Houston hotel, Alex watched the woman saunter across the expensive Persian carpet. She was a walking advertisement for the latest cosmetic advancements, from the hair extensions that made her short blond hair reach well past her waist, to the large, plump breasts rising out of her low-cut silk blazer. Her lips were full and sensual, thanks to collagen injections and a cherry-red lip stain her plastic surgeon had recently begun to offer his patients. Her legs were smooth from laser hair-removal treatments, and tan from frequent trips to a salon. She was as perfect as money and vanity would allow, but she would quickly fade.

She'd managed to put off the aging process, but she couldn't stop it.

He could, though.

His gaze traveled the length of the woman—down her shiny golden hair to the pink-tipped toenails peeking from her strappy Italian stilettos—and his body tightened in response. His blood rushed and the familiar heat of desire threatened to overwhelm him.

Her appearance had nothing to do with his lustful reaction, though. She could be gorgeous or homely. Young or old. Blond or brunette. A natural beauty or the surgical triumph who now stood near enough that his heightened senses could taste the moist heat of her in the air. His reaction would have been the same. It was *always* the same.

He wanted her.

Alex Daimon wanted *all* women.

It was his duty. His nature. His curse.

His ears prickled with the sound of the blonde's deep, even breathing. Her scent—an enticing combination of expensive perfume, warm female, and quiet desperation—drifted across the lobby and urged him nearer.

Yet he didn't approach. He would wait until he was certain the time was right, until he knew that this woman was ready to be a willing participant in the coming exchange.

Willingness. That was the only rule in the game of seduction he was about to play. His lover had to want him as much as he wanted her, and be willing to walk into darkness on her own two feet.

They always did, though. He was a master at his craft, and he could twist even the most principled to the point where she begged him to take both her body and her soul. Which he always did.

A brief wave of longing swept through him, but it was quickly lost—lost to the lust that now burned in the place where his soul once lay.

"A sweet piece, isn't she, my friend?" The question preceded a clap on Alex's shoulder.

He glanced behind him to see Caine. Clad in a T-shirt and faded jeans, the man looked far removed from the Viking he'd been centuries ago, before he'd made the fatal mistake that doomed him to ever-burning lust and an eternity of slavery as one of the Devil's Own. He was a demon now, like Alex. And not just any demon—one driven by lust, filled with need, overwhelmed by desire.

He was an *incubus*.

"Sweet and very eager," Alex agreed.

"But she's not to be yours. The Evil One wants you." Caine clapped his shoulder. "Sorry, friend. This one's mine."

Without another word, the ex-Viking crossed the lobby and slid into the elevator behind his prey. Alex caught a glimpse of the woman's surprised but pleased smile, and of Caine's look of hunger, before the doors slid shut.

His body throbbed, empty and unsatisfied. Not that anything could sate the lust inside him—not one touch, one kiss, or fifty thousand deep plunges into a woman's flesh. There was no refuge from it, and so he moved from one victim to the next, his search for peace endless.

This is true damnation, he thought.

Just as the notion filled his head, his surroundings started to swirl. The colors faded into an absolute blackness that consumed him for a long, breathless moment, wrapped around him like a death shroud.

"Where in the Hell have you been?"

Alex blinked several times, his senses slowly focusing in on the voice. Coldness seeped into the soles of his feet, working its way up his legs, through his groin to his torso, down into his hands and at last consuming all of him. The stench of death and decay burned his nostrils. The crackling and popping of an inferno filled his ears, then abruptly silenced. He had been transported.

"*Texas,*" he answered. "Or have you forgotten your most recent orders?"

An eerie chuckle filled the pitch-dark chamber where the Evil One—and now Alex—stood. The Devil was clad in loose black pants and a jet cape, and the ensemble was completed by a red waist sash. The silk rustled as he turned. At his glance, a fire sparked to life and rose in a full circle that surrounded him with crimson flames. Nodding in approval, the Prince of Evil said, "That's better. Step closer, Alex, so that I can see you."

Alex approached the blazing ring, his arms folded, a scowl creasing his features. "You know what I look like. All too well."

"How long has it been now, since you became mine? Fifty years? Sixty?" the Evil One asked. He always appeared as a devastatingly handsome man, and as he spoke one perfectly shaped blond brow inched upward. The nearby flames cast writhing shadows across his bare, muscular chest, his perfectly chiseled features.

"Nearly a century," Alex replied.

"And you do keep track, don't you?"

"Down to every hellish minute."

The Evil One smiled coldly, but no laughter eased the tension between him and his minion. "Tell me about the Texan."

"Let Caine tell you about her. She's his now."

"Yes . . . but I want your take on the situation."

"She yearns for eternal youth and beauty. You should have no trouble striking a bargain with her."

"Good. I so enjoy visiting the easy ones." The Evil One frowned, his ice-blue gaze raking over Alex with chilling thoroughness. "Is that the form you chose to do my bidding? No cloven hoofs or horns?"

"This one had normal tastes for a change. She fantasizes about *men*."

The Evil One smiled without mirth. "How lucky for you. I do know how you love to appear human." He trailed off and shook his head. "I would think an heiress would have much more . . . *creative* fantasies than one of some rock and roll hippie. I mean, really." He sighed and curled his lip in distaste. "Long stringy hair, a jaw full of stubble, a pair of raggedy jeans, and a ripped T-shirt? You look like you just stepped out of a music video." He made a tsk-tsk sound, his voice echoing through the shadowy chamber. "She might have asked for so much more."

"What? Something like the form you're wearing?" Alex asked. He knew his master was painstaking in his choice of incarnations. With long, flowing blond hair and deeply sun-bronzed skin, the King Devil resembled more an angel of mercy than a master of evil. But his eyes revealed the truth. They were cold, unfeeling, like the master himself.

"I'm vain, what can I say? A slave to frailties of the flesh, including a taste for beauty."

Indeed, the Evil One revered beauty—especially his own.

It is a deceptive beauty. . . .

Alex forced the thought away. In this unholy realm mortals called Hell, he was in no position to cast stones. He was just as deceptive and as beautiful, when he chose to be, as the ruler himself.

"This was her fantasy," Alex declared, hands outstretched. "And whatever my own wish, I comply with that of my prey." He cast a disdainful look at his tattered and much-too-snug clothing. Closing his eyes, he focused his thoughts for a brief but effective moment. He had lost none of his magic since his enslavement; he was still as powerful a sorcerer as when he'd been alive.

"Much better," the Evil One commented when it was done.

Alex touched a hand to his now-smooth jaw and opened his eyes to see that neatly tapered trousers now hugged his thighs, their cuffs tucked into gleaming black boots.

"Except for *that*," the King of Devils scoffed. His gaze was riveted on the red crest embroidered on Alex's shirt: the emblem of his family. "Why do you remind yourself of who you were? Why do you torment yourself, my boy? That's my job."

Alex turned away, the loose shirt he had donned fluttering as he did. Its fine material caressed his skin, reminding him of the fleshly form he wore and its heightened sensitivity. His blood pumped faster, burning with the lust inside him that had not been sated.

Yes, the Evil One was right about one thing. Alex did enjoy being human—looking and feeling the way he once had. This body, this image was his one connection to what he'd been. And his family crest was not a punishment, but a reminder of the mistakes he'd made.

He felt a moment of revulsion for what he'd become, but quickly squelched it. He could make the feeling vanish like the distasteful clothes he'd so easily discarded—though never for good. He would feel the self-loathing again—hadn't he for the past one hundred years? He had been a sorcerer, but he had never planned on eternal damnation. The darkness had taken him, but he had not been taken by the darkness. No, he would never have chosen this existence willingly, and so there would always be moments of regret.

Pensive, he rested his fingertips on the embroidery of his family crest, and turning to his master he asked somewhat vexedly, "Why is it you called me back?"

"I have another task for you." The Evil One motioned Alex forward, into the fiery circle where he stood.

"Why didn't you give it to Caine and let me finish with the Texan?"

The Prince of Darkness smiled, a dazzling display of white teeth that rivaled the predatory gleam in his eyes. "You'll see. Come." He beckoned.

As if Alex could have refused.

He wanted to. For a century, he'd longed to fight back, to ignore his master's orders. He would have, but the Evil One held all the cards. He held Alex's soul.

Alex moved through the flames, feeling their heat lick at his skin for a blissful moment. He yearned for more—but that craving was futile, he knew. There was a coldness inside him that was absolute, eternal, except for those few moments when he buried himself inside hot female flesh. Then, as he thrust towards climax, the warmth embraced him; then he could glimpse Heaven. But the feeling gripped him just long enough to make him yearn for more. It was never enough to completely dispel the cold. No lovemaking had ever done that.

"A virgin?" Alex guessed, arousal swelling in him no matter how he tried to steel himself against it.

"Yes," his master said. "But that isn't all. This one is special, Alex."

"Special?" The notion almost made him laugh. In one hundred years, the Evil One had never considered anyone special. The idea was ludicrous, yet the fire that blazed in the master's eyes told an altogether different story.

"Special," the King of Devils repeated, his expression stony. "And she requires your immediate attention. Come." His perfectly sculpted fingers flashed in the firelight, their razor-sharp nails gleaming white. "I've got a surprise for you."

Alex felt a vibration ripple through him, and a half-second later he found himself staring out of a full-length mirror into a shadowy bedroom, lit only by moonlight that spilled through an open set of French doors. Sheer white drapes billowed into the chamber, caressing the four-poster bed at its center.

Peering through the glass, Alex felt joy and rage whirl into a tempest inside of him at the sight that met his eyes.

She lay on the bed, one arm flung over her head, her silvery blond hair draped across the pillow. Her chest rose and fell beneath a white cotton nightdress with a neckline that plunged dangerously low to reveal an inviting swell of creamy flesh. *Warm flesh* . . .

Had he a heart, it would have been lodged in his throat. It was her! *Catherine!* The realization jolted through him like the Evil One's icy touch. But that was impossible! Catherine was . . .

Alex found himself drawn back through time, recalling a similar room long ago. He'd been so young—despite his power—and much too naive for the woman who'd sought him out.

She'd stood before him, close enough to touch, her hair a silvery cloud falling about her shoulders.

Those thick silver lashes had framed the most vivid sky-blue eyes into which Alex had ever gazed. Eyes that had drawn his heart, his soul.

Deceptive beauty.

He remembered her staring up at him, hunger simmering in those deep azure depths. Arms outstretched, she'd beckoned him forward, calling his body, his spirit, offering herself . . .

Alex had answered, his desire knifing through him, propelling him forward: giving him into the power of the most beautiful woman he'd ever seen. And the most deadly, he'd realized too late.

"Give yourself to me, Alex," she'd coaxed. "I need you beside me—inside of me. I want to feel you, my love. We were meant to be together. To join our bodies . . . our power. Join me, Alex. Forever . . ."

"Forever," he'd agreed, the one word changing his life for all eternity.

Alex jerked back, spinning around, searching for an escape from the memory. Pain suddenly held his body prisoner. There was no escape. *None!*

"Remembering, Alex?" The Evil One's throaty rumble brought him back to the present, to the mirror and the sleeping woman. A knowing light filled the eyes of the Prince of Darkness.

Those eyes were blue as Catherine's had been. As soulless.

"Who is this?" Alex asked, his gaze fixed on the woman in the bed.

"Don't you know?"

"It can't be her. She's been dead for a hundred

years, her spirit locked away, her body long since rotted."

"Indeed, her spirit has been locked away . . . until now. She has returned in this body. They are the same flesh, the same blood."

"No," Alex said, desperate, yet afraid to believe what he was hearing. Could this really be her, or was this another of the Evil One's tricks? "That's not possible. She's dead. She sealed herself in that tomb to escape us—to escape her family. How can it be that she's suddenly free?"

"You doubt my gift? For shame, Alex." Laughter and a chilling smile accompanied the King of Pain's words. "Here I offer you a chance at vengeance, only to have you question my sincerity. I'm truly wounded."

"Gift?" The word rolled off Alex's tongue with all of the bitterness suddenly swirling inside of him. "You aren't the generous sort—and I doubt a horde of archangels could manage to 'wound' you."

"So very true. How well you know me, Alex."

Alex knew him well, all right. Enough to know that very little could truly wound him. As a spirit, he was invulnerable. Only when occupying a physical body could he be harmed.

Harmed. But not annihilated.

Nothing could actually destroy this monster. If the body he possessed happened to suffer a fatal wound, the Evil One simply felt the pain. He hurt, like the body he controlled, but in the end—upon taking his last breath—his spirit would simply return to Hell, weakened yet not defeated. Such was his nature. Once he had time to recuperate, he would be back at his evil dealings, as powerful as ever.

"Doubt my intentions if you will," the Prince of Evil was saying, "but I *am* offering you the chance at vengeance. Carry out my orders, and you'll be condemning Catherine as you never had the chance before. All you need do is seduce this one"—he motioned to the woman on the bed—"and give her to me." A red glow fired the pupils of his eyes for a split second, then they cooled once more to blue.

"If it *is* Catherine, why don't you just step in and destroy her?" Alex asked.

"Always full of distrust, aren't you?" The Evil One shook his head. "This woman that Catherine possesses is pure. Extremely so. Catherine thinks that she can escape me by occupying a virgin, but she's mistaken. She will pay for fooling me . . . for fooling *us*." His smile flashed in the moonlight. "You will spoil her for me, Alex. But there isn't time for a slow seduction . . . as much as you might wish it. Time is of the essence. You *must do your part quickly*."

Amused by his master's seeming loss of control, Alex quirked a brow. The Evil One understood the look and a cruel smile spread across his face.

"I shall have her, Alex . . . as I have everything I want. Make no mistake about it. *Everything*—including you. Now, do as I command. Seduce her, spoil her, and then I shall take over. And be quick about it. Soon will come the anniversary of Catherine's death. That's when her possession of this new body will be complete."

Alex found himself asking, "How did she find a body that looks so much like her?"

The Evil One smiled. "I think Catherine has a sense of irony. When long ago that book she stole from you made her the most powerful sorceress around—safe even from your power and mine—her descendents banded together and were about to destroy her. She sealed herself in a tomb with the book, cursing her seed thenceforth.

"This girl, this Callie Wisdom, is Catherine's own flesh and blood. She braved the tomb to steal the book and break the curse—although I doubt she understands exactly what she got herself in for. She has certain . . . powers . . . but has been reluctant to use them. And they will be the death of her, for Catherine shall possess her as surely as anything."

"In seven days," Alex said.

"Yes. But once the possession is complete, you and I shall again be powerless against her. If Catherine is allowed to occupy the girl completely while the body is still pure, we won't be able to touch her. She's too smart to fall for your wiles, and . . . you know the rules about me touching virgins. If the body is pure, I too will be powerless. So you must—"

"Step in now," Alex finished. "But what if I refuse this gift?" He wanted revenge, but also—more than anything—he wanted to no longer be a pawn of the Devil. Though that feeling would fade, overcome by lust. It always did.

The Evil One seemed to know that. "You won't," he said with frightening confidence. "Rebellious you have been, infuriatingly so, but you've never failed me. Your hunger is unparalleled—for flesh, and now for revenge. Catherine promised herself to me, vowed her loyalty and obedience, then used my power and yours to cheat me. *She* destroyed you. *She* is the one who damned you . . . the one who cursed you with your fate, not I. And because you know that, you won't refuse me. Don't forget how well I know you, Alex. You are one of mine own.

"Besides," the Devil added with a cruel smile, "you *can't* refuse. I hold your soul in my hand."

The Evil One made a fist, and Alex felt a tightening in his chest. He managed not to flinch, but the effort cost him. He took several quick, painful breaths.

"Yes, you are unforgivably rebellious," the Evil One growled, his smile broadening. "But I know your darkest desires. You won't let your hatred of me interfere with revenge. You are a creature of the moment, looking only for the basest fulfillment. That's what you are."

"What you made me," Alex reminded him.

The King of Demons smiled again, his gaze icy. "Yes. You will seek revenge and serve me in the process. So it has been, and so it shall be." As he spoke, he lifted his hand and made a small motion in the air. "Which is why I put up with you."

Slowly, the blanket that covered the sleeping woman moved down, past her waist, hips, thighs, calves. The nightgown she wore slid upwards, baring long, shapely legs.

"Do you still doubt this is Catherine?"

Alex's gaze traveled up the sleeping female's body to the silver perfume flask encircling her neck. The piece of jewelry lay upon the expanse of flesh above the plunging vee of the woman's nightgown. He recognized it as Catherine's. His attention moved back down to the soft-looking skin of her thighs. He felt a renewed throbbing in his groin, the call of the beast that lived and breathed inside of him.

"Why me?" he demanded, his voice suddenly hoarse. "Any of the others could also spoil her."

"Does it matter why I give you this gift?" the Evil One asked, making another movement with his hand. The nightgown slithered further up to reveal white lace panties, the barest hint of silver-blond hair peeking out through the material.

Alex took a deep breath, his blood heating until his body burned as hot as it ever had. It grew hotter still as the gown traveled higher, until both breasts stood proud and beautiful, their wine-colored nipples swollen in silent invitation. The woman's precious perfume flask caught rays of moonlight with each rise and fall of her chest.

"She's beautiful, and I am offering her to you. Must you know anything else?"

"No," Alex breathed in defeat, unable to lie to He who commanded his soul. He was already hard, eager for a taste of this woman, and it was all he could do to maintain control.

Control? He almost laughed at the very thought.

He had no control, not since Catherine Drashierre had sold him to the Evil One and doomed him for eternity.

But now it was time for revenge. Finally he could achieve it, by touching her, tasting her, possessing her. He could finally curse her as she so deserved.

"I leave you to it," the Evil One said. And with that, he blended into the darkness like a wisp of smoke.

Alex stepped from the mirror. Moving to the foot of the bed, for a long moment he watched its occupant. Almost as if she were aware of his presence, her nipples seemed to swell further. Her breaths grew shallower. She *did* feel him. . . .

Soon, he found himself thinking, she would feel his rage as well as his lust. She would be frightened, terrified—as he'd been so long ago.

With a deep breath, Alex let his physical self dissolve. His spirit rose and moved over the female's body, then slowly he allowed it to sink into her. As his essence became one with her, he found the experience almost as gratifying as actual sexual contact. More so, in this particular instance, for he'd never felt such an intense warmth. This Callie Wisdom was definitely pure—physically, anyway. If her spirit was indeed merging with Catherine's, there was no way to escape that taint.

As Alex felt the woman breathe around him, inside of him, he could certainly understand the fascination other demons held for possession. The spirit grew so cold, so numb as time wore on and the years turned to decades and centuries. Occupying living, breathing flesh was comforting. Extremely so.

Alex, himself, had never had much of a taste for possession though. For him, the pleasure was usually brief. The warmth of a body, ironically, was created by its purity. Most humans were useless in that respect, and for many, even if their bodies happened to be unsullied, the moment Alex entered them, he could see their imperfections and the joy subsided. But not this time.

This woman's mind, like her body, was clean, unblemished, and he could understand why Catherine had chosen to possess her. By the laws of Heaven, the Prince of Demons couldn't touch one who was pure. Only after a mortal had first strayed from the flock, could He step in. Only when Alex had finished with her.

Like a soft breeze blowing through a grassy field, Alex journeyed into her thoughts. If he searched deep enough, he would see she was like all the others, he knew. He fully expected to see some dream lover, some fantasy that waited to be revealed. Even the purest young women dreamed of earthly pleasures. How often had fantasy been the first step towards damnation for Alex's victims? How often had some young virgin given of herself in her dreams, never realizing that the seduction of her mind would soon be followed by a physical union that would tie her to darkness forever? Too many times to count.

At first, Alex had resisted such seductions, loathing the role he'd been condemned to play. But he had never been able to win out over his desire. He still hated what he was, but he couldn't change it; he simply could not resist the craving inside of him. This was no ordinary lust he bore, but want magnified a thousandfold. He couldn't fight it any more than a man dying of thirst could resist water.

Lust drove him. . . . Pure, carnal lust. It was the curse of the incubus. His curse.

Searching for a rent in the girl's purity, Alex drifted through the cool blue haze of his sleeping victim's subconscious. Soon, he went deeper, farther, into the darkest recesses of her mind, until he broke free into a brightly lit room. There he saw her, in the far corner, kneeling before a withered old man.

"Look at me, Daddy. Please!" she begged.

The old man shook his head, tears streaming down his face. "I can't, Callie. I can't."

"Try, Daddy. I can save you. I *will* save you! I promise! Just open your eyes and try. For me. Let me see if the incantation worked."

Slowly, the man's eyes opened to reveal empty sockets. The tears dotting his lashes turned a bright crimson. Drops of blood trickled down his cheeks.

"Daddy!" she cried, the word crossing the distance to Alex, cutting into him like a dull blade. Pain, real and so very intense, gripped him. Her pain. *Their* pain now, for at this moment the woman and he were one in mind, body and spirit.

"I'm sorry, Daddy," she wailed. "I tried to save you. I tried!" Frantic, she flipped through the pages of the worn book spread open on the floor beside her—the book Alex recognized, the one Catherine had stolen from him! "It isn't too late! Just hold on. . . ."

"Callie," Alex called. She turned to him, her hand poised in midair, her tear-stained cheeks shimmering in the dim, dreamy light. He saw then that the Evil One hadn't tricked him. This Callie was the spitting image of Catherine—the Catherine he'd fallen in love with, lost his heart to, given his soul.

It was overpowering, the urge to fly at the girl and tear at her spirit until he found that which was Catherine. But he couldn't frighten her. That would spoil his plans. He had to get this woman—Catherine's host body, he reminded himself—to offer herself willingly to him. She had to want him, not fear him.

With every ounce of strength he had, Alex focused on the love he'd had for this female, this Callie or Catherine who were soon to be one and the same spirit. The feelings were vague, distorted memories buried beneath the black spoilings of what had once been his soul. He concentrated harder, urging them forward, needing to remember, to trick and taint his prey as she'd done to him.

He held out his arms. "Come to me, love. Let me hold you."

The young woman looked startled, almost hesitant, a reaction which caught him off guard. He'd found most of his victims to be bold in their dreams, reckless in their acquiescence. But not this one. She was cautious and frightened. So very, very frightened.

As it should be, he reminded himself.

"Who are you?" she whispered.

"Come," he called again, his voice firm, refusing to be denied. "Take what I offer. Let me hold you. Comfort you."

Tears trickled down her face, and she shook her head. "No," she murmured, instead turning to bury her head in the old man's lap.

Ah, this must be her father—the man for whom this young woman had braved Catherine's tomb. Touched for the first time in a hundred years, Alex found himself stepping forward, the flames of his anger temporarily doused. He felt compelled to chase away the tears, found himself drawn to this young woman as he usually drew others to himself.

He floated across the room, closed his hands over her shoulders and forced her to look up. Glancing into her eyes, he saw again her resemblance to Catherine and he steeled himself to his task. "Don't deny me, Callie—nor what I offer." He could feel her hesitation, her confusion . . . and the beginnings of desire? What had kept this girl pure for so long? Fear? Pride? "Here in your dreams, you're free," he urged. "Free; do you understand?"

The young woman stared up at him blankly, then, "Go away," she cried.

Had she recognized his intent? Despite the ferocity of her words, the young woman's eyes begged him to stay.

He knelt down beside her and pulled her into his

arms. She was stiff at first, obviously frightened. But he'd dealt with such problems before. He ran his palm down the length of her spine and felt the tremor that rushed through her. He could sense what she wanted.

"Let me comfort you," he whispered, his tone seductive, full of false promise. "Let me face this nightmare with you, Callie. Let me hold you . . . help you."

She let out a grievous sob and buried her face in his neck, her arms snaking up to lock behind his head.

Alex felt a stirring deep within. Oddly, it wasn't triumph, but pain—*her* pain. Agony fierce enough to rival that of wanting her.

He steeled himself against the strange sensation, knowing that it was likely only a by-product of his possession of her body. He had none of his own feelings save lust, was incapable of anything more. With his soul had vanished his humanity, his empathy.

The young woman held him tighter, and he threaded his fingers through her hair—hair the exact shade of Catherine's. For a fraction of a second, he tightened his hold as fury washed through him. The urge to rip every beautiful strand from her head was nearly overwhelming. *Traitor!* his mind cried. *You betrayed me. Sacrificed me. And you will pay.*

She must have sensed something, then, for she turned her eyes up to him—and they were graygreen, not blue like the woman who'd damned him. Alex felt his fury fade. Here was the girl who'd braved all for her father. His hold on her relaxed. Suddenly, where before he had longed to destroy this woman in his arms, now Alex wanted to comfort her, to simply hold her here in her dreams.

For once, he might bring comfort instead of destruction.

Impossible. A silly musing that defied all he was. And he kept forgetting that whoever this woman was, she was being possessed by his enemy—a woman who would take more and more control of this body until she owned it completely. And she would destroy him again with her deceitful ways if he let her. But he wouldn't. Not this time. He was wiser now, and hardened. While Catherine had been moldering in her tomb, waiting for this moment to return to Earth, Alex had been dreaming of freedom. Condemned to learn the ways of evil, he had done so . . . and now was the culmination of all those years of schooling. He'd learned well, and Catherine would learn too.

He looked down at the girl, her lips parted, glistening up at him, waiting to be kissed. She was an innocent, he could tell by her face, by the look in her eyes, and yet . . . he couldn't do it.

He removed himself from her dream. Dissolving, he forsook the beatific warmth of possession and forced his spirit from her body. Escaped, he lingered over her corporeal body and watched as she whimpered in her sleep. Her smooth brow twisted in a frown as if she, too, regretted the parting of their spirits. Alex propelled himself away, coalesced in physical form at the foot of the bed.

Shaken and surprised by his weakness, he staggered toward the mirror and ducked into it. On the other side, he breathed in the chill rank air of Hell. He tried to calm the fire raging in his veins, the lust, powerful and all-consuming, that cried out for fulfillment.

Tomorrow, he vowed. Tomorrow, once the sun set and the shadows descended, he would return to this Callie woman and seduce her like he should have done tonight. He didn't intend to leave her unsullied, no matter how pure she'd felt. Catherine would grow within her. He'd already seen the beginnings, felt the vague familiarity of the sorceress's thoughts. The possession was in its early stages, and Catherine's spirit would only become stronger as the days progressed. So soon, she would completely control Callie. But not before Alex meted out justice.

"I *will* crush you," he swore, clenching his fists, the rage in his voice echoing in the darkness. "I will crush you and bring you back to Hell with me."

Chapter Two

"Callie!"

She bolted awake, the scream ringing in her ears. Leaping from her bed, she flung open her bedroom door and hurried down the darkened hallway. Her father's door stood wide open, his room pitch black. Empty. Panic gripped her, then she heard his voice again.

"Cal!" The cry echoed through the house. She followed the sound until she found him huddled on the floor in the bathroom.

"Daddy," she whispered, flipping on the light switch and rushing to his side.

He clawed at the floor. Fear etched his weathered features. His eyes were wide open, seeing yet not seeing. He saw only blackness, only pain and death. Nothing else. No light. Not even Callie herself.

"Daddy, I'm here," she murmured, dropping to her knees on the tiled floor beside him. "I'm here," she said again, louder; his hearing was deteriorating rapidly, like his sight and other senses.

"I—I slipped. I couldn't see the sink. I tried to hold myself, but I couldn't see it. . . ." He slammed a fist against the floor. "Dammit, I couldn't see it!"

"It's all right, Daddy." She gathered him close. His arms came around her waist, and he clung to her as if she were a lifeline.

She *was* his lifeline, his hope, his eyes now that the curse had destroyed his vision. His other senses were diminishing as well, would continue to go until he remained just a shell of a man. And soon he wouldn't even be a shell; he would be dead. So her mother had explained.

Callie forced the thought away and clamped her eyes shut against burning tears. In the blackness of her mind, a figure materialized: Her father, the way he'd been six months ago—before her mother had died, before Callie herself had moved back here to be with him, when work had brought her back for the first time in ten years. Her father in his studio, sunshine streaming through the open windows, brushes scattered everywhere, emptied tubes of paint strewn across the floor.

"Bring me that cobalt, will you, Callie?" her father had asked, his attention riveted on the canvas before him. "This sky needs a little more blue." He leaned forward, dabbing the silvery clouds with the tip of his brush.

"It's beautiful just the way it is, Daddy. You

worry too much." Still, she turned and walked to a row of paints. They were arranged in order according to shade, exactly the way she remembered though she hadn't been in his studio for many years. She knew the room by memory, every nook and cranny, every chip in the white stucco that covered the walls, every scuff on the marble floor. Everything was the same. It was as if time had stood still in the small chamber. Picking up the tube, she pivoted and headed back to her father.

"Clients won't pay for shoddy work. They want colors—lots of vibrant colors." He paused and took the paint tube. "Thanks, honey. Where's your mother?"

"In the garden." Callie smiled, surveying the half-finished canvas in front of her father. "The Dupree estate never looked so good. Beau Dupree had better give you a bonus for this."

"He's already paying me plenty. Besides, the exposure he gives me is well worth the effort. I contracted with three new clients because of that portrait I did of him last year. He's very good for business."

"You've definitely got an eye for detail," Callie said as she watched him swirl in the cobalt. The color brought the sky to life and Callie marveled at how her father could have been blessed with such talent.

"You know, sweetheart, you might try your hand at a little painting yourself while you're here visiting us. I still have the paint box you had back in grade school."

"That old thing?" She laughed. "I can't believe you saved it, especially considering how awful I was."

"You've never been awful at anything. You were just a beginner—"

"—who couldn't even paint a banana."

"Fruit has never been my specialty, either." He gave her a wink. It was as if she'd never been gone. "You might try some other still life. A landscape, maybe a house . . ." He put down his pallet to go and rummage in a nearby closet. "Here it is," he murmured a few seconds later as he dusted off an old pink case shaped like a tackle box. "Ready and waiting for your creative talent."

"It'll have to wait a lot longer, Daddy. I'm only going to be here with you and Mom for today. The rest of the week is committed to my work, remember? The CPA convention downtown?"

He frowned. "You work too much. You haven't taken a vacation since you started that job. What has it been now? Five years?"

"Six, and the agency is really busy. Since they made me a partner last year, I've taken on two new accounts," she defended. "I don't have time for a vacation."

He gave her a knowing look. "At least not for any that bring you back to New Orleans."

She averted her gaze and shook her head. He'd never faulted her for running away from her life, going to Texas. But he'd been hurt by it, she knew—even if he had encouraged her to go. "That's not it. I'm just really busy."

"Busy running away." He crossed the room and took her hands in his own hot ones. "You can't change what you are, Callie."

She relished the heat for a long moment before pulling away. With the warmth came the memories. Chilling recollections that could freeze the happiness of being home again and leave her cold and alone and frightened—so very frightened. She remembered living with her parents, the happiness she'd known. But she also remembered her failures, was reminded of the powers she was no longer willing to use.

"You're right, Daddy," she said cheerfully. "I can't change what I am. A certified public accountant. A busy one."

He shook his head. "Stubborn girl. Just because you deny something doesn't make it go away. Like your mother. She thinks that because she's given up practicing the *sight* that she's no longer what she was . . . but we both know that's not true. Like you. She just putters around that old novelty shop of hers, pretending like nothing's wrong."

Callie hadn't believed him at the time. But now she understood the truth. Her father had known he'd married a seer, though he never spoke of her abilities. And when Callie's mother had vowed to lead a normal life with him, devoting her time to raising prize-winning roses and running a small shop devoted to angel memorabilia in the French Quarter, he'd let her do what she wanted.

But it was Callie's mother's power that had saved them for so long. Now both Callie and her father understood that. Her mother's love had kept him healthy, strong, alive. She'd magically staved off the curse on Catherine Drashierre's descendents and their spouses. Now that her mother had died, Callie's father had taken ill.

The day after her mother's funeral, Callie had watched her father destroy his studio, his vision so cloudy he could barely stumble from canvas to canvas.

Rage, at losing his wife and his precious sight, had fueled an eruption of violence that had left the room in shambles and Callie in tears.

She hadn't believed in the curse, then. Despite her mother's deathbed explanation, Callie had fought the truth, calling in every specialist in the state—in the whole damned country—to oversee her father's care. She knew her mother had been an empath, but tales of spells and sorcerous relatives had been too much to swallow.

And yet, despite the doctors, her father's condition had worsened. In the six months since her mother's death, Callie had watched her father go from a thriving fifty-five-year-old to a broken old man who seemed one hundred and fifty-five. His senses had all deteriorated. Death would follow, her mother had sworn. . . . Soon, likely on the exact day Callie's grandfather had died, the very same day her great-grandfather had died as well, her father would die. It was the day Catherine Drashierre had cursed her descendants and buried herself alive. . . .

But, no. Her father would be the exception. Callie wouldn't lose him. He was all she had left. He'd given her life, pulled her back from the other side when the knowledge of what she was had almost destroyed her. He'd told her to leave home, to go stay with relatives in Texas when her life had been too much. He and her mother had even offered to move with her, but she'd said no. She knew how much that had hurt. He'd saved her.

She would do the same for him.

"I'm sorry, Callie." Her father's voice drew her from her memories, her thoughts, back into the darkened bathroom and the nightmare of her life. She gazed into his sightless eyes, willing him to see her, knowing he wouldn't.

"Forgive me," he said again. "Your mother warned me about this. She told me not to love her, that this curse would eventually destroy me. But I couldn't help myself. One look and I was lost. I guess I didn't believe in curses, even though I knew what your mother . . ." He paused, unwilling to speak the words. "She told me time and time again what she feared. I refused to listen, told her what nonsense such superstitions were. But it's happening. What she predicted is actually happening. The same as it happened to her father."

"No," Callie whispered. "Maybe it's not all this hocus-pocus. You still have to see that other specialist. Maybe this is some rare disease and there's some medication to reverse your condition." She knew he couldn't hear her. He was talking not so much to her, but to himself—just as she was. As if they could make some sense out of what was happening. . . .

She held her father tighter, letting her embrace reassure him, grateful she didn't have to say any more. She was terrified inside that her mother was right, that some crazy curse from an evil ancestress was going to destroy him. That all she'd done so far—moving back here, going to the tomb, stealing the book—all would be for naught.

No! She couldn't fail. She wouldn't! First there was that specialist Dr. Grammer had told her about. An internist. Maybe he could do something. Curses had to have physical cures, too, didn't they?

Even as she grasped at the hope, it fluttered out of her reach. Medical science could never cure what ailed her father. She knew that.

"I could face this if your mother were here. If only she hadn't . . . But then, I wouldn't have to face it if she were here, would I? She would have kept from happening. That slip of a woman protected me for thirty-five years, and I didn't even know it."

"Miss Callie? Is everything all right?"

Callie glanced behind her at the thin, wiry man who appeared in the doorway. Burgess Connelly was the only friend she'd had since this nightmare started. A faithful butler to her mother and father for over thirty years, Burgess had been Callie's one shoulder to lean on the past six months. He'd wiped away her tears and helped with her father.

She managed a smile for him. "Fine, Burgess. Daddy just took a little fall."

"Here, let me help." Burgess rushed forward, his silver hair mussed from sleep, his thick eyeglasses lopsided, obviously donned in a hurry.

Grateful, Callie smiled as the man took one of her father's arms. She held the other, and together they helped him stand.

Once they had her father back on his feet, Callie turned to the butler. "Thanks, Burgess."

"Sorry to wake you," her father murmured, embarrassed.

"No trouble, sir. Glad to be of help."

Callie patted the old servant on the back. "Go on back to bed now, Burgess. It's late and Dr. Grammer's coming first thing in the morning. I can see Daddy from here."

The butler hesitated. "You ought to be sleeping, Miss Callie."

"I ought to be, but I can't. You go on," she urged. "I promise I'll tuck myself in as soon as I get Daddy resettled."

Burgess straightened his eyeglasses and gave her a wary glance.

"Promise," she said, crossing her heart.

"Go on, Burgess," her father spoke up in falsely cheerful tones. "You know how I hate the two of you fussing over me. I could see myself to bed if it wasn't for my damned eyes. . . ." His voice faded.

"Goodnight, then." Burgess gave Callie a sympathetic glance, then disappeared down the hallway.

"Come on, Daddy. Let's get you back to bed." Callie held tightly to her father's hand and led him back down the hallway to his bed.

Tucking the blanket around him, she sank to her

knees and rested her cheek against the back of his hand. "Rest, Daddy," she murmured, listening to his raspy breaths, watching the irregular rise and fall of his chest.

Closing her eyes, she remembered again the man he'd once been. Big and strong, he'd swept her into his arms and onto his shoulders, his deep voice crooning to her, always singing.

"This old man, he played one. . . ."

He'd saved her with his love. Now she would save him. She wouldn't stop fighting until he was able to see again and resume his painting. She'd find a way to make this curse just a silly thing of the past and happiness the only possibility for the future. She'd comfort him until—

"Let me comfort you." The words drifted through her mind, stirring another image: the stranger from her dreams. He'd been a man of shadows, but surely beautiful—even though she couldn't quite remember his features.

She felt him again, a mixture of raw power and strength that seemed to enfold her, fuel her courage, and stir something else as well. He'd made her feel things she'd never allowed herself to feel before: need and desire and longing. A physical, breath-stealing heat.

A heat she longed to feel again.

Yet he'd frightened her too, as much as he comforted. She had never dreamt of a man before, not the way she dreamt of him.

Rising, she took herself back to bed as if in a dream. Lying down, she felt herself drift, floating into another realm where sensation ruled and no nightmares haunted her. The world and all its troubles slipped away. At last she saw him, a silhouette really, but she knew who it was. He drew her with invisible fingers, beckoning her closer, calling to her soul.

Fear rushed through her, along with desire, and Callie found herself propelled toward him. The incarnation was not as clear as before, as if he were just a memory and something was missing that had been there earlier.

He didn't speak, didn't talk, but Callie found herself tingling as she moved into his arms and finally allowed herself the oblivion of true rest. Tomorrow she would think about her father; tonight she would allow herself to dream.

The following evening Callie pulled the reading glasses from her face and rubbed her burning eyes. All day she'd been cooped up in the back room of her mother's novelty shop, her shoulders hunched forward over the antique rolltop desk, her gaze fixed on the yellowed pages of the thick book she'd taken from her ancestor's tomb.

She was surprised she'd gotten it. She'd seen many creepy things in her lifetime, but she'd never gone poking around a mausoleum in the middle of the night. And she'd never stuck her hand inside a coffin that had been sealed for over one hundred years. Then again, she'd never had a reason to be so bold and desperate.

She shook away the goosebumps that even now chased up and down her flesh.

"Time well spent," she told herself for the hundredth time. She had the book.

Now, if she could just figure the damned thing out.

The volume was over three inches thick, with page after page of almost indecipherable writing—spells, she assumed. She'd been at it all day, reading, yet she'd barely covered twenty pages. She'd started at the beginning, staring at each word, each symbol, trying to comprehend some meaning that would jump out at her as a clue to her father's condition. All day she'd looked, and she was no better off than she'd been six months ago.

"What am I going to do, Mikey?" She glanced at the figurine that sat near the edge of the desk and stared back at her.

Mikey, or rather the crystal representation of the archangel Michael that Callie had commissioned for her mother many years ago, had tiny chips of sapphire for eyes and gold-dusted wings. It had garnered sizable offers from many of her mother's shop's customers, being just the sort of thing that patrons of a novelty store called "Angels in Our Midst" would love. But the piece had never been for sale.

Callie's mother had adored it, not only because she was a fanatic collector of angel paraphernalia herself, but because it had been Callie's parting gift before leaving Louisiana to live in Texas—far away from her past and her parents. Callie's mother had often called the statuette her inspiration, a little piece of Callie that she could keep with her, no matter where Callie went or how far apart they were.

Well, it didn't do any good now, Callie found herself thinking. Death was a gap far too wide for a crystal angel statuette to bridge.

Her attention shifted from Mikey to the legal pad where she'd been scribbling notes. An entire day spent and she'd only managed to fill up half a page with passages that she hoped might help. At this rate, she'd die of old age long before she ever found anything to save her father. Part of her found herself wanting to cling to the idea that there were no such things as spells; in accepting her mother's explanation, Callie had given up on the only reality she'd come to know over the past fifteen years. Part of her screamed this was just a rare disease, as several doctors had suggested.

She knew otherwise, though. Her mother's words resounded in her mind. "Please, Callie . . . take care of your father," she'd said, and Callie recalled the tiny hospital room, the stark white walls, the smell of disinfectant.

"Promise me," her mother had begged, her voice barely audible above the respirator pumping precious oxygen in and out of her weak lungs. "Ask him to forgive me."

It was then Callie had clutched her mother's hand and had the visions. They'd fought their way into her head at the contact . . . a black casket . . . a freshly turned grave. She'd begged her mother to live, but it had been no use. Her mother had died, but not before admitting, "My heart is worn out. It's my time, Callie. Please, listen to me. I can feel myself slipping away. It's up to you now. I never did him any good. I just buried my head in the sand and tried to ignore what I knew deep in my heart, but my heritage, who I am, caught up with me. The curse will take your father—"

She'd tried to cut her off, but her mother wouldn't be swayed. "You know it's the truth," she said. "And you want to run away."

Callie shivered, remembering her hands clamped tight around the door handle to escape, its metal cold, biting into her flesh. "I *had* to leave before, Mama. I didn't want to; I had to. I thought you understood."

She heard her mother's voice as if she were in the room, the scene replaying itself.

"I do. You saw your power and the true responsibility then, and it scared you, so you ran, as if you could leave it all behind. But you couldn't, Callie. Could you?"

Callie's head bobbed up and down vigorously. "I *did*. No one knows about me in Texas. I have a house, a flower garden, nice neighbors, a good job."

"But the power is still there—inside of you. You didn't leave anything behind. It followed you to Texas. This will always be with you. You can't change what we are. What *you* are—"

"Stop!" she'd cried, whirling to face her mother, her hand out, pleading. "Just stop. Please. I'm not the same as you, Mama, and I don't believe all that nonsense you told me about Daddy dying. Gran was old and senile—"

"Don't talk about your grandmother that way, Callie. She was a wonderful woman. Good, kind, strong. She knew what she was, and she accepted it. She didn't run away. She was never ashamed like me." Her mother's gaze dropped, and Callie saw the self-loathing creep across her features.

"She was senile, Mama, and everything she told you about Grandpa's death and that stupid curse was nonsense. Just silly susperstition." Oh, if only her words had been true.

"And is it silly superstition that makes us what we are?" her mother had asked.

"What you are, Mama."

A knowing light glimmered through the pain glazing her mother's eyes. "You're more like your old mama than you think, baby." Her mother held out her hand and beckoned Callie closer. "You can't keep running. Face the truth. The past. I know you don't want to, but ignoring it, pretending it doesn't exist, won't make anything go away. Trust me."

Callie had nodded, tears streaking down her cheeks, the respirator keeping time with the pounding of her heart as she listened to her mother's awful account of things to come. Things that had all come true.

Then her mother had said, "Read your grandmother's diary, Callie. It explains everything. Your father will die, like your grandpa and your great-grandpa did. *Read*."

That night, Callie had gone back home and rummaged through her mother's drawers until she'd found the faded burgundy diary. Returning to the hospital, Callie had kept a vigil at her mother's bedside, reading the tome from cover to cover, then again. The story that had unfolded, of her evil ancestress who'd cursed all her descendents, was unbelievable.

Yet Callie knew her mother believed.

After ten years of running away, Callie hadn't wanted to accept her past. She'd fought against the truth. She still fought, sort of; some rational part of her was still entertaining the hope that her father's illness was a freak coincidence, that the curse was just what she'd originally believed—a silly superstition.

But Callie knew the truth now. She was willing to accept it. She'd seen the proof every day as her father grew weaker and weaker right before her eyes. She heard it in the deep rasp of his breathing, felt it in the hopelessness that gripped her every time a doctor shook his head and told her there wasn't anything the medical world could do.

When she'd read in her grandmother's diary about the grimoire—the book of spells that the evil Catherine Drashierre had used to curse her descendants, the book she now read—Callie had lit upon the idea. If the book had held the curse, then maybe, just maybe, it held the cure, as well. It had been a long shot, but it was all Callie had.

Now she held the book in her hands, had found it in her ancestor's tomb.

So soon . . . Callie pushed her glasses back on and attacked the grimoire again, determined to find the answer she so desperately sought. Time was running out. . . .

You won't save him, a voice whispered in her head. *I won't let you.*

Callie felt a tingling in her stomach, spreading outward, sweeping through her body, the same feeling she'd had the night when she'd slipped her hand into Catherine Drashierre's coffin and retrieved the witch's book. Callie's eyes burned, and she clamped them shut. The air closed in around her, thick and smothering. The smell of musty earth assaulted her senses, and she grasped the perfume flask suspended about her neck.

" 'This old man.' " She recited the familiar nursery rhyme, hearing her father's voice, trying to ignore the words in her head. " 'He played one. . . .' "

Already you can feel me, Callie. The feeling will grow stronger. I will grow stronger, and soon I'll swallow you.

Callie fought the strange sensations surging through her. She gasped for air, forced her eyes open, and concentrated on the text in front of her. The writing seemed a black blur, moving from side to side, the words dancing around the page.

" ' . . . he played two. . . .' "

She held her mother's perfume flask tighter and focused her thoughts.

" 'He played knick-knack on my shoe.' "

Slowly, Callie's vision returned to normal. Her

heartbeat slowed. The strange tingling in her body subsided to a slight tickle in her middle.

Callie took a long, deep breath and glanced at the closed door leading to the alleyway behind the shop. She wasn't locked in anywhere, she told herself. There was plenty of room. Plenty of light. Not like the time when she'd been plunged into darkness with those damned visions: her power out of control, her mind filled with that little girl's pain. . . .

No, she wouldn't think of that. This time was different. She was in control now. She would always be in control. No one would ever take that away from her again. That's why she'd gone to Texas. Here in New Orleans things were different, her power was manifesting itself again—what else could this be?—but she would maintain control. She would.

At last her nerves returned to normal, and Callie chided herself for her silly claustrophobia. It had never been this bad. She usually could be in small rooms without feeling such terror, but apparently not today. Maybe sitting in the same place all day had brought on the attack. Yes, that had to be it. The whole episode hadn't been a manifestation of her power, but simply her mind going stir-crazy. This back room where she sat *was* pretty small. Unbearably so.

As for the attack being so strong, well, she couldn't explain that. Any more than she could explain why she'd heard a strange voice. Obviously her superstitions had been aroused by holding this book of her evil ancestress.

She ignored the unease which crept up her spine, and forced her attention back to the book. Picking up her pencil, she jotted down several more notes, losing herself in one particular passage that seemed comprehensible. Maybe this was it. . . .

A few minutes later—or maybe more, she couldn't tell—the bell on the front door chimed. Annoyed, she slammed the book shut and shoved it, along with her notes and Mikey, to the far corner of the desk, then rolled the lid shut over them. She'd come here today to get some time to think, not deal with customers. Still, since Alice, the girl who usually helped out in the shop, was off weekdays, Callie saw little way around it. Luckily, it was near closing time.

Leaving her chair, she picked her way around several stacks of books and headed for the front of the building.

"Kids," she muttered after a quick glance around the empty store. Angels in our Midst stood in a neighborhood filled with children, and pranks had been more than common. Callie had been the object of many since she'd taken over the shop—especially by young boys. Yes, this was certainly a far cry from her old position crunching numbers for a top-ranked accounting firm in Texas.

Walking to the front of the store, Callie peered out the door. "Hey, lady! Watch this," a young teen called out as he sailed past. He did a handstand and then flipped, landing on his skateboard with an ease that awed Callie.

She looked on and smiled, watching the skater

zoom across the street and duck into an alleyway behind a small bakery. For a moment she let herself be flattered by the boy's antics, then she flipped the switch for the neon sign that hung in the store's front window. The bright pink flickered, then died, the light's filaments glowing brilliantly before complete darkness set in.

The shrill ring of the phone drew her attention, and when she didn't answer, the answering machine clicked on.

"This is Callie. You've reached Angels in our Midst, a store specializing in all types of angel paraphernalia. I'm unavailable right now, but if you leave a name and number, I'll return your call. Also, if you're looking for a special book or video on angels, please leave the title so I can check on it. Thanks, and be sure to wait for the beep. . . ."

She expected it to be Burgess with an update on her father. She'd hated leaving him, but she'd needed to concentrate and had known the store, slow during the week, would provide solitude for her to study the book of spells.

Instead of the familiar rasp of Burgess's voice, Callie heard a distinct Cajun accent. "Miss Callie? Detective Guidry here. I know you don't want to hear from me, but I really do wish you would consider giving us a hand. We've got several missing persons—two women—and now that you're back in town . . . Well, we think the perp is the same guy responsible for a few other murders in a nearby parish last month. He's smart and dangerous. I know you got out of this business a long time ago—heck,

I wish I had—but if you'd at all consider using your talents . . . call me at the stationhouse. Extension 214."

Callie ignored the shiver that crept down her spine, her attention going to the closed door behind the counter. It led to one of the back rooms. It was a *seeing* room, where she and her mother had occasionally used the *sight* to help the authorities— mostly helping people find missing loved ones. Her cases had included a runaway teen and an old woman with Alzheimer's who'd forgotten her way home. All had been recovered safe and sound, and all because she had provided key clues as to their whereabouts. But it was that power she'd fled, that was why she'd run off to Texas and left her parents. It had been too much, she had seen too much.

Callie had been young, only five years old when she'd first discovered she could see things, get psychic impressions by touching inanimate objects. At first, she'd been thrilled. She'd found her own missing doll, helped her neighbor to find a lost puppy. Then Callie had discovered that when she touched an actual person, held their hands and concentrated, she could see things that were important to them, could see their pasts.

An adventurous five-year-old, she hadn't been scared by her abilities; she'd been amazed and delighted. She'd helped her friends find missing toys, pets, all kinds of things. Then one day a nearby neighbor's daughter had disappeared, and the distraught parent had come looking to Callie's mother for help.

Her mother hadn't been at home, but the young Callie had offered to stand in. She'd helped the man find his daughter. After that, her reputation had been made. She'd become the object of special news reports, newspaper articles, scientific papers.

As she got older, she'd gained a measure of local fame for her help in finding missing children, and she'd formed a relationship with Detective Guidry. Eventually he'd come to her for help with a child murderer. His colleagues were stumped, and Callie had more than welcomed the dead-end case. She hadn't realized she wouldn't be up to the task, hadn't realized she would fail. She'd liked being the last hope, the saving angel.

Eager to help, she hadn't hesitated to sit down with the latest missing girl's parents. And they'd found her. But that was when Callie learned that happy endings weren't guaranteed. What came next would haunt her forever. She'd failed miserably, been unable to help the police the way they needed. . . .

She couldn't think about it! Even now it made her gut twist with regret and anger. That case had been the last time she had used her *sight*. Her world had crumbled. She'd fled New Orleans, fled her family, fled who she was.

Over the past ten years, she'd managed to piece what she could of it back together, had managed to build herself a new life. Now, somehow Guidry had tracked her down, found her. Now, when everything was at its worst—her mother was dead, her father was dying—he wanted her help again. Well, she wouldn't do it. She *couldn't*. Not if she was going to help her father.

Callie clutched the tiny flask around her neck and traced the filigree with the pad of her finger. The piece of jewelry was all she really had left of her mother—that and Mikey—and like the woman Callie had loved so dearly, it gave her some small sense of hope. She felt the skin-warmed silver and closed her eyes. She accepted the truth now, and she wasn't running anymore. She *would* save her father somehow.

In her mind, his image materialized as if a television set had been switched on. The *sight* was often like that, like watching a movie screen. Events that had happened, or were happening, just unfolded right there in her head.

Tonight's vision of her father was the same one that had haunted her for the past few months. He huddled in front of a fire, gripped by chills though the temperature outside was in the eighties. He clutched a blanket around himself and stared into the flames, his eyes open but unseeing.

A tear slipped down Callie's cheek and she dashed it away, giving herself a mental shake. She hated these visions, but perhaps one of these times she would see something different. Maybe.

She stared through the storefront window, out into the night where the skater had disappeared. Most of the businesses on Toulouse street had already closed. A few had their outside lights on. Callie turned the shop's hanging sign to CLOSED, pulled the shade down, and locked the door.

"Closing time already?"

She swung around at the sound of the voice. It was low and utterly disturbing, and a chill crept through her. She glanced warily at the shadow of the man who'd spoken. He stood near the rear of her store, and Callie wondered how he'd gotten inside.

As he moved forward, the light from the lamp on the counter bathed him in a pale yellow glow, and all Callie could think was that she was asleep on her feet. The man before her was too handsome to be real.

Chapter Three

He was beautiful in a dark way, with a deeply
tanned complexion and short dark brown hair that
had been combed back from his face. He wore a
black silk shirt that flowed over his well-muscled
torso, its tails tucked into fitted black slacks. At well
over six feet, he seemed to dominate the room, ex-
uding a raw strength that crossed the distance between them and enfolded her until she had to
struggle for a breath.

As if aware of her inspection, he stepped even
closer, affording her a better view of his face. His
features were classic, from a finely sculpted nose to
a strong, clean-shaven jaw. He was handsome, more
than she could have imagined. Perfect even . . .
almost too perfect, as if he were some carefully
carved statue come to life. And his eyes . . . He had

the most incredible eyes. Their depths were a rich warm brown with tiny gold flecks that seemed to spark, to glow, as he gazed back at her.

He stopped a few feet away, his abrupt halt jarring her from her thoughts. "Interesting," he commented as he fingered a row of potholders embroidered with angels. He turned then, the action almost in slow-motion as he absorbed the room with his eyes. His attention finally riveted on a large bookshelf to his right. "*A World of Angels,*" he read, pulling a volume from the shelf and skimming through its pages. "Is this one any good?"

"No—I mean, yes," she stammered, searching for the words that had suddenly escaped her. "I didn't see you come in. How long have you been standing there?"

He ignored the question, his attention fixed on the book. "Do you believe in angels?"

"Excuse me?" she asked, his question catching her off guard. Her mind was reeling, her thoughts racing as she tried to figure out where in the world this man had come from.

"I asked if you believe in angels." His gaze stayed glued on the book. "It says here that for every person there are at least ten guardian angels. Do you believe that?"

"N-no." Her voice shook, and she swallowed nervously. Nervous? She had nothing to be nervous about. So this man had slipped in without her seeing him; she didn't have to see every customer come in and out of the store. And she had been preoccupied.

"You don't believe in guardian angels?"

"I didn't say that. I just don't know about ten of them for each person. I think that with all the war and famine in the world, at least nine of those angels could be better used elsewhere instead of following me around."

His lips hinted at a smile, and he glanced at her then. It was just a glance, but he might have actually touched her the way her senses fired to life. She felt warmth on her face, her neck—everywhere his gaze passed for that fleeting moment before he became engrossed in his reading once again.

"Is that what you're after?" she asked. "A book about angels?"

He gave nothing as simple as a "yes" or a "no." Instead, he stared up at her with dark eyes and took a step back, as if he waited for her to join him near the bookshelf.

A part of Callie wanted to move forward, but her legs seemed made of stone. "Any particular angels you're interested in?" she asked, keeping her distance. "Guardian angels, archangels—"

"*Fallen* angels," he cut in, and the words caused in Callie a ripple of fear.

"Fallen angels," she echoed, swallowing against the sudden tightness in her throat. "Okay. Well, we really don't carry much on that subject. An occult bookstore might serve you better."

"Don't *you* have anything?" he asked. "I'm already here."

Yes, she thought, all too aware of his presence. He emitted a magnetism that was almost palpable, and Callie's body responded as it never before had. Her nipples tingled, the insides of her thighs burned. It was as if this man had physically touched her. Stroked her . . .

She forced the ridiculous notions away. Her naivete was always getting her into trouble. She'd always kept her distance from everyone, especially men, unwilling to let anyone too close. After fleeing New Orleans, she'd never really felt comfortable with people, never really felt as if she belonged. Even back in Austin, where she had a good job, drove a nice car, and lived in an attractive house, it was clear she just wasn't like the rest of her neighbors and co-workers—no matter how much she wanted to pretend that she was. She'd tried at first, even fooled herself into thinking that maybe by not using her gift, she'd somehow become normal.

But it had been deep inside of her, waiting. She'd always known that . . . no matter how much she pretended otherwise. There was no changing who she was, no matter what she did. And the idea of having to explain to someone what she was, what she'd run away from . . .

Distance was better. Safer.

She was anything but safe now. Only a few inches separated her from this dark, handsome stranger, and she was desperately aware of just how close they were. This, however, was a different sort of discomfort than she usually felt. Normally around men Callie felt afraid to reveal too much, afraid that her friends and others might find her attractive and she would have to reject them. She felt fear as she thought of all the different scenarios that could happen when they found out who she really was.

No, this was different. It was physical. This was the kind of discomfort a woman felt around a drop-dead gorgeous man.

Her sex drive had finally decided to rear its ugly head—after how many years? Surprised and intrigued, Callie was all too aware of every incredible inch of this man, so close she could reach out and touch him. If she wanted . . . "I—I think we might have one or two books on the subject," she said at last, desperate for a distraction from her disconcertingly lustful thoughts. She pointed to another bookshelf near the back of the store. "You're welcome to have a look. But I doubt you'll find all that much."

"I'd be eternally grateful for your help," he said, a silent challenge glittering in his eyes. *Your help, and anything else you want to offer*, his gaze seemed to say.

Oddly enough, as much as Callie wanted to be rid of this man, to shift her mind from the dangerous path it was taking, she couldn't resist stepping forward. She edged past, careful not to touch him despite her desire to do just that.

Several feet away, she stopped at the bookshelf she'd indicated and scanned a row of spines before pulling a book free. "Let's see. There might be something here. . . ." She flipped through the pages. "But I still think you'd be better off at an occult bookstore."

"I rather like this little shop." The words sounded

right next to her ear, and Callie jumped. The man stood behind her, his shoulder blocking her escape when she tried to turn. He'd moved so quickly, so soundlessly, it was as if he'd floated the distance to her.

Nonsense! her reason screamed, yet she couldn't shake the strange quivering that rolled through her—fear and something else. Excitement. Hot, lustful excitement.

"I think I remember something about fallen angels in this one," she said, throwing all of her attention to another book and busying herself pulling it from the shelf.

"Let's have a look then," he answered. His hand closed over hers. "That looks heavy."

"It isn't—" she began. The protest lodged in her throat as her gaze went to his hand—large, flawless, with firm fingers and perfectly manicured nails. Too perfect, she thought again. Much, much too perfect.

She glanced up at him, and regretted it immediately. He was so close she could feel his warm breath on her face, see the long sweep of dark lashes that framed his eyes. The irises gleamed with a brilliant gold fire that bathed her face in warmth as his breath and touch turned her skin to gooseflesh.

When he caught her stare and held it, Callie could have sworn she saw surprise in his gaze. "Your eyes," he marveled, his voice so low she almost thought it her imagination. "They're *gray* today."

"Since the day I was born," she said, eager to put up her defenses, to use sarcasm to put some distance between them. She failed. She was too busy trying to control the pounding of her heart to come off sounding anything but informative.

At the moment she was hard-pressed even to remember her name, much less the dozen or so reasons why she shouldn't be standing there, much too close to this man, having thoughts that would make a Jezebel blush.

"Don't you like gray eyes?" Even as she asked the question, she couldn't believe she was doing it. She wasn't the flirting type, never had been. She'd always been more comfortable with books instead of boys, the one sitting at home on Saturday night, studying or reading. *Hiding.* Now here she was making a fool of herself despite every self-preserving bone in her body that screamed for her to shut up.

"It doesn't matter what I like or don't like," he replied cryptically. The strange glimmer that lit his eyes passed and he stiffened, as if he'd just remembered something important. "You've been very helpful." His voice was hard and much cooler than before. "I'll take this." He indicated the book he held.

"But it might not have anything on the subject you're looking for."

"I'm sure it will be fine."

"We haven't even looked at the Table of Contents. I wouldn't want a dissatisfied customer. You should get exactly what you came for—"

"I came for *you.*" And before she could so much as breathe, the man leaned forward and captured her mouth with his.

Callie didn't get a chance to think about what she

was doing, much less stop herself. She couldn't. One instant, she was a disjointed fragment, alone, isolated, and the next, she became a part of this other being, fitting with him to make a perfect whole. She softened. Her lips parted. Her tongue met his, its insistent demand.

He tasted of mystery, of dark secrets and erotic dreams. Overwhelmed, she found she couldn't deny herself, couldn't think. He surrounded her—his scent, his taste, the raw strength of him—and Callie was lost and damned at the same time, for she knew better than to let a stranger get so close to her. A stranger who made her burn and ache and crave things she hadn't even let herself imagine in her wildest, most private thoughts.

But was he a stranger? The thought snaked its way through her mind and kept her from resisting when all common sense ordered her to stop, to back away, to turn and run for her life if she knew what was good for her.

He sucked and nibbled at her bottom lip. Then his tongue stroked and tangled with hers until her blood pounded faster. A tingling sensation rushed to her head, and heat flooded between her legs.

Suddenly his hands were at her back, pulling her flush against him. The feel of him, rock-hard and throbbing, sent a jolt of panic through her. Reality surfaced. She pushed at his chest, just a fraction, enough to tear her lips from his and catch her breath.

"Stop," she murmured, gasping for air. "We can't do this. I mean, *I* can't." She shook her head.

"I think you'd better leave." She stumbled backward, staring up at him, the boiling in her veins subsiding. She regained control of herself despite the heat which blazed in the man's eyes, searing in its intensity as his gaze roved over her.

"I'm not ready to just yet," he replied. The words were coolly spoken and his voice was disturbingly familiar.

The realization stopped her cold, and she stared long and hard at him. "Do I know you?"

"Do you?" he echoed.

You do, a voice whispered. *From your dreams, Callie. Your dreams . . .*

Her heart seemed to stop as she remembered the warm embrace, the murmured words of comfort from the dream stranger last night. But it couldn't be! Absolutely, unequivocally, not. There was no way. Dreams were dreams, and this was reality. Or had last night's dream been a vision of things to come?

"Maybe we've passed each other on the street at one time or another," he said, as if reading the emotions warring inside of her. "New Orleans is a small city, especially down here in the Quarter."

She grasped at the thought, a lifeline when she found herself drowning in strange sensations, insane urges. "Of course," she said. "That must be it. . . ." The words were lost in a wave of dizziness that washed over her.

She blinked, trying to focus as the man's face blurred into two, then three. A moment later her vision sharpened again, his image became distinct, and her legs went weak.

He stood before her, his hair slightly longer, wearing a flowing white shirt with a blood-red insignia—what looked like a family crest—embroidered on the pocket, black pants and black knee boots, looking like an image straight off the cover of one of the historical romance novels that filled her mother's bookshelves at home.

More unnerving than the sudden shift in clothing was the fact that she recognized him like this, the way he was dressed, and also the way he touched her in the next instant.

He was beside her, surrounding her, almost instantaneously. "Are you all right?" he asked. His hands were at her arms, pulling her close, cradling her in a warmth that felt too right, and much too familiar.

She clutched at the bookshelf behind her, closed her eyes and nodded. "Fine, fine. Just give me a minute."

"You look as if you've seen a ghost."

The comment brought her eyes wide open. The blurriness was gone. Everything was clear, distinct, including him—he wore the black shirt and trousers again, his hair short, his touch cold. Unnervingly so.

Frightened, she shrugged away from him, relieved when he let her go without a struggle. "I—you looked different for a second there," she blurted.

"Different? How so?" He leveled a stare at her, his dark gaze drilling into her, stripping away every piece of clothing, every frivolous thought, until she would have sworn he saw her very soul. "What exactly did you see?"

He voiced the question innocently, yet she had the distinct impression he already knew the answer. "You were . . . I mean, everything just went blurry for a few moments." She attempted a smile, knowing she couldn't tell him exactly what she'd seen. He would think she was crazy.

Then again, what had she seen? Had it been her *sight,* showing her a glimpse into his life?

The question sent a shiver through her. It couldn't be. She hadn't used the power to see into anyone's life in over ten years. She wouldn't let herself. Sensing things when she touched inanimate objects, like the book of spells, was one thing, but touching an individual, prying into that person's life, was entirely different. She'd vowed never again to touch another human being like that.

And she wouldn't.

But had she done it subconsciously, inadvertently?

She glanced away from his probing gaze, wanting to reach out, to touch him and see all that he was thinking, feeling. Backing away, she tried to distance herself from his compelling presence. He was a stranger, for heaven's sake, and she'd never been drawn to strangers. To anyone, for that matter.

Until now, a voice reminded her, her flesh still burning from his kiss. She touched a hand to her trembling lips. Heat seeped into her fingertips.

"What did you see just now, Callie?"

"Nothing," she lied. "I guess I should've had a bigger lunch. I always feel a little light-headed when I'm hungry."

They stood so close she could hear his heartbeat. Impossible! It had to be her own, which disturbed her even more. Almost as much as her response to his touch. What was wrong with her?

Distance. She needed distance.

She eased back a few inches and took a deep breath. That was better. She would pretend none of this had happened. "If you're ready, I'll ring you up—"

"I'm not." He placed the book on the shelf and ran his thumb horizontally, touching the spines of the volumes next to the one he'd set down. "*Walking with Angels*," he read. "And all this time I thought angels flew." He laughed, a deep chuckle that slid into Callie's mind, burned through her body to infuse her blood. "Didn't you?"

"They can walk, fly or drive a Mercedes for all I care," she replied, suddenly feeling annoyed. "As long as they do it during business hours. It's past closing time."

"You want me to leave." He raised one dark brow.

"Yes. Please," she admitted, the word so soft she wondered if he could even hear.

"Liar," he replied, his sensuous lips curving into a half smile that did dangerous things to her heartbeat. "You don't really want me to go, Callie. You just think you *should* want me to go. You're a nice girl. One unaccustomed to being kissed by strange men." He trailed a fingertip down the curve of her jaw, and as much as she wanted to pull away, she couldn't. His touch was entrancing, his eyes magnetic. "You're pure . . . so very pure, Callie. So new to all the feelings pushing and pulling at you."

"What is it you really want with me?" she managed to ask, rocked by his words and doubly upset by the truth in them.

"You tell me. You're the seer. Tell me what you see."

The truth crystalized in her mind and her temper flared. How had he known her name? How did he know anything about her? "Did Guidry send you? If he thinks he can get me to cooperate by sending in some . . ." She closed her eyes and grappled for control. *Calm, breathe.* Her eyes snapped open and she glared at him. "You can both go straight to hell."

The man smiled then, actually smiled, as if she'd said something witty. "Thanks for the sentiment, but you're too late, pretty Callie. I've already been there."

"Tell Guidry to leave me alone."

"When I meet the man, I'll be glad to. Is he bothering you?"

"Not any more than you. It's past closing time, and I'm tired."

"Meaning?"

"Meaning, get out. I'm not interested."

"Really? You seemed interested a few moments ago."

Callie felt heat creep into her cheeks. What *had* come over her?

The answer stood right in front of her, an intense look in his eyes, a smile on his face. *He* had come over her—this dark-haired stranger who affected her like no one she'd ever met.

She shook the feeling away. The last thing she needed right now was to lose her wits to some man. She had to stay strong, controlled, focused; her father's life depended on it. "Just take the book and go." She thrust the hardback he'd chosen at him and started to move away. A firm hand on her arm stopped her.

"I told you, the book isn't what I'm looking for."

"Then look for whatever it is you want somewhere else."

"*You're* what I want."

"Look, I don't know who you are or—"

"Alex," he interjected. "My name is Alex Daimon."

"Okay, Alex Daimon. I don't know what bus you just rode in on, but you don't just walk in off the street and tell women you don't even know that you want—" The rest of her words were cut off by a swift knock that came from the storefront.

"Ms. Wisdom? Callie?" a voice called. "Are you in there? It's Detective Guidry. I need to talk to you. It's an emergency."

"Just pick out what you want and take it to the register," she snapped, moving past Alex Daimon, never so grateful for an escape in her life. She rounded the bookcase and headed for the front, glimpsing Guidry's pale blond hair, his navy suit, through the door.

"Thank God you're here," the detective said as she unlocked the door and pulled it open. "I went by your house but your butler said you were here. I really have to talk to you."

"The answer is no."

"I see you got my message."

She nodded, but he went on. "Well, there's only one missing woman now. We found one of them." From the grim expression on his face, Callie knew what had happened before she heard his next words. "One of the women kidnapped last month was found strangled a few weeks ago. The body discovered this afternoon was also strangled. I think it's the same guy, and if it is, he still has the other woman. A few of us are hoping that she's still alive. . . ."

He paused to wipe a hand over tired-looking eyes. "We thought maybe you could give us a handle on this bastard—pardon my language. He's slick, and we haven't got a clue. I was hoping you might take a ride with me to the area where we found this last body."

When Callie started to protest, Guidry held up a hand. "I know you don't want to, but you're all we've got."

"Find someone else."

"Hold on and let me finish before you say no."

"I already said it."

He gave her a frustrated look. "Give me a chance to change your mind, then."

"I don't think so."

"Mrs. Bodine," he called, motioning behind him. That's when Callie noticed the small woman who waited quietly just inside the doorway. Her long hair was jet black, pulled back in a tight bun, her face devoid of make-up. She looked young and vulnerable, but a graying at her temples and the first sign of crow's feet around her eyes betrayed her age. She clasped her hands together, her dark gaze anxious as it lit on Callie.

"This is the lady I was telling you about," Detective Guidry said to the woman. "She can help us find your daughter."

"No," Callie argued, shaking her head. Hope remained in the woman's eyes, and Callie cast an angry glare at Guidry. "Thanks a lot."

"I'm just doing my job."

"Your job is harassing innocent citizens? Making them—"

"I'm not harassing you. I'm simply asking for help."

"Right!" She threw her hands up. "Can't you just leave me alone? I don't want any part of your investigation. I can't help you!"

"You won't help me," he rejoined.

"I *can't*. You don't understand. I don't even know if I can do it anymore."

"Please." Mrs. Bodine's soft voice was like a sledgehammer to the carefully built emotional wall Callie had erected so many years ago. The woman's soft touch on Callie's shoulder drew her around. She turned, hating herself all the while. She knew, even before she looked into Mrs. Bodine's desperate gaze, that she wouldn't be able to resist. Years of pretending the *sight* didn't exist, of hiding her power from everyone, seemed pointless in the face of this woman's despair.

"My baby could be alive out there," Mrs. Bodine said.

"But what if . . ."

Callie's words trailed off as the woman shook her head. "I need to know for sure: if there's hope, or if the worst has happened—" The words caught on a sob.

Callie found herself pulling the woman into her arms, stroking her back. Sobs shook the small body and Callie held the woman tighter.

"Please. You have to help me find out the truth," came the muffled plea. "Please."

"Damn you, Guidry," Callie hissed, her rage directed at the police detective. The man merely shrugged, a victorious gleam in his eyes.

"It's okay," she whispered to the woman, tearing her gaze from Guidry's. "Let me just deal with this last customer and then we'll go." Callie let go of the mother, who sniffled and dabbed at her red-rimmed eyes. She turned, but Alex Daimon was nowhere in sight. He was gone, as if vanished into thin air.

Impossible! She moved to the bookcase where he'd been only moments before. She touched the book he'd left sitting on the counter. The leather was still warm from his touch and her hand tingled. She took a few more steps and rounded the bookshelf. The door to her office stood wide open.

The office itself was empty, the back door closed and locked. Callie examined the dead bolt. He had to have gone out this way; there was no other explanation. He couldn't just vanish. . . .

"Is something wrong?" Detective Guidry moved into the office doorway, his watery blue gaze sweeping the empty room.

"Uh, no. Did you by any chance see a tall man, dark hair, go past you?"

"Not a soul."

"But there was a man here not two minutes ago." She whirled, her gaze searching. "He must have left, but I don't see how he did without one of us seeing him." Her next words were cut off by the static from Guidry's walkie-talkie.

"—*Guidry, the lieutenant wants you back at the crime scene. Pronto.*"

"Will do," the detective replied, giving Callie an impatient glance. "Ready?"

"I owe you for this, Guidry," she snapped.

He caught Callie's arm as she moved to go past him, gave her a truly grateful look. "No, I owe you. Thanks."

Softening, she reminded him: "You could be thanking me for nothing. It's been over ten years."

"No, I meant thanks for not punching me in the nose for bringing Mrs. Bodine here." He grinned.

She glared at him. "I intend to have that pleasure as soon as we get back."

His smile widened, but she could see some uncertainty in his eyes. Good. Let him worry about it, because she'd meant it. She owed him, and she always paid her debts.

She couldn't resist one last glance around the darkened store, her gaze lingering on the bookshelf where she'd left Alex Daimon. He was really gone, disappeared without a trace. She ignored the tiny twinge of regret, pulled the door closed, and locked it. She pushed the mysterious customer from her mind and climbed into Jack Guidry's patrol car. Later, she could figure out how Alex had slipped past her. Right now, she had more pressing things to deal with.

One missing woman, and one dead one. . . .

She clutched her hands together. Her palms burned, the skin still wet with Mrs. Bodine's tears. She cast a quick glance behind her at the woman huddled in the backseat. Desperation was evident in the way she gripped the door handle, her eyes fixed straight ahead, seeing yet not seeing as she prayed for her daughter's life.

Callie turned back around, hoping with all her heart that she wasn't making a terrible, terrible mistake.

Maybe things would be different this time.

Maybe the girl wouldn't yet be dead.

"Over there, near the lake," Detective Guidry said, motioning to a small area where a policeman stood, snapping photographs, while another knelt down, combing the grass surrounding the body.

They'd dropped Mrs. Bodine off before coming. This remote area near Lake Pontchartrain was heavily wooded, the perfect place to dump a body. It had been three days since Mrs. Bodine's older daughter had been strangled, and from what Guidry had told Callie, the body had been here the entire time.

Lanterns lit the area. Mosquitos swarmed. The sound of dogs barking penetrated the steady chirp of crickets. The police were searching for evidence. Clues. Anything to lead them to the killer.

Callie glanced at the black body bag stretched out on a gurney not two feet from her. Two black-suited men from the coroner's office stood at attention nearby.

"We were waiting for you," one said. "The eyes are still intact. He didn't do a job on this one. Not like the first. Lucky for us." He took a deep breath and leveled a stare at Callie. "Are you ready?" When she nodded, he turned to lead her to the body.

"What we think happened is that he brought her out here, still alive, then killed her with that." Guidry pointed to a filthy piece of rope that an officer was stuffing inside a plastic bag labeled EVIDENCE. "Then he took off, maybe scared by some local hunters or something, not realizing he'd left the rope behind. Not that it'll do us a damn bit of good. That stuff's available at any fishing shack along the bayou, not to mention every tackle shop from here to Texas and back. Hell, even the grocery stores carry the stuff. Of course, there's enough blood for DNA testing, but that's only good if he's on file—and if it's *his* blood . . ." Guidry's voice trailed off as they walked.

A putrid odor—a mingling of damp earth, death and rotting fish—filled Callie's nostrils. She struggled for a breath and focused her attention on the detective's shoulders.

"I'll try, but I don't know if it'll work. Everyone I've ever touched has been—" The words died in her throat the moment the detective stepped aside. Callie looked at the corpse's feet, the ankles tied together, toes blue and swollen.

"I can get you a pair of gloves." Guidry was beside her, hands shoved into his pockets, his mouth a severe line. Absently he slapped at a mosquito on his cheek.

"No. It would hinder the contact."

He nodded, his eyes trained on her rather than the body. The moment Callie forced her gaze up to survey the rest of the dead woman, she understood why.

Grass and mud smeared parts of the bloated and bruised body. Flies and mosquitos hovered about, drawn by the smell and the sight despite the efforts of the photo-snapping police officer who tried to shoo them away.

Callie's gaze moved up, over a bruised and battered torso, past the purple strangulation marks around the woman's throat, to her face. The lips were a purplish color—the only color in the stark white face save the bulging, red-rimmed eyes.

The moment Callie stared into the lifeless gaze, another part of her seemed to take control. Determination pushed aside fear and disgust. She dropped to her knees and took the ice-cold hands in her own. Ignoring the wave of revulsion that rolled through her, she tightened her fingers around the woman's and stared deep into the dead eyes.

A image rushed at her like a gust of frigid wind: a woman's figure, vivid, strong, begging to be seen, heard, saved.

"Help!" The cry knifed through her, and Callie saw a woman's tear-streaked face, eyes filled with pain and fear.

She felt herself sinking into the ground, deeper into the cold mud. Then she heard another voice. A different woman.

"Don't hurt her! No!" A wail pierced her ears and Callie clutched the icy hands tighter. At this moment they were her own hands.

"Shut up, bitch!" came the deep growl. It was human, yet not. "Do as I say, or you get the same thing as your sister here." And then she saw the silhouette of a man, features hidden in the darkness as he leaned over her. Mosquitos swarmed. The sound of water lapping against the shore kept time with her frantic heartbeat. Fingers circled her neck and squeezed, tighter, tighter. . . .

Blackness swallowed Callie. The voices faded. Cold seeped into her. It was too cold, too dark, almost as if the earth had swallowed her and she was glimpsing the world beneath.

Then a lightbulb flickered and she found herself in a sparsely furnished room containing a double bed made of wrought iron. The mattress was stained, and a nightstand and a worn-looking chair were nearby. A single mirror hung on the dingy cement wall, a crack jagging its way across the silvery surface. The room was frigid, with the steady growl of an air conditioner in the background. She heard the drip-drop of condensation; it played on her nerves, making her flinch.

Light filtered in from a small rectangular window near the ceiling. Dust whispered in the thin shafts of light, the air tainted with cigarette smoke and something else—the vile scent of blood.

Callie saw dark crimson stains on the wall: fingerprints.

A voice rang out. "Your time's coming soon, whore. You'll end up just like your sister. Like the others." It was the same unearthly voice, low, harsh, rumbling in her ear, sending chills through Callie's body.

"No!" came the faint whimper from the corner where she huddled.

A silhouette appeared in the doorway, bright daylight outlining his powerful frame as he entered. When the door slammed shut behind him, the room was shrouded in shadow once more. He advanced on her, fists clenched. Closer, closer he came, until the flickering lightbulb illuminated his face.

Callie froze. Her heart stopped, and she fell into a nothingness so bleak, so absolute, it must be oblivion.

Surely it was, for Callie had no doubt she'd just glimpsed Death, himself—and he'd scared the life right out of her, just as he'd squeezed it right out of the woman in the swamp.

Chapter Four

"Ms. Wisdom?" a voice called.

Callie felt a nudge at her shoulder, pulling her from the darkness, from the death.

"Are you all right? Ms. Wisdom?" Detective Guidry's voice seemed louder, closer, followed by a slight pressure on her arm.

Callie opened her mouth but no sound came out, only several short gasps as she tried to draw oxygen into her lungs. The smell of stale cigarettes and musty earth burned in her nostrils, and she gasped for clean air.

"Blanchard, get a doctor!" the detective ordered, his voice booming.

Reality returned to Callie like an icy douse of water. She felt the soft earth at her knees, damp, soaking through her slacks. The pressure on her skin was warm, however, and very insistent, where the detective's hands covered her shoulders and provided the support that kept her from slumping to the ground next to the dead body.

"I said to call for a doctor, man," Guidry shouted again. "Don't stand there staring at me. Do it!"

"No," she managed to croak, blinking her eyes, desperately trying to focus. For a moment the blur of lights merged into one, then slowly they distinguished themselves into two, three, a multitude of lanterns scattered throughout the woods: policemen searching for missing clues that would lead them to the other woman if she was still alive.

And she *was*. Of that Callie was more than certain. But for how long?

The question hammered in her head as she held the woman's dead sister's icy hands, her own knees pressing into the soggy riverbank, next to the exact spot where the woman had been killed. Callie could still feel the warmth of the woman's body when she'd been held prisoner in the room. . . . And the absolute cold of her death now.

"Ms. Wisdom?" Detective Guidry repeated. "Can you hear me?"

"Yes." The word came out in a rush of air as she let the corpse's hands fall back into the body bag. She grasped the detective's fingers, which rested near her collarbone, and stared up at him. "You were right. He did kill her here."

"Are you sure?"

"I saw it. Felt it." She touched a hand to her neck,

her skin tender, her throat muscles sore from the killer's deadly fingers.

The policeman swore.

"What's wrong?" She glanced up.

"The first body was killed in an abandoned warehouse out near the airport. I was hoping to place this body there, maybe find a link."

"The other woman is alive," Callie whispered. "I saw her. She's still alive."

"Where did you see her?"

"He's keeping her in a room—a small dark room."

"Where?" Guidry demanded. "Do you know where?"

Callie shook her head, a drop of perspiration sliding down the side of her face. She swiped at the moisture with the back of her hand, suddenly realizing how sweltering the night air was. The room had been cold. So cold, like the body.

"I just saw the inside. Not much furniture, the whole place was really dirty, and the walls . . ." Her words trailed off as she lifted her hands, which still tingled, to caress the night in front of her. With every stroke of her fingers, she felt a rough, uneven surface. "Concrete," she murmured. "The walls were made of concrete, and they were stained."

"Stained with what?"

Blood-red fingertip trails danced in front of her eyes. "Did he strangle all of the others?" she asked instead of answering.

"No," the detective replied. "And we're not sure it is a 'he.' It could be three different people, for all we know. Or two. That's why you're here. I was looking for some solid connection between these three deaths. The MO's are slightly different for each. And the DNA from the crime scenes . . ."

"But there *is* a connection," Callie said. "Something you're not telling me. Why else would you . . . ?" She fixed her gaze straight ahead as she stared into nothing and saw more than she cared to. Much, much more. A black silhouette, the flash of a silver blade, scarlet drops of blood.

"Do you see something?" the detective asked, yet he knew the answer. Callie heard it in his voice, felt it in the tightening of his fingers on her shoulders.

"I mean he didn't just kill them, Guidry. Did he?"

"No, he didn't," the policeman replied, his voice quiet. Mosquitos hummed a haunting melody around them. "The first two bodies had small lacerations at their wrists." He knelt down and pulled the dead woman's arm up. He indicated tiny slash marks, nothing more than scratches really. "The coroner said this could be a coincidence. . . ." He shook his head. "But it's just too friggin' weird for this to be three different killers."

"It's the same man," Callie agreed. "And those marks *are* the connection. He drained some of their blood."

Excitement lit Guidry's eyes. "I was thinking that maybe he's some sort of ritual nut," the detective grunted, glancing around at the swampy area that surrounded them, the thick foliage that stretched for hundreds of yards, so thick it seemed one could lose one's soul in the black shadows. "There's so much stuff that goes on around these parts at night. Voodoo, witchcraft—all sorts of hocus-pocus. We suspect this guy's into something like that."

"Maybe. I saw some of the blood on the wall where he was keeping them. Like fingerprints, arranged in an odd sort of pattern."

"Ritualistic?"

"I'm not sure."

Guidry's gaze went past Callie, to the dead woman, and a haunted look filled his eyes. "It has to be the same man, no matter about the different MO's."

"It is," Callie insisted, though unsure how she could be so absolutely certain. But she was. She hadn't seen the perp's features clearly, not in any of her visions, but it had all been the same man.

Maybe she had seen more than she realized. Sometimes when she went into a trance, she couldn't make heads nor tails of what she saw. It was only slowly, as she remembered and relived the visions, that the pieces would fall into place until she had a completed puzzle before her.

"How can you be so sure?" Guidry shook his head, his jaw clenched. His excitement had given way to suspicion.

"I saw him."

"But not clear enough to give a description."

"No, but I know it's the same guy."

"How?"

"I—I felt it." She shook her head. "Look, believe what you want, Detective. It's up to you. I'm just trying to help."

"What else did you feel?" Guidry pressed, passing a hand over his haggard face.

Callie closed her eyes, a chill sweeping through her. "He'll kill the other one. Soon," she added, the word trembling on her lips. "Very soon."

Guidry muttered an expletive, quickly lost in the buzz of insects, the water slapping the shore, the crunch of leaves as what seemed like half the New Orleans police force combed through the trees, searching for something they wouldn't find. There would be no clues, other than a few drops of blood found on the victim that weren't her own. Nothing else, though. No tire marks, footprints, nothing. It was as if the killer had swooped down, killed his victim, then escaped on the night breeze.

"Guidry, the lieutenant wants you on the car radio," an officer said, coming up to them.

"Dammit," he muttered. "Tell him I'm busy."

"He said to tell you to stop embarassing this department, that he didn't care if you worked with this woman before. He said to cut the psychic bullshit and bring him a killer."

Guidry glared at the patrolman, who shrugged and then turned to head back to his police cruiser.

"It isn't bullshit," Callie said softly when the officer was out of earshot. She wished it was.

"I know. I remember." Frustration etched Guidry's face. "But my boss doesn't. Those days we worked together are long gone. I need something concrete. Any details that might help us identify this bastard?"

"The room smelled really funny—damp, kind of

moldy. There was a lot of dust, too, and smoke—cigarette smoke."

"So he's a smoker." Guidry laughed. "Him and a million others in this city. Anything else?"

"The window," she said.

"How many did you see?"

"Just one, but it was strange."

"Strange? How so?"

"High," she replied. "Very, very high. Too high. Close to the ceiling."

"Could the room be a cellar?"

"Not a cellar."

"What makes you so sure?"

"It didn't feel like a cellar . . . but maybe." Annoyed, she shook her head. "I don't know. Maybe."

"Maybe's not good enough. *Think,* Callie."

But she couldn't. Her temples throbbed with each word she spoke, each thought that fought its way into her head. Callie touched fingertips to her aching forehead. "I'm trying, but I can't. Maybe after a few hours, once things have had a chance to gel." She glanced up at him. "I'm sorry."

Impatience and exhaustion played a tug of war with his features. Ultimately, exhaustion seemed to win out. He sighed. "No need to be sorry," he said, grasping her hand and helping her to her feet. "This was a long shot anyway. Maybe forensics will come up with something."

"They'd better, Detective," Callie said, taking the handkerchief he offered her and wiping her hands—as if she could erase the chill crawling through her bones. "That young woman doesn't have much time."

He closed his eyes, a look of pure frustration twisting his face before he turned and glared over his shoulder. "Blanchard," he called to a uniformed officer nearby. "Tell the lieutenant I'm taking Ms. Wisdom home, and keep these men searching this area all night if necessary. No one leaves until we find something; do you hear me?"

The officer nodded, then gave the okay to the two men from the coroner's office. As they wheeled the body away, Guidry stuffed his used handkerchief in his pocket and steered Callie back to his car.

A man rushed at them before Callie could climb inside. He snapped a few pictures, questions pouring from his mouth. "Detective, what's the deal with you bringing in a psychic? Hasn't the police department wasted enough taxpayer dollars? Can't you guys find any of your own clues—"

"Blanchard!" Guidry roared. "Get this piece of crap away from here."

"Come on, Detective. What's the story?" the journalist called out. "Did she stare into her crystal ball and give you a name—"

"Come on, Walters," Blanchard said, coming over, grabbing the reporter by the arm, and confiscating his camera. "Detective Guidry isn't ready to make a statement now. You'll hear an update at City Hall when everybody else does."

"This is the *third* body. People are entitled to know what's taking you guys so long to find a suspect. And now you're falling back on the hocus-pocus that—"

"Out of here, Walters," Guidry ordered. "And if you don't go quietly, I'll have you arrested for obstruction of justice."

"You can't do that. I know my rights. I'm not obstructing anything."

"Then I'll think of another charge. Either way, you'll be sitting in a jail cell tonight." He grabbed the confiscated camera, pulled out the film and tossed it into the backseat of his car before helping Callie inside.

"That's private property!" Walters cried as the uniform hustled him away. "You can't . . ." The words faded as the reporter was shoved into the back of a police car.

"Who was that?" Callie asked after Guidry had slid behind the wheel, beside her.

"The local media maggot." He turned and gave her a look. "You would do well to stay away from him if he tries to talk to you. He dug up the old file on you and me. He thinks . . ." His voice trailed off and he looked pensive.

Callie felt annoyance. "Don't worry, Detective. I won't embarass you or your department. I don't even own a crystal ball."

As if she'd read his thoughts, he turned away, a telltale flush creeping up his neck. Briefly, she wondered how it had affected his career that she'd stopped helping him, stopped using her powers years ago. He *had* tried to get in touch with her several times. . . .

Her thoughts were interrupted as Guidry said, "I'll drop you at home and call you later tonight. I'll ask some questions, maybe they will open things up for you."

"It's already pretty late," Callie pointed out. "Will you still be up later?"

"I don't get much sleep these days," he replied.

Indeed, she could tell he didn't. Dark circles shadowed his eyes. The attractive, easy-going man she remembered from ten years ago, with his short blond hair and clean-shaven features, had all but disappeared. His hair now brushed the collar of his uniform, the pale locks thinner and tousled, as if he'd raked his fingers through his hair time and time again. His entire body seemed tense, tired. Very tired. She didn't have to use the *sight* to know that.

Callie stifled a yawn as she remembered her own past few sleepless nights. And when she did sleep, the nightmares came . . . the visions. She could certainly sympathize with Guidry's exhaustion. She battled her own, just as she was battling fate.

Her attention fixed on the silver thermos resting on the cracked blue seat between them.

"Thirsty?" he asked.

Callie swallowed, her throat suddenly burning. A wave of heat washed over her, stifling, like a thick wool blanket had been pulled over her head. She fought for breath as a tingling in her hands began.

"Ms. Wisdom? Callie?"

She clutched at the window knob and rolled the glass down. Sultry night air rushed through the window and she drank in the oxygen, but it wasn't enough. She needed air, space, freedom. . . . What was happening?

Callie gripped the perfume flask around her neck and the tingling subsided. Her fingers began to feel normal again.

"Are you all right?" The detective cast an odd look at her. "I'm sorry if Walters upset you—"

She shook her head frantically. "No, no. I'm fine. I just hate being closed up, that's all. A little claustrophobia." But it was more than that. She knew it. She'd felt it. Something wasn't right. She'd dealt with the claustrophobia her entire life and never had it ever felt like it had just now, except earlier in the bookstore.

"So, how does your wife feel about all your sleepless nights?" she asked, eager to distract herself from the strange feelings coursing through her. Talking was much better.

"No wife. She left me. I'm married to my job, now."

"Sounds lonely." Callie felt awful for the man. Did he have no one, now?

"My thirst for justice keeps me warm at night. I have to bring this guy in. I *will* bring him in. It's all I want. All I ever think about."

"I hope you do."

"I will," he said, the vow seemingly more for himself than Callie. His grip tightened on the steering wheel as he stared straight ahead.

She glanced out the window at the woods still dotted with pinpoints of light. Searchlights. Futile searchlights. The police wouldn't find anything.

Callie knew it deep down inside, just as she knew the girl would die. Very, very soon, unless she could remember something more. . . .

Her thoughts turned to her father, and she wiped at a stray tear that wound its way down her cheek. He would die soon, like the girl, unless she could find an answer for him, as well.

"Detective?"

"Yes?"

"Could you drop me back at the store? My car's there and I have a few things to pick up."

"Sure thing," he replied, and Callie settled back into the seat. She would retrieve Catherine Drashierre's book of spells and head for home, then stay up all night pouring over every page until she found something. *Anything*.

Not much time left. . . .

She shot a glance at her watch.

But how much time would be enough? How could she know how long it would take to uncover answers she didn't understand? There was no comfort to be found; it was fleeting ever since her mother's death. Well, not last night . . . when the dream man had come to her: She'd felt comfort then.

She let her eyes drift closed. What she wouldn't give to escape to the peaceful oblivion of sleep, where the problems of her life could sometimes be left behind. Sometimes. Perhaps she could rest in that dream man's arms and forget everything apart from him and the strange feelings he stirred.

But this time the dream would be different. The

man had a face now, and in the dark recesses of her mind Callie pictured Alex Daimon, felt his strength. Her lips burned. Yes, her dream comforter was no longer a man of shadows. He was *real* now.

Callie's eyes snapped open to take in the dark interior of the police car. The steady hum of the engine filled her ears and she smelled the faint odor of exhaust blowing in with the air conditioner. Damn her stupid hormones! She didn't have time for them.

Only her father and, now, the missing woman.

Only life and death. Salvation and destruction. She had no time for some sinfully handsome man with penetrating eyes and an indefinable wildness that entranced, overpowered her.

She pushed all thoughts of Alex Daimon away and concentrated on the passing scenery. She couldn't think about him. She *wouldn't*. If only her subconscious would cooperate, for she could still feel him, see him at the far edges of her mind. He was waiting for her to sleep, she knew. Then he would come to her.

"You need to eat, Miss Callie," Burgess said from the doorway of her bedroom.

Callie glanced over at the tray on the desk in front of her and smiled. Her stomach gave an involuntary grumble. "Stop worrying, Burgess. I'll eat." She picked up her fork and took a bite of the shrimp creole the housekeeper, Mrs. Beauville, was famous for. Her recipe had garnered first place in many local cooking contests, and normally Callie would have gobbled down every delicious bite.

She forced herself to swallow, fighting back a wave of dizziness that swept over her. She managed a smile for Burgess though she felt self-conscious beneath the man's scrutiny. "See? I'm eating, so you can stop worrying. How's Daddy?"

"Sleeping now. He missed you at dinner."

"It couldn't be helped, Burgess. I had to go with Detective Guidry."

If her reacquaintance with the detective surprised the butler at all, Burgess didn't show it. "Any clue about those women?"

Callie shook her head. "Nothing that really helps." She closed her eyes against a sudden swell of tears. "I couldn't tell them much of anything they didn't already know." Except something about a high window and lots of cigarette smoke. Fat lot of good that would do them!

After a moment the old servant spoke: "Are you sure this is wise, Miss Callie? Don't you think you should've turned the detective down? You need your strength for your father."

"Oh, Burgess, I've run so long. I couldn't turn my back this time. I had to help."

"And who will help *you*, Miss Callie? You can barely sit up right now."

True, Callie thought as she touched a hand to her aching head, the action taking every ounce of energy she had. Her arms, her legs, felt numb, heavy, weary.

"I had to help, Burgess. I have to help." She searched her brain for any clues, recalling the scene in the dark room with the woman and the silhouette over and over, hoping for something she'd missed earlier.

"Take care, Miss Callie. There's only so much you can do, and your papa needs you now."

Callie nodded, knowing Burgess spoke the truth, yet unable to deny the woman's frightened voice, calling to her, reaching out for help, for hope. And Callie was her last hope.

"I'll look in on Daddy later," she murmured. "It's late." She glanced at the brass mantel clock on the fireplace in her room. "Nearly midnight. Why don't you turn in?"

"I'll stay up and take your tray downstairs."

"No, no. I can do it. You go on. You baby me too much, Burgess."

"Old habits are hard to break," he said, giving her a sheepish smile. "I was around when you were an infant, and your mama and papa were the proudest parents around."

She smiled. "I know, and I appreciate you looking after me, but I'll be fine. Go."

Burgess shot her a doubtful glance, then stifled a yawn. "If you're sure?"

"Completely. Just run on and leave me to my work."

"You doing the books from the store?" he asked as he turned to go.

"Sort of," she said, casting a quick look at the bag that he was looking at. It held a book, all right, but not an accounting ledger as Burgess assumed. It held a book that required her complete, undivided attention.

He shook his head, a smile tugging at his mouth. "Your mama never did like doing them. Used to push it off on me every chance she got. Her and your daddy weren't the accounting types. Creative spirits, your mama used to say. And creative spirits don't do bookkeeping."

"Tell me about it. It took me weeks to figure out the store's bank balance, and I still haven't put everything in order. But I'm trying."

"I'll see you at breakfast, then. Six A.M. I'm close by if you need me." He turned and Callie listened to his footsteps as he shuffled away, down to the bedroom next to her father's.

She took a deep breath and turned back to her food. Grabbing her fork, she took a rather large bite. Her stomach twisted in response. Callie reached for her napkin, the white linen seeming to weave in front of her. She spit the food out and leaned back in her chair. The churning in her middle calmed to a slight queasiness once she'd rid herself of the food. She couldn't eat. She couldn't sleep. What was wrong with her?

The once delicious aroma upset her already uneasy stomach. She pushed away from the desk to sink onto the edge of the bed and reach for her bag. Retrieving the book inside, she tossed her slippers to the floor and scooted back to lean against the headboard, a pillow propped at her back. Her small nightstand light cast a faint yellow glow across the dingy pages.

She scanned line after line, running her fingers over the text, praying for some sort of recognition, hoping to *feel* something. Strangely, her power seemed useless where the book was concerned. There were no memories evoked by the tome. She sensed nothing familiar, nothing that would help her determine which page held the right incantation or its cure. There was nothing.

As she stared, the book became a blur and Callie leaned her head back, exhaustion claiming her despite her best attempt to fight it.

Her dreams were memories of retrieving the book.

"Beware the keeper of the Power. . . ."

The warning whispered through Callie's brain and stopped her cold. Fear slithered into her bones, settled in and sent a chill through her despite the sweltering night air. She cast a glance around her. Only pitch black darkness stared back. Nothing else. Nothing human, at least.

"Get a grip," she told herself, pushing any supernatural imaginings away before they took root. It was probably the wind playing on her overactive imagination. Being in this godawful place near the stroke of midnight was no help. Then again, she'd had little choice in the matter. She'd had to wait until her father went to sleep.

Determined, she blocked out the voice in her head, the wind, the small part inside of her that told her she was stupid to be venturing to a graveyard in the middle of the night. She clutched the handle of the crowbar and heaved again. The cement door of the mausoleum creaked, the sound grating on her nerves like this door that had gone too long without oiling. One more heave and a black space the size of a handspan gaped at her.

Air sucked and swished past her. Dust billowed out and the smell of long-rotted flesh and dried bones burned her nostrils. Callie smelled something else as well—something sinister that rushed at her like a frigid breath being expelled—and it almost made her throw the crowbar to the floor and run from the mausoleum. The place was so small, so stifling, its walls so thick. And the voice in her head, calling her . . .

No! There was no voice. Only her imagination.

" 'This old man,' " she whispered, recalling the familiar old song, trying desperately to recall the peace her father had instilled by singing it to her. All she had to do was concentrate on her voice and ignore everything else. " 'He played one. He played knick-knack on my thumb. . . .' "

Her flashlight flickered, casting dancing circles across the mausoleum's floor. This place had stood undisturbed for nearly one hundred years, but as she walked forward Callie's footprints smeared the accumulated dust and left a sign of life that seemed to rail against the presence of death that permeated the room.

And the presence of evil . . .

" 'With a knick-knack, paddy-whack, give the dog a bone . . .' "

Approaching the sarcophagus at the center of the

room, Callie ran her fingertips over the letters etched into its lid. IN DEATH LIES ETERNITY

A shiver rippled through her, and she yanked her hand away.

" ' . . . this old man came rolling home.' "

Steeling herself, she pushed open the coffin and peered inside. A blue satin nightdress, faded and yellowed at the edges, drew her eye. She looked closer, saw the bones of a once delicate hand resting against the crimson lining of the casket. Faded black leather peeked from beneath the folds of the gown and relief rushed through Callie. She'd found it, the book mentioned in her grandmother's diary!

Relax. Breathe. So she'd found it. So what? Maybe it would prove as useless in helping her father as the doctors had. But deep down, she knew the truth, even if she wouldn't admit it to herself.

" 'This old man. He played two. . . .' "

She gathered her courage and dipped her hand inside the coffin. Her flesh brushed bone, and a tremor swept her insides. Callie clamped her eyes shut. A sick feeling rose in her throat as she eased her hand beneath the dead woman's nightdress sleeve, under the edge of the thick book.

" 'He played knick-knack on my shoe—' "

The words caught in her throat as bony fingers closed around her wrist.

"Mine!" a voice shrieked. A furious gust of wind slammed the mausoleum door fully open. Dust and cobwebs whirled into an angry cloud that swallowed Callie.

Pain streaked up her arm. Her head swam. The

surrounding darkness turned to a frenzied dance of shadows, and she shut her eyes. This couldn't be happening. This couldn't be real.

Only it was. As real as her father who lay dying in his bed at home. Dying, and Callie couldn't let him down. Maybe this book wouldn't help, but maybe . . . She couldn't ignore even the most remote possibility. She wouldn't.

"No!" she shouted back. Grasping the book, she pulled. The skeletal fingers seemed to clamp tighter, cutting off her circulation. "I need it," Callie cried, forgetting how crazy this was to be wrestling with the skeleton of a dead ancestress for a book of spells, forgetting that this might all be her imagination. "Please!" she cried.

Traitor! the word seemed to pierce her ears. You have betrayed me. You will pay. I will not go back. My spirit seeks vengeance. You are my flesh . . . my blood. . . .

The bones bit into her wrist, and Callie struggled. The wind lashed at her. Cold fingers drifted down her bare arms. A draft of air snaked around her ankles. The cold surrounded her, gripping, threatening to crush her courage and send her screaming from this place.

Her knees buckled, and she started to sink to the floor. Terror was overcoming her. "Daddy," she whispered, and her father's face appeared in front of her like an angel come to snatch her from Satan's clutches.

" 'This old man, he played three. He played knick-knack on my knee.' " Her father's deep voice

sounded in Callie's ear, comforting, allowing her to regain her wits.

Traitor! the other voice hissed again. A voice that had to be Catherine's. *You are mine now. Mine!*

Frantically, Callie shook her head. Scrambling to her feet, she yanked the book away from the skeletal fingers and fled.

"The book is mine!" The wail followed her. "Mine!"

Callie raced through the door and out into the darkness, flying over neglected graves, trampling flowers and leaves, stumbling as she darted around grave markers. She raced past the caretaker's shack at the edge of the cemetery, and fled into the woods beyond.

A shadow passed over the moon, obliterating even the tiniest sliver of light. Blackness closed around her. Callie ran faster, the wind chasing her like a rabid dog snapping at her heels. Unseen fingers gripped her by the throat, and she lost her footing.

Her heart seemed to stop in the next instant. A tingling rushed through her as she slammed into the ground. *Come back,* came the urgent whisper, the voice inside of her head. *Return the book to me. It's mine, just as you are mine.*

Callie tried to clamp her ears shut, but the voice wouldn't go away. It was inside of her now.

She struggled for breath. The book, like lead in her arms, weighed her down. An invisible force pulled at her as she struggled to get back up.

No! her mind blazed, drowning the compelling

whisper. She had to keep moving, for her own life. For her father's.

" 'This old man, he played four,' " she breathed, catching sight in the distance of the white columns of her family's manor house. " 'He played knick-knack on my door.' " Desperately, she held the book and rose to her feet.

Then she was running again. Faster, faster . . .

Callie's eyes snapped open, jerking her from the nightmare to the dimly lit bedroom and the tome open on her lap. None of that had happened when she'd retrieved the book, had it? She couldn't remember. She stared down at the book and her trembling hands. Tingling spread up her arms, through her chest. Then came a heat that had her gasping for her next breath.

She flung the book aside, scrambled from the bed, and hurried to the balcony. Throwing open the French doors, she drank in the night air, grateful for the faint breeze that surrounded her. The house had seemed so stifling, the room closing in on her; the velvety sky was endless, with no beginning, no end.

Endless, timeless, she thought as she walked out onto the balcony and gripped the railing. Her head tilted back and she stared at the moon, a welcome change from the horror of her dreams.

Looking into the sky, Callie waited for the strange tingling to pass, for the claustrophobia to subside. It didn't. The tingling switched to a burning, and Callie clasped her hands together, her own touch strange, almost like the touch of another. . . .

You are mine now, Callie, the night whispered, the words creeping into her ears, spiraling through her body, wrapping around her heart and squeezing. She gripped the balcony railing as a pain seized her middle.

We are one. The same flesh now. Soon, the same spirit.

"No," Callie managed to whisper, desperate to deny the strange voice and all it implied. She sank to her knees, the pain that ripped through her body nearly unbearable.

For a moment she believed she was dying. She had to be. Nothing short of death could feel so paralyzing, so all-encompassing. Opening her mouth, she tried to scream, to call for Burgess. Not a word passed her lips, only a rush of breath, a whimper, as if her body had stopped taking orders from her brain. Yes, she was dying. . . .

"In death lies eternity. The phrase echoed in her head, and then she saw the speaker. It was herself, almost. The woman had the same white-blond hair, the same high cheekbones. But the eyes glittering back at Callie were ice blue, not gray-green, and Callie knew instantly that she gazed upon Catherine Drashierre—her ancestress who was as evil as the Devil himself. Callie would have screamed, but her mouth wouldn't cooperate. Her voice wouldn't work, either. It was as if her body wasn't her own anymore, but a strange shell she was locked inside, unable to get out.

The vision of Catherine stepped closer, arms outstretched, her ice-blue eyes sparkling with deadly intent. *Soon we shall be the same spirit, the same eternal spirit. Eternity waits for us, dear Callie. Eternity and power.*

"Callie," a new voice called. It was deep, soft, cutting through the thunder of Callie's heartbeat and Catherine's chilling words. Catherine stopped advancing. Callie saw fear flash in the woman's eyes, then her image vanished. Callie's hands cooled, and she managed to grab the balcony railing and climb to her feet. Her head was still spinning.

Blinking, Callie tried to focus. Her attention was drawn to a pale human silhouette in the far distance, standing atop a house that rose tall and proud against the black velvet of night. The mansion's white columns were thick and sturdy, its roof flat, and an iron railing spanned the roof's perimeter.

Callie shook her head and wondered why she'd never noticed the manor house before. She'd stood on this balcony, gazed at the surrounding plantations many times, but she had no recollection of the place or its owner. The house was large, rising up well beyond the tops of the magnolia trees that filled the area, and it seemed to emanate an aura of power and mystery.

Icy rivulets of fear trickled down her spine as Callie forced herself to turn around, to flee the open air which had been her salvation only a moment before.

But the voice, too, had been her salvation.

Callie . . . Its deep rumble echoed in her ears, following her as she stumbled back inside to her bed. She collapsed on the eyelet comforter, her hands at her temples.

Callie . . . Callie . . . Callie—

The ring of the phone cut into her thoughts. She reached for the receiver on the nightstand. "Hello?"

"Did you remember anything else?" came Guidry's familiar voice.

"I—not really. I haven't had much chance to think." Callie managed to focus her eyes on the mantel clock. Two A.M. She did a double-take. Two A.M.? It couldn't be. Had she slept so long? Maybe the clock was fast.

Its steady tick magnified, keeping time with her heartbeat, and she closed her eyes. Where had the time gone? Had she been on the balcony for over an hour? She couldn't have—

"Nothing? Not even a small detail?" Guidry's voice disrupted her thoughts.

"Nothing," she echoed.

"Tell me everything again."

"You already know what I saw."

"Again, Callie. Sometimes people leave out details, unintentionally of course. You might have, too. Tell me again, just to be sure we know everything."

"Okay," she replied, closing her eyes, willing her mind to relax.

She walked a dark tunnel until she emerged into the dim room, saw the concrete walls again, the blood-red fingerprints. Cigarette smoke assaulted her senses, and she found herself huddled in the corner, a silent observer to the scene playing before her eyes. She was powerless.

With as much thoroughness as she could, she described her surroundings, the lump in her stomach turning to a solid fist, the killer's face a shadow that refused to be lit. She saw only his outline, a figure as black as his soul. The shape was as bleak as death.

This *was* death. . . .

After finishing her description, Callie hung up the phone and fled. She passed through several darkened hallways, fled down the stairs, then she was outside, her bare feet flying over cool grass as she headed for her flower garden.

Once there, she dropped to her knees in the freshly turned earth and surveyed the pansies and rhododendrons and other colorful flowers. While moonlight caressed the blossoms, giving them an unearthly glow, they were of this earth. They were freshly sprouted. Growing. Alive. *Real*.

Her fingers brushed the silky petals, and she closed her eyes, inhaling the fragrance, relishing the feel of something real, something so small, yet so natural at her fingertips.

Callie thrust her hands into the dirt and closed her eyes, relishing the feel of soft earth. This was reality. Long ago she'd planted this garden, sitting next to her mother on the bare grass, starting it with a plastic pink shovel. "Helping," her mother had called what she'd done, but Callie knew she'd made more of a mess than anything else. Still, she'd helped begin this place, loved seeing her mother plant seeds and smile, loved cultivating what grew here. Her mother had kept it alive while Callie was in Texas, and now Callie tended it with love. It held only memories of happy times for her.

Callie withdrew her hands and patted the earth. Noticing a few wayward weeds, she knelt beneath the midnight sky and tore at them. Doing so, she felt the warmth of the sun, saw her mother's smiling face, and took comfort.

Hours later Callie washed her hands and collapsed onto her bed. As she slumped back onto the pillow, her face streaked with the silent tears the memories had brought, she reached for the book of spells. She was intent on finding something; the events of this night seemed to make that necessity apparent. But as she took the book her hand seemed dead weight, her eyelids heavy. She managed to pull the text closer, to touch it, but her eyes drifted shut.

Just a few minutes, she told herself. She had a right to be tired and would sleep a few minutes. Real sleep. Not nightmare-riddled exhaustion. Then she would continue reading and reading and reading until something made sense.

As she sank into the oblivion of slumber, she vaguely heard the voice from outside in her subconscious, soothing, pulling her into slumber.

Callie . . . Callie . . . Callie.

She realized it was Alex Daimon's voice just before she fell completely, deeply asleep. She was sure it was him. He'd been waiting for her, and now the waiting had ended.

* * *

Alex stepped from the full-length mirror, his gaze fixed on Callie stretched out on the bed before him. With a glance, he dimmed the lamp on the night-stand, then moved to the foot of her bed. The white sheers that covered the French doors billowed around him, caressing his skin, making his blood burn hotter.

Moonlight spilled through the windows, illumi-nating Callie's pale features, and suddenly Alex longed to see more. He stared at the white blouse she wore. Slowly, the buttons slipped from the buttonholes. One after the other they popped open until the silk shirt slithered open to expose lace-covered breasts. Next came the button of Callie's jeans, then the faded denim crept down her thighs, her calves, until it eased past her feet.

Alex took a deep breath, his nostrils flaring. Lust had roared to life, hammering through him until it was agony not to touch this woman, to be inside of her, invading her mind and her body until he felt only her heat. He stepped closer.

Then he heard it: "Alex." His name was a whis-per on her parted lips. She arched her back, her breasts jutting into the air, the nipples swollen be-neath the confining lace of her bra. Alex froze.

She was dreaming of him—freely. He hadn't yet invaded her thoughts, and she dreamt of him of her own volition. The realization was staggering.

"Alex," came the breathless call again, and Callie tossed her head to the side, her hands moving to the creamy skin of her thighs. Slowly, tortuously, she slid her hands up over the mound of silver curls peeking through the lace of her panties to her abdomen, her fingers making delicate circles that played on Alex's senses as if she were touching him rather than herself.

It wasn't enough for him to simply watch. He could sense the moist heat between her legs, already taste her essence on his lips, feel her skin soft and warm beneath his fingertips. And the knowledge that she wanted him urged him forward, eager to enjoy her delicious body. Just one sweet taste to sate his raging appetite. . . .

Her hands moved higher, her palms caressing the rosy nipples visible through her white lace bra.

Alex reached out, yet something stopped him. Some invisible force even more powerful than the lust.

Impossible! Nothing was more powerful than the beast inside of him. He was what he was. An incubus, a spoiler, a deceiver. A few more inches and he would be touching her. He wanted to touch her, ached for it, more so because she already called him of her own free will.

Just an inch more! his lust cried. His hand started to tremble, and he balled his fingers.

He couldn't do it. She was too warm, too different from what he'd imagined. He'd felt her heat last night, then again in the bookstore, and minutes ago when she'd been on her knees in the garden. He'd been watching, waiting. But he couldn't just give in to his appetite. She was too pure. Soul-saving pure. Despite her lust, he could taste her innocence—and it both drove him wild and repelled him.

It was a difficulty he hadn't anticipated.

He had been depending upon her eyes to steel him. She looked so much like Catherine in every other respect that Alex had expected her eyes to be the same. Blue. Cold. Evil. But Callie had soft sweet eyes that could send his blood racing with just one glance. And they'd done just that twice now. No; Callie Wisdom didn't turn Alex cold, despite the fact that her ancestress's spirit was inside of her, somewhere, battling for control.

It was already a furious battle; Alex could tell by the dark hollows beneath Callie's eyes. Catherine was trying to weaken her body, then her spirit. Only when Callie was powerless could Catherine take complete control. But Callie had a strength about her. A kindness. A vitality that would make her cling to life, face the darkness, and fight. She revered life—all of it. Whether it was a loved one or a stranger. He had seen that in her choice to use her *sight* and face a darkness that had come so close to consuming her once before.

Suddenly Alex felt disgusted—with himself, what he was, and what was happening to her. And he couldn't stop it, any more than he could stop himself from wanting her. Any more than he could stop the Evil One from destroying her when the time came.

And the time would come soon. Alex felt the fire in his veins, the urge to sink inside of her nearly overcoming him. One stroke of her satiny skin, her heat licking at his icy flesh, and he would be powerless to stop himself.

He would be powerless, and so would she, then, for the Evil One would come for her and she would be as damned as Alex. And the Evil One would have her before he condemned her.

So what? he told himself. Catherine deserved Hell for selling him out. But Alex was having a harder and harder time convincing himself that the warm body on the bed was enough of Catherine to destroy. Callie looked like her ancestress, but her purity was unquestionable. Maybe if she were different, he could hate her, destroy her. If only she'd been less focused on others, or if she'd stared up at him in the bookstore with freezing blue eyes instead of gray-green. If he'd felt greed or lust or any other jaded emotion when he'd been inside her thoughts the night before, if he hadn't felt sympathy, desperation, love . . .

Her lips parted and a soft moan escaped. Alex felt his sex lengthen, throb, ache. Oddly enough, as much as he wanted to step forward—to drift into her thoughts and see what dream played havoc with her senses, to *become* that dream—he couldn't bring himself to perpetrate the invasion. The temptation to satisfy his lust would be far too great then.

To take her.

To condemn her.

To relinquish her to the Evil One, and there would be no turning back. If he took her once there would be no possessing her again, no loving her. . . .

Loving her? He gave himself a furious shake. What was wrong with him? He was here to tempt and seduce, to sate his lusty appetite and spoil a woman in the process. Nothing more. Demons were granted nothing more, and he was what he was.

She wants you—deep inside, slamming into her, pumping hard and fast and—

Get on with it, a voice told him. *Now, while you have the chance. While she burns for you. Then she will burn for all eternity, as she is meant to.*

For the next few moments, Alex let himself remember Catherine. Her love. Her betrayal. Her condemnation. He recalled the deep-seated hate he'd carried nearly a century for this woman responsible for ruining his life. Soiling his soul.

"Catherine." The name rolled from his lips, and he found himself sucked back through time.

He stood in the familiar garden behind the Daimon mansion, the moonlight casting an ethereal glow on the lush surroundings and the angel-like woman in front of him.

Catherine smiled, reached out, and grasped his hand. The night wind whispered through the magnolia trees, the air slightly chilled, but Alex felt nothing except the heat of his body. Fire burned through his veins for this beautiful creature who clasped his hand and touched it to her breast.

"Share your power with me, Alex, and I will be yours. I know you want me. I see the way you look at me. And I know that a man with your appetite can't wait. You're young, hungry, and burning for me. I feel the heat. I have since the moment we first met. Share with me," she repeated again, "and I'll give you everything you want. Right here. Right now."

He'd heard the rumors about her; she sought only power. That was, of course, what had led her to him. Looking into her eyes, he could almost believe she sought him. But he was a link to power; he knew that. His own magic was unsurpassed, and his family book of spells. . . .

If only he didn't want her so badly. He'd never wanted a woman so, not in all his thirty-two years, and he couldn't think straight. She filled his thoughts, his soul—or so it seemed. And he'd always wanted a soul mate, someone to share the duty that had fallen to him as the oldest Daimon son.

Like his father, his grandfather, his great-grandfather, and generations before that, Alex was a protector. He was a guardian of *The Divine Power*. It was the book of spells, his family's book.

As a powerful warlock, Alex had been burdened with that great responsibility, and when he chose a mate, she too would learn all his secrets and help him see the family's duty continue. His helpmate would share the burden.

Now, he found himself thinking, who better to fill that role than Catherine Drashierre, a powerful sorceress in her own right? Together, Catherine and Alex would see that *The Divine Power* would remain untouched, the book's sacred words of good and evil, light and darkness, hidden from all prying eyes.

The Divine Power held the essence of man. It linked good and evil. In this world the two were seen as opposites, but they were so very close it frightened Alex. The book made that very clear. The recitation of a few words could invoke unspeakable evil, yet the fervent prayers on other pages could summon a chorus of angels.

Alex knew. He understood. Born to protect the book, he was destined to rear a son who would carry on that task when the time came. But to do so, he needed a wife. He'd been searching, and as he stared at the woman before him, he knew his search had ended. He would share all. Give all.

And not just because this woman burned for the power he held, but because he too burned—for her. He wanted Catherine, soft and pliant in his arms, her legs spread wide and him buried inside of her. Yes, he burned for her, like an inferno that raged out of control.

But was it wise to give power to those who sought it so desperately? His father would have said no.

"Right here, right now," she repeated, taking his hand, easing it up her skirts to the delicious heat between her legs.

In the space of a heartbeat, the peace and security of his father's teaching slipped from his mind. One touch and he was lost—mind, body and soul.

Now, staring at Callie on the bed, Alex again relived his pain and anger. Catherine hadn't wanted him. She'd been after the book. She'd used it to forsake him, curse him, and then she'd tried to outsmart the Devil, himself. And succeeded.

Only temporarily, he reminded himself.

Alex reached out and trailed a hand over the inviting curve of Callie's bare calf, his senses firing to life, magnified a thousandfold. He touched satin and velvet and silk and the agony that wrenched through him was almost the end of him.

This was nothing like what he'd felt with Catherine or any of the other legions of women he'd been with since her. This was different, and that very fact terrified and made him ache all the more.

Callie arched her back to follow his soft touch, another whimper passing her lips. Alex moved closer, his fingers higher, her skin sweet misery to his eager exploration. He traced tiny circles over her leg, up the outside of her thigh. Slowly, invitingly, she bent her knees. Her legs parted.

A cold fear shot through him, icing the blood in his veins—a cold so gripping and absolute that Alex snatched his hand away. His gaze went to Callie's face and he saw the frown that twisted her features. Her dream had ended. She'd plunged deeper into sleep, into a nightmare. She struggled for a breath, her hands going to her throat as if she were choking, fighting the attack of some unseen villain.

Anger burned in him, and it was all he could do not to rush inside of her mind, defend her against the invisible forces haunting her. He forced himself away, turned and stepped back into the full-length mirror. With a single glance over his shoulder, he brought her wide awake.

A scream wrenched from her throat and she bolted upright, eyes wide, face and chest flushed, fear glittering in the liquid green of her eyes. At that moment, she looked nothing at all like Catherine.

No, Callie Wisdom looked every bit the frightened, vulnerable innocent she was, and Alex fought back another wave of revulsion at what he was, what he'd been commanded to do.

Beauty can be *deceptive,* he reminded himself.

Callie *was* Catherine. Or would be. Their spirits were slowly merging, and nothing would stop that. He gazed at the perfume flask nestled in the deep cleavage between Callie's quivering breasts. He remembered the cherished piece of jewelry so well, it was as if he'd given it to Catherine yesterday instead of one hundred years ago.

Callie's gaze darted wildly around the room, and Alex sank back into the shadows of the mirror. Still he watched, and waited.

He would seduce her next time. He *would.*

And in doing so he would damn her soul.

Chapter Five

The darkness embraced Alex with a stifling intensity as he started to leave Callie, and something shifted deep inside him. Regret? Impossible! He hadn't felt regret—not true, gut-wrenching regret—since he'd been mortal. Not since those few seconds of horror when he'd lost his soul for an eternity.

He'd felt nothing since but hatred and revulsion. And lust. Never regret—until now.

Whirling around, Alex watched the moonlight as it filtered through the mirror that served as a huge gateway to the mortal realm. He glimpsed Callie, her frightened eyes, the tears glistening on her cheeks. She rounded the bed and moved toward the French doors, driven by her claustrophobia and something else . . . something wicked that haunted her dreams and sent fear racing through her body.

Suddenly Alex needed to alleviate her fears. He took a step forward, toward the moonlight and her pale silhouette.

A deafening roar reverberated around him, a joining of dark voices that told of pain and torment and death. They were his reality. The air stirred and whirled around him with a life all its own. Then the darkness sucked at him, drawing him backward until the mirror grew smaller, smaller, until it became only a pinpoint of light.

Like a candle flame snuffed out, the light at last vanished and Alex found himself drowning in the blackness, as if someone had dropped him into a bottomless pit. He fell harder and faster, with no end in sight. He clutched at nothingness, searched for a lifeline he knew didn't exist. There was only emptiness and pain, so much agony that his thoughts clouded and he wished for death. . . .

Death? But he was already dead. At least his spirit was. His soul had been snatched from his body before his mortal life had ended, and condemned to everlasting service in Hell. He'd been a victim of greed, a slave to his own lust.

Alex's fall slowed, then he found himself propelled sideways through a sudden burst of flames and into a dimly lit chamber beyond. Invisible fingers jerked him to a stop, and he stumbled, yet he managed to keep his footing, though his senses were still reeling.

The smell of rot and filth assailed his nostrils, and he grimaced. Had he been thinking clearly, he would have wondered why the awful stench bothered him now when he hadn't noticed it before. Not since he'd first been damned.

"Time for a progress check, Alex," the Evil One's voice crackled through the chamber.

Alex glanced around, searching for a face, but he saw nothing save the wall of flames and the darkness which caged him.

"Fill me in," the Prince of Darkness demanded, his voice louder, more grating, as if it came from inside Alex's head. "Have you finished with her?"

"You know I haven't," Alex bit out.

"Indeed, I do," came the harsh grumble. "What I am dying to know, if you'll pardon the expression, is why not? I told you time is of the essence." A burst of brilliant blue fire jagged its way through the blackness, striking the stone floor a few feet from Alex, testament to the Evil One's displeasure. A shower of azure flames erupted. Sparks flew. Alex flinched at the liquid fire that spewed at him, but he didn't step back.

"She must surrender herself willingly," Alex replied, his voice deadly calm, revealing none of the strange turmoil that raged within. "That takes time."

"Time we don't have," his master replied. "Go to her. Play your part, Alex, until you have her begging for you. Don't waste any more time. I won't brook any disobedience."

In the next instant, a jolt of electricity ripped through Alex. The pain was fleeting yet so intense it forced him to his knees, and it left him panting in the putrid air surrounding him.

"I won't have it," the Devil repeated, his voice rougher, more guttural. "Don't even think about defying me, Alex. Greater, more powerful spirits than yours have tried and failed. I can make you miserable." At Alex's pained smirk, the Evil One added, "*More* miserable than you already are. I can fire the lust in your veins . . . intensify the hunger, until you become nothing but a mindless slave to your appetite. More than you already are. You are my pawn, Alex. Accept what fate has given you, what gifts I have favored you with."

"You mean condemned me to."

"Oh, Alex. There are certainly worse fates—such as what I have in store for our dear Catherine."

"And what of Callie?"

"The innocent Catherine possesses?" The King of Evil's laughter rumbled through the hall. "She'll face the same fate as Catherine. They shall be one and the same, and they'll both suffer my punishment."

"But—" Alex started, but his voice died the moment he felt invisible fingers grip him. They squeezed.

"Don't disagree with me, Alex. I'll crush you and send you into the fire. Eternal damnation."

"You mean this isn't it?" Alex muttered once the pain subsided. His palms flat on his thighs, he tried to harness his energy and force himself back to his feet.

"You know the difference, Alex. There is no true suffering as one of my minions. Not like those other souls down in the pit. There is no true torment as one of the Devil's Own."

"Like hell there isn't."

"Most of my demons enjoy the roles they play. I must say you're an ungrateful bastard, Alex. I own you. If I were so inclined, I could have sent you into the pit instead of giving you so much power."

"You sought to *use* my power. That's why you didn't send me down then, and why you won't now."

"Au contraire, my naive friend. If you fail me this time, I don't care how powerful a sorcerer you were in life, or how vital your spirit. You *will* be cast down. Now, do as I command."

"I will," Alex agreed, hating himself as he consented. He should hate Catherine—Callie, too, reason told him. He did—hate Catherine, that is. If only he could hate Callie, as well.

"When?" the Evil One demanded.

"Soon."

"It had better be. You must move quickly or this project will be your last. I'll toss your spirit into the pit and devour that flesh-and-blood body you insist on occupying, and I'll enjoy each bloody bite. Understood?"

"Go to Hell," Alex hissed.

The Evil One's laughter rumbled all around, making the darkness tremble, the flames vibrate. "Oh, my boy. Since you seem so inclined to forget, let me give you a little reminder of what Hell is truly like."

The flames shifted, streaked toward Alex and circled him, like a pack of vultures moving in to pick clean his bones. Their heat engulfed him, severe, scorching. Alex gritted his teeth as his skin caught fire, melted, the stench of his burning flesh stifling. He clamped his lips together against a scream.

Serve me, Alex, a voice roared inside his head. Was it the Evil One, or his own damnable lust?

Touch her. Taste her. Spoil her. . . .

"Yes," Alex vowed, his voice a pained whisper.

The flames dissolved and cold of undeath again closed around him, extreme, biting, and he wondered if the flames weren't the lesser of the two tortures.

He closed his eyes, willed himself numb to the forces around him. The pain in his body subsided, and he opened his eyes. He ran his hands over his arms, his gaze sweeping the rest of his body where the flames had devoured his flawless flesh. Soon, not a trace of the Evil One's punishment lingered. He was whole once more, yet empty inside. The irony of it nearly made him laugh.

"Soon, Callie," Alex whispered, surprised at how easily her name rolled from his trembling lips. It should be Catherine he thought of. Catherine who was meant to be punished. Instead, he saw a pair of warm green eyes, felt the mixture of tenderness and hunger that had gripped her body when he'd touched his lips to hers. He heard the soft whisper of his name as she arched into an unseen lover in her dreams. He had been that lover.

Her image vanished as a roar of laughter deafened him, the sound like a mad hellhound shrieking through the bleak underworld. It reminded him that this task was his fate, regardless of the strange feelings he'd been having lately. He was a creature of the Underworld. And he had a job to do.

Out on her balcony, Callie pulled the ends of her blouse together and stared out over the treetops that blanketed the surrounding area. A breeze blew, making her shiver although her skin felt hot to the touch. She'd started off dreaming about her father, seeing her usual vision of him, but then Alex Daimon had appeared. He'd pulled her into his arms and . . .

Her face burned hotter. Memories of his touch, his kiss came flooding back. He'd touched her, kissed her places no man had ever even glimpsed. Worst of all, she'd enjoyed every caress. So much, she'd shed her own clothes in her sleep, she realized, glancing down at her bare legs, her open blouse. Hadn't she'd fallen asleep fully clothed?

She felt a shudder crawl through her, slightly ashamed as she was to be dreaming about a man she hardly knew. It was inappropriate, especially when so many other things clamored for her attention. Her father, the missing woman . . . There were things far more important than a much too vivid dream in which she'd been having much too good a time. Focused . . . She had to stay completely focused.

Well, at least her subconscious knew that she had to keep her focus. Surely that was why Alex Daimon had vanished and the black silhouette had materialized. The silhouette had started to choke her, and she'd forgotten her erotic dream as she fought for every breath. Surely the silhouette was her guilt.

She inhaled deeply and wiped at her watery eyes. This was what a person got for falling asleep when she should have been trying to help her father.

Callie started to turn, and her gaze slid past the nearby graveyard to the mansion silhouetted on its far side. The place seemed so dark, so lifeless against the full moon. No lights shone in the windows. The place stood empty. Dead. Callie fought back a shiver at the thought. She was letting her imagination get the best of her.

The house hadn't been recognizable before because the old mansion had been run-down while Callie had been growing up. No one had lived there. A thick wall of trees hid the house from the road, and warning signs kept trespassers away. And rumor kept the kids away.

She could still remember the stories about that house. Haunted, everyone said. Some people had even claimed to have seen the ghost. Callie had paid little attention. The house had never bothered her before—but then there had been two huge magnolia trees near her balcony, blocking her view.

The trees were gone, destroyed when Hurricane Ginny blew through. Now there was nothing to hinder her view. And Callie wished there were.

The house disturbed her. Standing there on the balcony, with the house staring back at her, the windows dark, like vacant eyes watching her, Callie's courage ebbed, became almost nonexistent.

She fought the feeling, steeled herself to do what she had to do.

Gripping the edges of her blouse together, she rushed back into her room. Flipping on the overhead light and both nightstand lamps, she grabbed the worn black book and went to her desk. She slid on her glasses then curled up in the high-backed leather chair, the book on her lap, and started turning pages. She drank in the text, her fingers trailing over the yellowed paper, searching as she'd been doing the past few days. She *would* see something, feel something that sparked her recognition.

The only thing she found, however, was a bone-weary exhaustion that made her limbs ache, her stomach cramp. Still, she stayed awake the entire night, reading.

Callie managed to stay awake all through the next day, through the usual Saturday hustle and bustle of the store, too. Customers came in and out. The cash register rang frequently.

Thank God she had Alice to help out, otherwise she would have gone out of her mind. As it was, the noise from the store distracted her from her reading. She almost closed the office door more than once, but a memory of her final dream stopped her. She still felt the fingers at her throat, her lungs barely able to drink in enough oxygen. Closing the door and confining herself to the office's small space was definitely out of the question.

A strange expectancy filled her as she searched the book, as if she stood on the verge of discovery. Then frustration would build when she failed to feel any familiarity with the words, and she realized she was as lost as ever. She stayed on edge throughout the day, her nerves frayed, afire with exhaustion. It made her want to scream in frustration, desperation, and defeat, but she didn't. She kept reading and hoping and searching, however futile it all seemed.

"Hey, Cal? You feel like catching a pizza with me?"

Callie glanced up at Alice. The young woman stood in the doorway, her brown hair pulled back in a ponytail, her dark eyes shining expectantly. "What happened to Roger?" Callie asked.

The girl shrugged and pushed a loose strand of hair behind her ear. Her eyes took on a faraway look that reached inside Callie to twist at her. "I told him another time."

"It's been over a year," Callie reminded her. "You're only nineteen, honey. You should be out having fun."

Alice looked up, her gaze locking with Callie's, begging for understanding. "I know. I just don't think I'm ready yet." At Callie's worried look, she attempted a smile. "I've kinda gotten used to being bruise-free."

The bruises *were* gone—the ones on the outside. But in Alice's eyes, Callie could see the marks on the girl's soul. Married at the tender age of sixteen, Alice had spent three years of her young life suffering at the hands of an alcoholic husband—one who thought smashing Alice's face against the kitchen doorknob was fitting punishment for accidentally serving him a lukewarm beer when he'd wanted an ice-cold one. The bastard would've killed her had some higher power not seen fit to wipe him off the face of the earth by sending a telephone pole crashing into his car while he was on his way home from some bar.

That had been saddest moment of Alice's young life, but Callie knew it had saved her life. Undoubtedly, she'd be dead by now if Jimmy Boudreaux wasn't. And she'd been helping the girl see that.

"Not all men are like Jimmy, Alice. I swear. There are some nice guys out there. Guys who don't use their fists to make a point."

The girl smiled, a sad expression that brought tears to Callie's eyes. "Maybe, but I don't think I'm up to putting that to the test just yet. So, how about it? You game for a fun-filled Saturday night with just us girls?"

"I'd love to, but I really need to get home. My father's waiting for me."

Alice shrugged and nodded. "No problem. *Casablanca*'s on tonight. I guess I'll see you tomorrow. You want me to lock the door?"

"Give me a minute and I'll walk out with you." Visions of the past night, of Alex Daimon and his disappearing act, flooded Callie's mind. The sun had already set and the last thing she felt like was being alone in the store. Alone anywhere, for that matter. She'd almost taken Alice up on her offer because of it—and because she didn't like to think of Alice alone on another Saturday night. But duty called, and the thought of pepperoni and cheese had made her stomach do an involuntary flip.

After seeing Alice to her Volkswagen parked out back, Callie tossed her black satchel onto the passenger's seat of her own car. Climbing in, she keyed the ignition, revved the engine and started her car into the flow of traffic down Toulouse, through the French Quarter, headed toward the freeway. She rolled her window down, settled back in her seat, and flipped on the radio. With the wind and the noise, she almost started to relax. Almost. Still, the expectancy remained, sitting in the pit of her stomach, refusing her any peace. Something was going to happen. She felt it.

A half hour later, Callie turned onto one of the winding roads that bypassed a handful of plantation homes, the last of which, situated near the end of the road, belonged to her family. Only a few of the houses she passed could be seen from the road; most were partially obscured by the huge trees that marked each property's edge. The trees grew thicker here, the darkness more encompassing. Callie flicked her headlights to high-beams, wondering why in the world the parish hadn't yet managed to put any streetlights in this area.

Then again, most of the houses were too far from the road to benefit from streetlights. These manor homes each had many outside lights; they didn't reach out to this isolated stretch of road. Strange. She'd driven this same stretch of road time and time again, during the day and late at night, and she'd never felt so uncomfortable before.

The street's darkness had never bothered her.

Even the abandoned mansion that bordered the cemetery adjacent to her family's property had never bothered her. But it did now. She pressed the gas harder when she neared the desolate plantation she'd seen last night, the place from which Alex had called to her. Thick moss-covered oaks lined the road, fortunately blocking most of the dilapidated shell from her view. She wondered if—

The car sputtered, then died, and Callie braked to a stop. Turning the key, she listened to the click. Once, twice . . . Dead.

What on earth? She glanced at the gas gauge. It was full. The glow of her headlights assured her it wasn't the car's battery either. She tried the ignition again. And again. Nothing.

"Unreliable piece of junk," she mumbled, slamming her palm against the steering wheel. She sat for what seemed like an eternity, staring at the darkened road ahead. Her headlights cast shimmering rays into the blackness. She contemplated the distance home. A few more yards, and she would probably be able to see the porch lights through the tangle of tree branches.

A creak of rusty hinges drifted on the night breeze, and Callie glanced over at the sign marking the cemetery. It was close. Her home was just on the other side.

Callie flicked her car's headlights off, opened the door, then climbed from the seat. With her satchel slung over one shoulder and her purse in a death grip, she started out. Darkness closed around her and she walked faster, her heels tapping a steady click against the pavement.

After she'd gone a few feet, she spotted the cemetery's iron gate peeking through an army of thick trees. She trudged on, her footsteps a steady echo. Then she heard something else. A sound. Another's footstep. She stopped and strained to hear.

Nothing now. Fear rippled up her spine. The hair on her nape stood on end. She felt a presence, even before she turned around. Even before she heard his voice.

"It's a little late to be out walking."

Callie whirled, bumping into a man who stood directly behind her, close enough so that she felt the warm brush of his breath on her face, the raw strength of his body only a fraction from her own.

The heat . . . it started in her hands, rushed to every nerve ending and clouded her senses. Alex Daimon's face became a dark blur, and she heard nothing save her breathing and the insistent thud of her heart.

Chapter Six

"Callie?" She heard Alex's voice through the fog.

Strong hands gripped her shoulders, their touch pleasantly cool. The sensation made her want to press herself against Alex and put out the flames engulfing her, but she couldn't move. She could barely breathe.

"Callie, what's wrong?"

"N—nothing," she managed, touching a hand to her temple, willing the ground to stop shaking, and the heat to lessen. She felt faint, and suddenly she was sinking to her knees, her legs too weak to hold her. Her hands were on fire and she stared at them, expecting to see flames. Surely she was being consumed! She saw nothing, however—even though her flesh tingled and her hands burned. They were unbearably hot. . . .

A massive pair of arms closed around her, and Callie felt herself lifted. Oblivion descended and she was suddenly left to wonder if she'd only imagined the icy fear in her stomach, or the woman's voice inside her head screaming, *He can't win. Fight him. Fight him!*

Callie opened her mouth but felt the press of Alex Daimon's cool fingers to her lips.

"Ssshhh," he murmured. "Rest in my arms, Callie. Just take it easy and rest." And as much as she wanted to fight, she was too tired, her mind exhausted, her body so weary, weighing her down, drawing her into the blackness, until she ceased to feel the dreaded heat.

Peace, cool and so very soothing, drifted through her body, almost as if she'd fallen into a deep slumber. But she couldn't be sleeping; she didn't see any visions—not her father, the missing woman or the black silhouette. And the visions always came with sleep. Always.

She heard the smooth rumble of Alex Daimon's voice, felt the comfort of his arms and a strange familiarity, as if she'd been cradled by him before. Oddly enough, as much as the feeling unnerved her, it gave comfort, as well.

The comfort she needed, if only for a few blessed moments.

Wind whispered over Callie's bare arms, prickling her skin, pulling her from oblivion. Another gust of wind and she shivered, forcing her eyes open.

A single candle burned, its flame flickering, pushing back the shadows just enough for Callie to see the four-poster bed upon which she lay, the blankets bunched at her ankles, her denim skirt hiked up to her thighs.

She bolted upright and pushed the material down, her gaze darting around the strange room, searching. . . .

The wind whipped at nearby floor-length velvet drapes, whooshed past into the room and licked at the candle flame. Shadows danced across the walls and Callie hugged her arms tighter, not so much from the breeze, but from an unnatural chill in the air. Where was she?

Rest. . . . Alex Daimon's voice echoed in her ears. He'd caught her before she'd hit the ground. He'd held her, protected her.

He'd banished the heat, too, she remembered. She'd been on fire. Burning. Melting. Then Alex was there, his touch cool, his voice soothing, like a blessed rain shower in the dry heat of summer.

Callie gazed about at her surroundings. This bedroom was straight out of an antique dealer's shop. A scallop-topped cherry wood armoire sat against the opposite wall. A china washbowl and basin graced the top of a small table in one corner. The bed's hand-carved posters gleamed brown lustre, the knobs sculpted into dragon's heads. A sheer fabric of the palest yellow swathed the canopy and spilled onto the floor.

Crawling across the crisp linen sheets, Callie swung her legs over the side of the bed, her feet touching a very expensive-looking rug, a delicate weave of yellow hues that matched the bedsheets and canopy.

Her shoes had been placed nearby. She pushed her feet into the black flats, her attention going to her worn satchel on the floor near the nightstand. Panic surged through her and she grabbed the bag. Rummaging inside, she breathed a sigh of relief the moment her hand brushed the worn leather book. She'd gone through way too much to find it to have someone steal it away. Not that Alex would. He didn't seem like a thief. But then, she knew nothing of the man—other than the fact that he was a very experienced kisser.

He could be a thief.

Or worse—she remembered her skirt pushed up to her thighs. He could be a . . .

Nonsense! reason argued. Callie remembered the comfort of his words and the protection of his embrace and instantly dismissed the notion. Alex had kept her from collapsing on the street. She should be grateful. She'd undoubtedly kicked off the covers while she'd been passed out. Obviously, her skirt had worked its way up her legs when she'd tossed and turned in her sleep. Her thoughts went to the previous night when she'd awakened to find her blouse unbuttoned, her jeans in a heap on the floor. It had been her own doing then, too, hadn't it?

Besides, had Alex Daimon wanted to take advantage of her, he certainly could have done so already. She'd just been dead to the world. He could have done a lot more than just look at her bare legs. So much more . . .

She closed her eyes at the wicked thought, unable to keep herself from imagining what it would be like to be touched by the man. *Really* touched.

Her breath caught as she felt the play of fingertips near her ankle. Her eyes snapped open, only to drift shut when she realized that no one was there. Her imagination, she concluded, though her skin still tingled from the contact.

Contact? There'd been no contact. Only her stupid libido playing dangerous games with her peace of mind. A game that still wasn't over.

Callie leaned back into the bed's soft pillows, her back arching as she felt the velvety fingertips on her calf. Soft, purposeful strokes suddenly had her lips parting, her breath coming in short gasps.

Delicious was the word that came to mind. Alex's touch would be delicious, even more than she had imagined. It would move higher, up over her kneecap, up the inside of her thigh, until he touched the part of her that ached for him—

Callie's eyes snapped open, and the sensation dissolved. She wiped the beads of sweat lining her forehead and damned herself for having such a vivid imagination. What was wrong with her? This was a stranger she was fantasizing about. Granted, he was a good-looking stranger, but a stranger nonetheless. *A dangerous one,* a voice whispered in her head.

So why did she have the inexplicable urge to crawl back into his bed, to burrow beneath its cool linen sheets and indulge herself in a dream like she'd had last night before her guilty conscience had intruded? That dream that had seemed as real as the hands stroking her only moments before. Perhaps it was because this room felt so familiar, as if she'd been here before. As if she belonged here now.

And Alex Daimon . . . Well, he felt much too familiar as well, and his embrace felt much too good.

She was losing her mind, she decided. She had to be. That could be the only explanation for her crazy feelings. Familiar, indeed. Callie had never met the man before finding him in her bookstore, and here she was dreaming about him. *Wanting* him. She was definitely having a nervous breakdown—one she didn't have time for. She had her father to think of. He and Burgess were probably worried sick about her.

"Hello?" she called out. There was no answer. She strained her ears, but she heard nothing except an occasional gust of wind, a rustle of the drapes, the beat of her own heart like a drum inside her head. "Mr. Daimon?"

Surely he wouldn't have left her alone in his home? He didn't know her any more than she knew him. Yet no one answered her call. There came no sound, save the wind, disrupting the eerie quiet. Callie moved to the doorway, then a slow creak found its way into the room and she stopped.

The sound persisted and she crossed the room to the window. Pushing the drapes aside, she stared down and out over Drashierre Cemetery, to Wisdom House on the other side. Fear gripped her then as she realized where she was—the abandoned mansion that had stared at her last night with its empty, lifeless windows.

She shook her head. It couldn't be! She had imagined him here, but . . . Another glance around the expensively furnished room showed everything to be immaculate, without even a trace of dust. Her fear magnified. Something was definitely wrong. This house had always been empty!

Callie rushed back across the room and snatched up her satchel and purse. She yanked open the door and hurried into the hallway. Fear and regret swirled together in her to make her hands tremble. A furious gust snuffed out the candle flame and slammed the door shut behind her, pushing her into the thickest, most stifling darkness she'd ever encountered, as if she'd been thrust into a pit with no light and no salvation. No hope.

Forcing herself to take a deep breath, Callie tried to calm her pounding heart. "Mr. Daimon?" she called out. There was no answer, except her own voice echoing through the massive hallway. Okay, so Alex Daimon had disappeared again, this time leaving her in an abandoned house that looked anything but. So what?

She would find her way out, then go home to her father. To hell with her savior if he didn't have the courtesy to stick around.

Her mind made up, Callie felt her way down the hall, her hands trailing against the smooth wall. Slowly, her eyes adjusted to the darkness. She discerned several closed doors on the opposite side of the hallway, the carved wood molding bordering the ceiling, the lifeless wall sconces.

Callie rounded a corner and caught her first glimpse of light. Hurrying, she reached the end of the corridor. A winding staircase led to a marble-floored foyer below. A warm yellow glow drifted from a room off to one side, its door wide open. So he hadn't abandoned her after all.

The moment she saw the shadow pass in front of the door, Callie had a wild urge to bound down the stairs and race for the front double doors. But Daimon would undoubtedly see her. That possibility made her hesitant, nervous, *scared*.

Scared? She shouldn't be scared. She should be grateful that he'd kept her from passing out in the middle of the street, in the middle of the night. She should be very grateful.

She was, she told herself, ignoring the voices that whispered otherwise. Squaring her shoulders, she reached for the banister. She would march down to the room, thank him for his kindness, and then say goodbye. Simple—

"I see you're awake."

Callie jerked around at the sound of his voice, her hand going to her chest. Her satchel thudded at her feet. Air bolted from her lungs as she stared up into the expressionless and much too handsome face of Alex Daimon.

"You scared the daylights out of me," she gasped, taking a deep gulp of air. "How did you get up here . . . ?" Her voice faded. She glanced back down the stairs at the light spilling into the foyer. She'd seen his shadow not more than a minute ago. *Downstairs*. Hadn't she?

Her gaze darted back to him. Her mind had to be playing tricks. There had to be someone else downstairs, for Alex was standing on the stairstep above hers. And she hadn't even heard his approach, as if he'd materialized from the darkness.

At that moment, he seemed a part of it, his hair such a deep brown, almost black. His onyx eyes were fired with gold flecks; his gaze drilled into her with an intensity that made her swallow and forget all about shadows and darkness—everything save the man standing so close to her.

"Is something wrong?" he asked, his voice deep and rich, sliding into her ears to wind through her body and tease her senses.

"No," she replied. "I—I just thought you were downstairs. It must have been someone else."

He stared beyond her. "There's no one else here. Only us." He eased past her down the stairs, then paused to grasp her hand and tug her with him. "But we can check to be sure."

"No one in here," he said as he led her down to the room she'd seen, aglow as it was with candlelight. Several candelabras had been placed at strategic points throughout the chamber—one on the fireplace mantel, one on the grand piano in one corner, another beside an exquisite cherry-wood divan near the far side of the room. "Maybe you only imagined it," he said, turning to face her. "I bet you have quite an imagination."

It wasn't so much the statement that made her

cheeks flame, but the knowing gleam in his dark eyes. She could still feel the purposeful stroking of those imaginary fingers up her calf, her thigh, and higher still. . . .

Reining in her thoughts, she cleared her suddenly dry throat. "Uh, maybe it *was* my imagination."

"Are you feeling better?"

"Much," she replied, grateful for the change of subject. "I should say thanks. If it wasn't for you, I'd be passed out on the pavement right now."

"I'm glad I was there."

She gathered her courage and leveled a stare at him, a swirl of questions whirling in her head. "What were you doing there, Mr. Daimon?"

"Taking a walk," he replied easily. His mouth curved into a delicious smile that did dangerous things to her blood pressure. Her courage faltered, but she fought for every ounce, determined to keep her wits about her, to get some answers.

"In this neighborhood?" she asked. "There's nothing out here except private plantations. Unless you live nearby—"

"I do."

"The families that live up and down this road have been here for years. I know all of them. Unless . . ." The sentence trailed off as another possibility struck her. "Here?" But she knew the answer even before he nodded.

His smile vanished. His eyes burned a brighter gold, and Callie yearned to look away, to break eye contact, but she couldn't. Far greater than her desire to maintain her sanity was a strange need to see him, to feel the intensity that surrounded this man.

"I thought this place was vacant. How long have you lived here?"

"A long, long time, Callie."

"But the outside looks so run-down, and the yard is overgrown. And—"

"Obviously the house isn't abandoned." With a sweeping gesture, Daimon indicated the room's lavish furnishings. "My home is very well kept. I'm sorry if outside appearances had you fooled. It's my own fault. I like my privacy."

"But I've never seen any lights."

"So, you've been keeping an eye on this place?" One dark brow slid upward.

"I can see it from my balcony."

"Tell me what you've seen."

"Nothing. Absolutely nothing. That's why I thought no one lived here."

"Had I known you were looking, I would've given you an eyeful, Ms. Wisdom. Funny, but I never pegged you for the—" He stopped himself and she knew he'd meant to say nosey. Instead, he finished "—*curious* sort." His voice held a teasing note, and his mouth curved into an enticing grin.

Callie's heartbeat skidded to a halt, then pounded on, louder, more insistent. Heat crept into her cheeks. "You make me sound like a Peeping Tom or something."

"Are you?"

"Of course not," she replied. Then they plunged into a dead, almost spellbinding silence where he simply watched her with those fabulous eyes—eyes that held so many secrets and stirred so many unspeakable things Callie couldn't begin to explain. She could only feel, and Alex Daimon made her very warm in all the wrong places, positively uncomfortable.

After an endless moment, she cleared her throat and searched for something—anything—to say. "I knew I'd seen you somewhere before. You've lived here a long time, you say?"

"Too many years to count."

Callie glanced at the portrait hanging above the white marble mantel of the fireplace. Alex Daimon seemed to stare back at her, the painting almost as real as the man standing beside her. It was so real and lifelike it unnerved her. And the clothes . . .

She did a double-take, and found herself staring at Alex Daimon pictured as she'd seen him the other night for those few strange moments when he'd been wearing the flowing white shirt with the strange insignia, the black breeches, the black knee boots.

"Are you sure you're all right? You look extremely pale." Alex's hand moved to her forehead, his touch cool, dispelling her fear, easing her worries.

"Fine," she murmured, her lips suddenly thick. "Just an aftershock from passing out, I guess." And from seeing the portrait, she added silently. Then, of course, there was the man standing next to her, his shoulder so close one slight movement and he would be touching her again. "A very good likeness of you," she said, turning back to him, careful to keep an inch of blessed space between them. "The artist must have been a genius."

"Genius, indeed," Alex retorted, his words fueled with a bitterness that didn't go unnoticed. "It's my grandfather," he said, as if he sensed her discomfort at the uncanny resemblance. "All the Daimon men look alike."

"Ah," she said.

"You look tired," Daimon said. "Why don't you sit down?"

Callie shook her head. "I have to get home. My father is waiting for me." His image pushed its way to the forefront of her mind. Urgency filled her. Yes, she had to get home. Soon. She had so little time left to help. . . .

"Surely you can spare a few moments to sit down and gather your strength. You're only five minutes away from home."

"Why didn't you tell me we were neighbors when you came into my bookstore?" The question tumbled from her lips, her gaze snapping up to search his.

"Like I said before, I like my privacy."

His curt reply, like a freezing wind, surrounded her. She stiffened. "Of course. Sorry to trouble you. I'll be going—"

"*No.*" As he clasped her hands in his, all thoughts of Callie's father vanished and she saw only Alex Daimon.

He blurred, then focused, then blurred again. She blinked and found herself staring at the man from the portrait. But he wasn't paint and canvas. He was real, and standing right in front of her, the soft folds of his white shirt brushing her arm where he held her hands, the crimson insignia so close she could see the tiny lines of painstaking embroidery.

Alex.

"You're trembling, Callie. Are you cold?"

She wasn't cold. Terrified was a much more accurate description—especially as he bent his head, his lips murmuring against hers, "Let me warm you." Then his mouth captured hers.

Heat unfurled inside her, chasing all fear and rational thought from her mind. Time stopped. Callie's reality became the feel of strong muscle, fierce hunger, and a desperate need to touch and be touched.

She didn't give another thought to the strange things she'd seen, nor did she see any more visions of her father. Her senses blazed to life, thrived, pulsed at the nearness of Alex. He incited such an incredible heat inside her, it wasn't enough to simply be kissed. She felt compelled to return that kiss and revel in it. Without hesitation, she eased her arms around his neck.

In doing so, she wasn't sure whether she surrendered to him or herself. But when she kissed him, oddly enough she felt like she was the victor.

Chapter Seven

Callie found herself pulled into Alex's embrace. His arms locked about her waist, his strong hands insistent at the small of her back. His lips were satin fire against her, his tongue delving into her mouth with an intoxicating persuasiveness to stroke and caress until he seemed to become a part of her—a part of her that felt so good, so right. . . .

She tangled her fingers in the silky hair at his nape. He was a cool stream on a hot day. She drank from him, letting his touch soothe her senses and set her ablaze at the very same time. His hands moved up and down her spine, softening her, fitting her against him.

They fit so well together. Her breasts pressed eagerly against the muscled perfection of his chest, her thighs pushed flush against his. The proof of his desire probed the softness of her abdomen to send tiny electric shocks through her body, leaving no doubt in her mind as to the extent of his arousal.

She knew he was on fire for her, yet oddly enough his fingertips were cool against her jaw as he swept her hair aside. She arched her neck, giving him free access to the smooth flesh there. He tore his lips from hers to kiss a path down the column of her throat to the pulse at the base. Her blood raced, throbbed beneath the caress of his lips which spread liquid fire over her skin like flame over gasoline.

He trailed long, lean fingers over her collarbone. Lower, over the fine silk of her blouse to trace the swell of one breast through the fabric. She gasped, sucking in a quick breath when he moved to her cleavage, the cool pad of his finger welcome on her feverish skin.

She opened her eyes to gaze up at him. Candlelight reflected off the dark brown hair that framed his face. The flames cast dancing shadows across the perfect planes of his jaw.

Too perfect. The thought was fleeting; it stirred only a moment of unease that quickly dissolved as his stare captured hers.

The gold flecks in his eyes caught the light, glittered brighter, a dazzle of stars against a velvet black sky. Heat crept up her neck. The only contact they had at that moment was his hand at her waist and the other at the hollow between her breasts, yet he surrounded her. His raw strength, like a potent aphrodisiac, enfolded her, pushed its way inside until she could see nothing save him. Smell nothing save him. Feel nothing save him—and the strange ache between her thighs.

He swept a glance downward and her nipples hardened. Her breasts throbbed and strained against the lace of her bra. His attention went from her chest, back up her neck, to linger at her lips, and she craved another taste of him. Then their gazes met and she saw the raw hunger simmering in the now golden pools of his eyes.

A delicious expectancy settled in the pit of her stomach. Nervously she licked her lips, waiting, anticipating. He smiled, as if he understood what she wanted. But he didn't seem ready to appease her. Not yet. His stare burned a path back down her neck to the opening of her blouse, and she could have sworn she stopped breathing altogether.

Almost of their own accord, her hands moved to the buttons on her shirt. One by one, she slipped them from their openings until the garment hung open. She slid the silk aside to allow Alex's searing gaze a glimpse of the flesh beneath. She struggled for a breath, suddenly desperate for air.

Not because of anticipation.

Nor relief.

Oddly enough, her reaction came from a deeply buried fear, one he stirred to life with his touch. A shiver worked its way through Callie's body and the urge to grasp her blouse and cover herself was nearly overwhelming. Yet her arms were now dead weight at her sides, as if Alex commanded her acquiescence just as he'd commanded her blouse to open.

Callie's body screamed in desire, responding to Alex's nearness, yet her mind fought against him. It wasn't because he was a stranger taking such intimate liberties with her, she knew, but more because of the man himself. He seemed more than a man, with eyes that set her blood ablaze and frightened the daylights out of her at the very same time. The man stirred her fear as easily as her desire and he was bent on possessing her. And that made her fight.

"Beautiful," he murmured, flicking the front clasp of her bra open. He shoved the cups aside to touch one soft pink nipple.

Callie flinched, wanting to lean away from this unnerving, and oh-so-dangerously delicious touch, but she couldn't. His gaze held her immobile, entranced.

She breathed in and out, her chest rising and falling as she sucked for air. He coaxed her nipple with his finger, watching it plump into a taut, quivering wine-colored peak. His gaze gleamed brighter, taking on a wild light until he looked ready to devour her.

When he leaned down and flicked his tongue over her breast's sensitive tip, Callie's lips parted and she managed one word: "No."

He didn't heed her protest. "Yes," he breathed as he drew the swollen bud into his mouth and suckled, grazing the tender flesh of her breast with his teeth. He sucked harder, the heat of his mouth sending jolts of electricity through her body, chasing away all fear. Desire pummelled Callie's senses, so keen she thought surely she would die if he stopped.

She closed her eyes and would have slumped to the floor had he not held her. Both his hands claimed her back now, urging her breast into his greedy mouth. His touch was no longer soothing. His fingertips burned into her, like hot brands that sent waves of heat rushing through her to feed the fire between her thighs. It burned so deliciously hot.

She clutched at the carved perfection of his biceps and willingly arched her back, letting the sensations that Alex Daimon stirred override all else.

Then she felt the cold silver of her perfume flask as it slid from outside her blouse to dangle against her flushed skin. The touch brought her eyes open, not to the dim candlelit library or the man so ardently suckling her. Instead, she opened her eyes to her father's image, his lifeless eyes, the blood dripping down his face. And then she heard her father's voice—*"Callie!"*—and sanity returned like a bolt of lightning.

"Daddy!" she cried, pushing at Alex with a strength that seemed to surprise him.

His head snapped up, and he left off his suckling her breast. His gaze drilled into her with nothing short of murderous intent.

"I—I have to go," she stammered. "Please—I have to." She pushed at him, but his arms were like steel bands.

His eyes blazed hotter, the gold flecks brighter, and she thought he meant to kiss her again, no matter how much she resisted.

Fear knifed through her, of him and herself,

quelling her desire. All at once, she realized the gravity of her situation. She was half-dressed in the arms of a stranger and she liked it. And this man *was* a stranger, she told herself, ignoring the voice that tried to scream otherwise. How could she have let herself get into such a predicament? Because she was stupid, gullible, and crazed with lust, and now she would pay. . . .

Her thoughts scattered when Alex released her. It was with a suddenness that sent her reeling backwards, and she grappled for the dangling ends of her blouse, jerking the material in front of her, all the while keeping her gaze fixed on him.

"I'll walk you home," he snapped and she heard his anger, saw it in the taut muscles of his neck, his arms bulging beneath his black silk shirt. But there was more than just anger battling inside of him.

She stared into Alex Daimon's eyes, and what she saw there disturbed her even more than her brazen surrender to him. Regret gleamed back at her. Oddly, she felt she shared the emotion. When he turned away from her, she felt an inexplicable loss so profound, she had to struggle for a breath.

No more understandably than why she'd given in to him in the first place, she stepped forward now, her hand going to his shoulder, her lips trembling as she formed the words, "I—Alex, I'm sorry. I just have to go." She didn't know why she apologized. He'd been the one bent on seduction, taking advantage of her, yet it had felt anything but that. She'd encouraged him. She'd wanted him. . . . Truth be known, she still did—so much that her legs quivered, her breasts throbbed, her nerves screamed. . . .

Tears welled in her eyes. "I—" she started, only to feel the first few drops slide down her cheeks.

He glanced at her, a startled look on his face.

"Sorry," she murmured, dashing away at the tears that kept coming. "I didn't mean to cry. . . ." Her words faded at the strange look he gave her, as if he felt her sorrow, her frustration, her confusion.

His expression was one she didn't have time to further contemplate. In the next instant, he was beside her, wiping away her tears, cradling her in arms that had sought only to possess her moments before. In the blink of an eye he went from lover to comforter, and Callie needed a comforter. Her mind craved comfort, almost as much as her body craved him.

"I'm here," he whispered. "Tell me what makes you so sad, sweet Callie. Tell me. . . ."

Callie found herself transported back into her dreams, to the first time he'd appeared, in her dreams. Alex felt just as she remembered: strong, virile, possessive. She leaned into him, compelled to take what he offered, her fear a forgotten memory next to the enormity of the future. "My father," she said. "I—I have to get home. He's . . . ill." Her tears flowed faster, freer. "He's dying." There, she'd said it, and it felt as awful as she'd always known it would. Awful and hopeless, the truth weighed heavily on her. But Alex Daimon was there to lift the burden.

"I lost my own father," he told her, his fingers smoothing her hair, his words soothing her soul. "I

149

was young, barely thirteen. I know it hurts. . . ."

"But I don't *have* to lose him," she whispered into the curve of his neck, misery and despair overriding reason that screamed for her to pull away and get the hell out of there. As much as she knew she ought to leave this house, to leave Alex, she wanted to stay. Maybe more, because she couldn't bring herself to give up the one place of solace she'd found over the past few months.

"I—I can help him," she went on, her lips brushing the smooth skin of his neck. She tasted the salt of her own tears. "I know it sounds crazy, but I can really help him. I'm trying to, God knows I am."

"We all do what we can, Callie. You love him. I'm sure you're doing everything you know how—"

"That's not enough," she cried. "I can't simply *try* to help him. I have to *do* it. I can't stand by while he gets worse, not when I might learn how to stop it." The admission about the book was there on the tip of her tongue, but she couldn't make the words form. He would really think she'd gone over the edge. Then again, he just might believe her. That possibility frightened her too—and she didn't want to be frightened anymore. "I—I just have to save him. I have to do more."

"Don't be so hard on yourself. There are things we have no control over. Life. Death. When we're young, we think we're immortal, but death is always there, waiting to snatch us up." He sounded almost bitter as he said those words, and she wondered what misery life had dealt him. Surely nothing as awful as what she faced.

"It doesn't have to be that way for my father."

"Everyone must face death sooner or later."

Callie pulled away enough to look up at him and see the turmoil brewing in his eyes. "You don't get it, Alex Daimon. Then again, how could you? You don't know me, my father, or our situation. You haven't the foggiest idea what I'm really talking about. You just don't know—"

"I know *you*, Callie. Better than you think." As he held her gaze with the same breathless intensity that reached out and gripped her soul, she knew he spoke the truth. Somehow, she and Alex Daimon were linked by more than a kiss, an embrace. They shared something else. She didn't know what, but she knew it as surely as she knew her father would die unless she found and reversed the spell that Catherine Drashierre had cast.

"We do know each other—" she started, only to hear his voice.

"You can't change fate or challenge death."

She stared deep into his eyes. "But I can, Alex. I can challenge death. Defeat it. I can *really* help my father. More than just being by his side to comfort him and see to his needs. I can *save* him. Can you understand that? I hold his life right here." She held up her hands and stared at them. Only she didn't see pale white fingers. She saw her father. "I feel his life slipping through my fingers, away from me, and the whole time I know I can stop it. I know I can, yet the answer is just out of my reach. So close, but so far . . ." Her voice broke and she buried her face in her hands, giving in to another bout of tears.

"Please don't cry," came his desperate plea a moment before his arms came around her again. "Please." The word seemed filled with despair almost as great as what Callie felt. For him she fought back her sobbing, but as much as she willed the tears away, they fell anyway. She couldn't stop their neverending flow.

Alex Daimon could. She felt his lips at her temple, his hands smoothing her hair. Slowly a peace drifted over her. Her sobs turned to sniffles, and then the faint sounds were lost altogether in the steady murmur of his voice. Callie did her best to discern his words, but she couldn't. The syllables ran together, indistinguishable. Not that it mattered. Whatever he said, she felt comforted. She felt it in his touch, in the numbing serenity that settled over her.

Once again, Callie found herself succumbing to the blackness while cradled in Alex Daimon's arms. She no longer thought him a stranger. They were linked, somehow, some way. If only she knew, for it was the not knowing that kept the seed of fear deep inside of her, made her regret the comfort of his embrace and wonder if she would ever wake up again.

If she did, would she find a stranger, a comforter, or a lover beside her? At this moment, she couldn't decide which she wanted—no, which she *needed*—the most.

Then he caught her nipple in his hot mouth, and Callie forgot everything save the lust burning through her body.

Chapter Eight

"Miss Callie?" She heard Burgess's concerned voice, followed by a slight nudge of her shoulder. "Wake up, Miss Callie. Please."

Callie's eyes fluttered open to find the butler leaning over her, worry evident in both his wrinkled forehead and his glimmering eyes.

"Praise be!" he exclaimed. "I was beginning to wonder if I should call the doctor back out here. That Daimon fella said no, but—"

"Alex Daimon?" she asked, struggling to her elbows. She darted a glance around her bedroom. It was empty, the corners a gathering of shadows beyond the reach of her bedside lamp.

"Yes. Alex Daimon was his name. Nice fella. I had the phone in my hand, ready to call and file a missing-persons report on you, when he knocked on the door with you in hand. Do you know what time it is?"

"He knocked on the door?" She willed the fuzziness away and tried to focus on the past few hours. Her stalled car. Alex's help. The abandoned plantation house that had turned out not to be abandoned at all. Her brazen surrender in Alex's arms . . .

"Yes. Awful nice fella. He said he found you a few blocks away. Said you had car trouble and decided to walk. He figured that the heat must have done you in because you passed clean out on the side of the road a few feet from the car, which is where he came across you. I knew you weren't eating enough," Burgess accused. "What did you have for lunch?"

"I—I don't remember. Where did Mr. Daimon go?"

"Nowhere. He's downstairs. You've only been here about fifteen minutes. He loaded you back into the car, fixed whatever it was that stalled that unreliable piece of junk and drove you home. I offered him something for his trouble, but he refused. He said he would wait around to see how you were."

Downstairs? Callie's heart catapulted. She could still feel the heat of his mouth, see the hunger in his eyes. She was grateful that he'd left their little encounter out of the story he'd told Burgess.

". . . call Dr. Broussard," Burgess was saying. "You still look extremely pale."

She said another silent thank-you. As hot as she felt, she was surprised her face wasn't flaming red, with the words 'woman in heat' branded across her forehead. What the hell had gotten into her? "Forget Dr. Broussard, Burgess. I'm fine. I—I didn't have any lunch at all. I'm sure that's what caused the fainting spell."

The *first* fainting spell, she silently corrected. The one she'd had before she'd regained consciousness in Alex's home. Before she'd thrown herself at him in a totally uncharacteristic display of lust. Before she'd burst into a fit of uncontrollable tears.

Callie knew she hadn't passed out in his arms when she'd been crying over her father. Something else had happened. Something strange, disturbing, as if Alex Daimon had willed her unconscious with the brush of his fingers against her skin, the softly murmured words she still couldn't recall.

"I told him I could call him, but he insisted on seeing you first thing when you woke up. That man's a determined one."

Callie shook away the disturbing thoughts to concentrate on Burgess. "I'm sorry, what did you say?"

"I said Mr. Daimon insisted on waiting downstairs." The butler's frown deepened. "Maybe I ought to take you into the city, to the hospital. You're not acting like yourself—"

"No," Callie cut in. "I'm fine, Burgess. Just tired, that's all. Tell Mr. Daimon I appreciate his kindness, but I'll talk to him another time. Please, Burgess. I really don't feel up to seeing anyone right now."

"All right," the butler agreed after a moment. "I'll be back in a few minutes."

A few minutes turned into many as Callie tried to calm her frantically beating heart. If only she could forget Alex's kiss, his touch, the strange excitement he stirred inside her. Strange, indeed, and frightening, for no man had ever affected her in such a way.

She tried to banish his face from her mind, but she couldn't. No, when she closed her eyes she saw deep brown irises, gold-flecked, and she felt Alex as keenly as if he were standing right next to her.

He did the most inexplicable things to her. He made her throw all rational thought to the wind. With one glance he could make her burn with lust. Never in her entire life had she ever undressed for a man, not the way she'd undressed for him. And never had she ever wanted anyone the way she'd wanted him. The way she still wanted him.

"You really should let me call the doctor, Miss Callie." It was Burgess again, the frown still creasing his face as he eyed her from the doorway where he stood with a large platter in his hands. "This food will help, but I'm not so sure the fainting was caused by hunger." He placed the plate on her desk and turned back to her. "I'd feel better with a professional opinion. I'm sure your father would, too. He was beside himself with worry."

The mention of her father forced Callie upright. She pushed the bedcovers aside, her hands trembling, her body shaking. She felt so cold. . . . Hearing her father's voice would warm her, reassure her that he was alive and well—that she still had time to save him. "Is he in his room?" she asked, straightening her skirt. She made her way somewhat unsteadily into the hallway. Burgess followed on her heels.

"Yes, and I didn't tell him you passed out. Only that you had car trouble. If he knew you'd fainted . . ."

"Thanks, Burgess. I owe you one. Daddy?" She moved into her father's room, crossing the distance to him. He sat in an overstuffed velour chair near a lifeless fireplace.

"Callie? My God, I was worried sick!" He held out his arms, his vacant eyes searching in the direction of her voice.

She moved into his embrace, returning the fierce hug he gave her. "It's all right, Daddy. I just had a little car trouble. The blasted thing overheated or something."

"To think you were out walking alone in the middle of the night. You're too young, and so pretty—"

"One of my customers at the bookstore lives nearby. He recognized me and gave me a hand with the car."

"Thank God. First thing tomorrow, have Burgess haul that car to a mechanic. I don't want this happening again. I never should've bought that flashy, computerized sports car. An older, more reliable car—that's what I should've gotten for you."

"Stop it, Daddy. My car is usually very reliable. With this awful heat lately, I'm not surprised it got a little hot."

He shook his head. "No, we have to be sure you're not stranded again." His voice was urgent. "My God, I didn't know what to do, Callie. I was sitting here, useless, while you were out walking in the middle of the night, with God knows what lurking about. You could have been attacked and there was nothing I could do. *Nothing!*" Tears rolled down his cheeks.

Callie held him, feeling his helplessness, and his revulsion for himself because of that helplessness. He'd always been so self-sufficient. So strong . . .

"Daddy, no. You can't watch out for me every second. I'm a grown woman, and things happen. The point is, I'm here now, so you don't have to worry anymore." She gave him a quick squeeze and pulled away to gaze into his face.

"I'm useless. I can't even help my own daughter." He lifted a visibly shaky hand to wipe at his tears. "Look how low I've sunk, crying like a baby when my baby girl needs me."

"Please, Daddy. You were always there for me. Now it's my turn."

"But you shouldn't be stuck with a sick old man. You should be out having fun."

"Dad, I'm an accountant. We don't have fun." The words brought a smile to her father's lips, but she could still see the turmoil in his expression. "It's late. Why don't you get some sleep?" Nodding, he let her lead him toward the bed.

"Sleep tight," she said, her voice louder than usual. He didn't seem to hear. The moment his head touched the pillow, his eyes closed.

Callie felt a scalding tear slide down her cheek. She smoothed the edge of the blanket and let her hand linger on her father's. He didn't feel the touch, didn't hear her whispered, "I love you."

Sleep had claimed him, just as death soon would.

Another tear wended a path down Callie's face. Then another and another . . .

"Don't cry, Callie." Alex Daimon's voice slid, so deep and intoxicating, into her ears. She jerked around to find him standing in the doorway.

"You're still here? But I told Burgess to—"

"Get rid of me?" He cocked one dark brow at her, his lips curving into a slow grin, his eyes obsidian. No gold fire burned in the depths, now. She saw only darkness, felt the fear of the night as his gaze drilled into hers. She slipped past him into the hallway.

"No—of course not. I told him to extend my thanks to you. I was tired and I didn't have the energy to tell you myself."

"The energy, or the courage?" He stepped forward, closing the distance until he stood a dangerous inch away.

"The energy," she stated, knowing she lied even as the words slipped from her lips. "About what happened," she started, only to have him press the cool pads of his fingers to her lips.

"Don't try to explain it. You don't have to justify your reaction to yourself. What happened between us just . . . well, it just *happened*. No apologies, no explanations."

"But I don't want you to get the wrong idea."

She almost laughed at her own words. The man had suckled her breast for God's sake, and she'd allowed it. Loved it, and she didn't want to give him the wrong idea?

"The only idea I have is that you taste wonderful, and you feel even better." His words brought a rush of heat to her face.

"That's exactly what I'm talking about. What happened between us shouldn't have happened. I shouldn't have let it happen because it can never happen again. There are a lot of things going on in my life right now and the last thing I need, or want, is a relationship."

"Then we agree," he said, his grin turning into a full-blown smile that did dangerous things to her heart. "It's not a relationship I'm after, Callie. It's you—soft, pliant, warm beneath me." He trailed his knuckles down the slope of her jaw. His smile disappeared as he added in a low, raw voice, "I want to feel you around me. Me buried deep inside you. . . ."

"But that's—"

"Not a relationship. That's pleasure. Pure, undeniable pleasure." To further his point, he grazed her nipple, bringing the peak to throbbing life.

"I . . ." Her voice was small, whisper-soft as she searched for a reply. "That's not what I want either," she finally managed.

"Liar." His gaze drifted to the top of her blouse, the cleavage there. "Your body tells another story. There's an attraction between us. One you're trying very hard to deny because you feel guilty for what you're feeling. Desire is nothing to be ashamed of, Callie."

"I hardly know you."

"You know me much better than you think, and I know you. It's what you feel inside that counts, not what you *think* you should be feeling. Don't fight what pulls us together. Don't fight me. . . ."

"Please leave." She inched backward and came up hard against the wall of the hallway. The small distance gave her some much needed courage. She stiffened, staring at Alex's shoulder, determined not to meet his eyes, knowing all the while what a coward she was being. But she couldn't—no, she wouldn't—let herself forget about her father a second time. "Please, Alex. It's late. I have a very busy schedule, and I'm afraid as much as you would like to believe you know me so well, you don't. Not at all. I'm not into sleeping with strange men."

"It's not sleep I'm talking about," he replied, his smile positively wicked. Then a somber look settled on his face and he stepped forward. His fingertips went to graze her breast and he murmured, his voice as soft as silk, "You sigh when I touch you here. And you feel the heat when I touch you here." His fingers moved lower, to skim the material over her abdomen. "And you ache for me here." His touch drifted even lower and she nearly reeled backwards. His arms were around her, steadying her in the next instant, his voice playing havoc along her nerve endings. "It's not a stranger who knows your body so well. You *know* me, Callie. In reality, and

Kimberly Raye

in your dreams. No matter that you deny it." With those words, he turned away.

Callie felt the strange urge to call him back. Instead, she clamped her lips shut and watched him leave, her body crying out silently at the lost sensation.

Even when he'd disappeared, his footsteps fading down the hallway, she still felt his presence, as if he'd left a piece of himself behind. Or had he taken a piece of her with him?

He *is* a stranger, she told herself again. A very insightful and honest one, and that was what bothered her more than anything. Every word from his mouth had been the truth. So little time together, yet he knew her as if they'd been more than acquaintances, shared more than a few kisses and intimate caresses. He knew her mind, her thoughts, her hidden desires—things no man had a right to know.

No man . . . But Alex Daimon seemed much more than a man.

Perfect. The word popped into her head. He was too perfect, too thoughtful, too caring, too inquisitive. Too everything, for a normal man.

"Miss Callie?"

Callie glanced up at Burgess who appeared in the hallway.

"Your dinner tray's waiting in your room. You really should eat something."

"Burgess, why did you let Mr. Daimon up here? I asked you to tell him to go."

A puzzled look crossed the old man's face. "But

I did, Miss. I told him exactly what you said to me. He smiled, scribbled this phone number for you"— he held out a crumpled piece of paper—"and left. I locked the front door behind him myself."

"When was that?"

"Over a half-hour ago."

A wave of dizziness swept Callie and she clutched at the nightstand. "But he was here not a minute ago," she said. "Didn't you see him in the hall-way?"

Burgess shook his head, confusion playing across his features. "Are you sure, Miss? I watched him leave, and all the doors are locked. He couldn't have come back. Not without me seeing."

"He did," she said, the words desperate. She couldn't have imagined it. Or could she? She'd been seeing some pretty spectacular things lately. "He was here a few moments ago. I was talking to him."

"I heard your voice. I assumed it was your father you were speaking with."

"You didn't hear Mr. Daimon? But you must have. . . ."

Burgess shook his head and gave her an odd look. "Why don't you come and have some dinner. Then you can lie down. I'll have the doctor come out first thing in the morning and take a look at you. Maybe you hit your head when you passed out or—"

"I didn't hit my head!" she blazed, "and I'm not imagining things, Burgess. He was here, I tell you. He was!"

"Whatever you say, Miss. I'll just go and check the front door." Burgess gave her another long curious look before disappearing down the hallway.

Callie clutched her trembling hands. Alex Daimon had been here, in front of her, entrancing her. There was no doubt in her mind. Yet Burgess hadn't seen him. He'd vanished, just like in her bookstore. Just like magic. . . .

Her thoughts collided. *Magic*. The book!

Callie rushed down the hall to her bedroom. Frantically, she began searching for her black satchel.

"Miss Callie, what's wrong?" Burgess called from the doorway. "I was headed downstairs when I heard you—"

"My satchel, Burgess. I can't find it. I had it back at the car." And in Alex Daimon's house, she added silently. She couldn't have left it there. She couldn't have!

"It's downstairs. Mr. Daimon left it and your purse in the foyer near the coatrack."

Callie rushed past the butler, down the stairs, and snatched up her bag. The moment she shoved her hand inside, she felt the worn leather and relief swept through her. It was short-lived, when she heard a woman's now-familiar voice.

"Mine . . ."

The satchel slipped from Callie's hands, its contents spilling across the floor. The book landed on the marble with a thud, its pages falling open. One fluttered free. Callie bent down and reached for the sheet, her fingers going to the yellowed page.

Heat sizzled through her fingertips, up her arms, followed by a strange tingling. She laid her palm flat against the page and the sensation intensified. Her gaze fell to the vivid black scrawl at the top.

In death lies eternity. The air rushed from Callie's lungs, her body tingled, and the floor seemed to vibrate. She knew in that instant, she'd found what she'd been searching for. This was the incantation, her father's last hope.

She went to read further, then realized the page was torn. Gone. The last precious lines of the page were missing.

Tears came then—tears of frustration, exhaustion, defeat. The words played over in her mind like a broken record.

In death lies eternity.

. . . death lies eternity.

. . . eternity.

Callie found herself propelled back through time, to Catherine Drashierre's crypt. She'd yanked the book from the tomb. Maybe the page had ripped then.

If there was even the slightest chance, she had to be sure, and in an instant, she knew what she had to do. Tonight, before any more time passed, before her father grew even more ill, before death took him . . .

Keeping the loose page, Callie stuffed the book back into her satchel, went into her father's library and stashed the satchel in the wall safe. Then she raced for the door.

Vaguely, she heard Burgess call her name, but she couldn't stop to answer him or give an explanation. Her senses were alive. The cemetery called to her—

a place of perpetual death, violated by the thin ray of hope shining from its midst.

Callie grasped at that hope, held it dear as she ran to the cemetery and eased open its creaking wrought iron gate. As she slipped inside, the night closed around her; a chorus of voices drew her near. Or maybe it was the wind. She couldn't discern.

She only knew she stepped closer to both death and salvation.

Chapter Nine

Callie pushed open the mausoleum door. Concrete scraped across concrete and she flinched.

I shouldn't have come back.

Even as the thought welled within her, she took a deep breath and another step inside. This was the only chance her father had.

Her hand went to the torn page in her pocket. Yes, he had a chance—one that she couldn't blow because it was a little too dark, a little too cold, a little too creepy.

A deafening silence enveloped her, disrupted only by the sound of her short, shallow breaths and thundering heart. Nothing moved inside the place; the air was unnervingly still. No night breeze drifted past the open doorway, as if the wind, too, were afraid to enter. Still, her skin chilled and her hands turned to ice, the cold coming from inside of her.

She trailed her flashlight beam along the far wall, staring at the curtain of cobwebs that covered the corners and draped across the walls like fine French lace. When the circle of light came to rest on the partially open tomb, her body went rigid. The small opening she'd made a few nights before beckoned to her. Challenged her.

Tightening her fingers around the torn page she carried, she moved forward and aimed her flashlight at the inside of the casket.

Relief surged through her as she glimpsed what she sought. The other half of the page was partially hidden beneath the faded nightdress the skeleton wore.

Mine! The word raged through her head and Callie hesitated, her skin smarting where the bony fingers had seized hold of her in her dream. It had been a dream, hadn't it? Visions of the corpse gripping her, pulling her inside the coffin flashed through her brain. Her hands started to tremble, and she stepped back. Fear rushed through Callie, tightening her fingers around the flashlight until the metal cut into her palms. She couldn't do this. Not again.

You can, a voice whispered inside her head, calling her courage forward. It was *his* voice, so clear and strong. And oddly enough her fingers relaxed. Her legs cooperated just enough to move her forward to the edge of the coffin.

Focusing on the scrap of paper, she dipped her hand inside. Her fingers closed around the missing page, and she snatched it from the coffin. Nothing happened. The skeleton did not move. Relief sang through her, dispelling her terror for a brief, joyous moment. She whirled toward the door. Now to get back to her fath—

Her flashlight beam went dead, plunging her into absolute darkness. She opened her mouth, a scream pushing past her lips, only to die when Callie heard the slow sizzle of a match.

Only there was no match. Simply a spark that flared into a flame that danced atop a tall white candle. Callie watched, terrified, as a candle lit against the far wall that a few moments before had been nothing but cobwebs and dust. Eyes wide, she stared around her as many candles lit, the long white tapers filling the room with an eerie glow. The room had been empty before, except for the ancient casket, but now it was filled by blazing candles.

Callie silently begged her feet to move backward while invisible hands urged her forward, toward the coffin, the blazing candles, and something else. Something evil.

In death lies eternity, Callie. My eternity, and you are my chance. Your soul is mine now that I'm free.

Callie clamped her hands over her ears. Her flashlight crashed to the floor. She whirled toward the door as laughter stirred the stagnant air inside the mausoleum.

Deny me, but you can't escape. I'm inside of you. I am you, Callie.... I know your fears, your desires. I feel them as if they were my own. We are one, Callie. The same flesh and blood. One ...

Just as Callie reached the door, it slammed shut.

Catherine's voice, low and seductive like the night, whispered in her ear. *There is no use in fighting. It's a waste of energy. My spirit is much stronger than yours. I've had over one hundred years to rejuvenate. Give in peacefully, quietly, and together we shall have everything we've ever desired. Everything, and everyone.*

The voice pounded at Callie's courage, pulled at her goodness, squeezed at her heart with merciless intent until her strength drained away and fighting seemed too much. She slumped back against the edge of the concrete tomb. Yes, fighting was too hard. She didn't have the energy, didn't want to go on when sleeping seemed a much happier alternative. She could give in quietly, leave her worries behind.

Father ...

Like a thin ray of light pushing its way through a violent storm cloud, her father's image fought past the overpowering presence surrounding her.

She couldn't leave him. He needed her!

Strength surged through Callie, and she grappled for control, hardening herself to the tomb's seductive whispers. Everything was becoming clear. Catherine Drashierre's desperate bid for possession would not work, for Callie knew now who and what was after her, just as surely as she knew she wouldn't give in.

Foolish, the voice hissed, its laughter gone as a cold draft snaked through the room, stirring layers of dust into a whirling gray mist. *I'll not let you steal my chance. Your spirit will be mine, Callie Wisdom. Mine!*

Callie blinked as the candle flames flared a bright red. White wax drizzled down the sides of each taper. The liquid turned crimson as the candles wept silent, bloody tears. Again, laughter shook the walls and the floor. The sound echoed inside of Callie's head, deafening, as if a thousand horses stampeded around her.

Through blurry eyes, Callie saw the vision: a shimmering black silhouette moving closer, closer. Then a coldness gripped her hands, pulled until she stood facing the apparition.

Callie blinked, once more stunned by her resemblance to this other woman. She might have been standing in front of a mirror. The specter had Callie's silver hair, her pale complexion, her exact features. Only the eyes were different, as cold, as chilling as the hands clutching her.

Mine! the woman's voice screamed, yet her lips didn't open. Instead, they curved into a smile that sent fear racing through Callie, seizing her bones until she felt as if a hurricane were beating at her senses, demanding to be let in. The apparition's touch grew colder, numbing, until Callie couldn't feel her fingers anymore, her hands, her arms. She opened her mouth to scream, but only a rush of air escaped as the numbness spread through her body. Whatever was beating at her gained the entrance it sought.

Mine! The word hammered at her, beating her down, until she slipped to the floor, prone to the

cold, laid bare to the apparition of Catherine Drashierre that was waiting to rip her soul away.

"Callie." Alex Daimon's voice reached out to her.
A high pitched wail followed, then the cold dissolved. Strong arms gathered Callie close and she
fought to open her eyes, to stare into his and feel the
warmth of his gaze . . . but the effort was too much.
Darkness screamed around her. Catherine's evil battered the invisible fortress Alex had erected. Death
circled, a thin gray ribbon of dust drawing tighter.

Callie locked her arms about Alex's neck and
held on as he swept her from the mausoleum, out
into the humid night. Away from the evil that
shrieked inside the tomb.

Through her sobs, Callie heard his voice, cool
and calm in her ear. "It's all right, love. I'm here,
and she won't have you this time."

With the vow came comfort, and fear, for the
thread of possessiveness in Alex's voice fed the terror already swirling inside of Callie. She fought to
open her eyes, succeeded, only to find herself
slumped against the wrought iron gate of the cemetery—alive, and very, very much alone.

Dread wrapped around Callie like a giant python
the moment she arrived back at the house. Lights
blazed from inside. Her gaze shot to Dr. Broussard's
BMW parked in the driveway, behind it a white
paramedic unit, its lights swirling in a red and blue
frenzy against the night sky. Her fear tightened
around her, cutting off her air as she broke into a
run toward the front door.

"Burgess!" she cried as she burst inside.

The old man appeared at the top of the stairs, tears streaking his crinkled face.

"Miss Callie. He's . . . he's gone."

"What?"

Dr. Broussard entered through the archway from the dining room at that moment and Callie whirled. "What's going on? What's wrong with my father?"

"Nothing anymore, I'm afraid." He put a comforting hand on her shoulder. "Let's go into the living room. I'd like you to sit down."

She shrugged away from him and mounted the stairs, taking two at a time, racing past Burgess for her father's bedroom.

"Don't go in there, Miss Callie. Please. It's better if you just try and accept this. He wouldn't want this to be hard on you."

Callie burst into the room and stared past the two paramedics unhooking a heart monitor, pulling out an IV. Her gaze went to her father's chest. There was no labored rise and fall. Nothing.

"Daddy!" the word escaped on a sob, and Callie rushed forward, her tears blinding.

"Sorry, Miss. You'll need to stand back. We're not finished with—"

"Get out! Just get out!" She shoved against the restraining arms, pushed and pulled until she was free. "This is my house, now get out!" She dropped to her knees at her father's bedside, frantically grabbing for his limp hand.

The skin was still warm against her lips. "This

173

can't be," she whispered. "There's still time. This can't happen now! Not now. . . ."

Callie felt the rush of cool air, heard the rustle of sheers, but she didn't look up. Not that she could have seen anything. She could only feel: the tears sliding down her cheeks, the air burning her lungs, her heart being ripped out of her chest.

"Callie." The deep, soothing voice slid into her ears and she managed to swallow, to blink and stare through watery eyes at the man leaning down next to her. Her father's hand slipped from hers and she turned, throwing herself into Alex Daimon's arms.

"It wasn't time!" she sobbed. "I still have time! This isn't supposed to happen yet!" The words were indistinguishable, sobbed into the crook of his shoulder.

"It's all right. I promise, Callie. It's all right."

"Nooooooo!" she wailed. "My father's gone. He's *dead!*"

"Callie." This time her name was nothing more than a weak croak. Her father's. Her eyes snapped open and she pulled away from Alex. She found herself staring down at her father, who stared back up at her, sick but alive. *Alive!*

"But, you were dead. . . ." She grabbed his hand, felt the faint thump of a pulse where there had been nothing before.

"I think they made a mistake," Alex offered. "Obviously."

"No. I saw the EKG. It was a flat line."

"So much for modern medical science," her father whispered. "Trying to knock me off before my time. Don't you know I'll put up a better fight than that, baby?"

The question was so typical of her father, Callie couldn't help but smile. Nothing had ever frightened this man, and though she'd seen him go from a strong, vital man, to a physically helpless one, his spirit was still alive and strong.

She shook her head and stared up at Alex. "I don't understand any of this."

"It wasn't his time," Alex replied, his knuckles grazing her cheek, wiping the tears away. "You said so yourself."

"What the hell . . . ?" Dr. Broussard appeared in the doorway, shock and disbelief etching his features.

"There was a mistake," Callie declared.

"Like hell there was, Callie. I checked him out myself." He pushed past to bend over Callie's father. "Burgess! Send the others up here." At his shout, the paramedics filled the room and Callie found herself shoved off to the side, the medical team swarming around her father.

In all the excitement, her attention focused on her father, and the next thing she knew, Alex was gone.

"Burgess, have you seen Mr.—"

"I'll need a complete statement of what happened, Miss Wisdom," Dr. Broussard told her, disrupting her thoughts and drawing her full attention away from Alex. "Let's go downstairs."

The wind soughed through the trees, sending chills up and down his flesh-and-blood body, but Alex

175

didn't feel the sensation. He felt nothing save lust. It ate at his insides as he watched Callie say good-bye to Dr. Broussard. The physician's car angled from the drive, then Callie turned to walk back up to the house.

She covered the distance quickly, her body nervous and stiff, but so damned enticing. Each step was a silent invitation, her hips swaying in a way that no one else might have noticed. Only Alex did, and the beast that lived and breathed inside of him.

He grew harder, his arousal so painful he had to relieve himself or explode. He moved closer, like a whisper of wind, and she whirled. Only she saw nothing. He was still too far away.

Yet not far enough.

The scent of her perfume carried to him, filling his head and making him think of all the things he so desperately wanted to do. Kiss her, taste her, savor her—her lips, her throat, her breasts and much more. . . .

The pain became unbearable, and Alex slumped back against the ancient trunk of an oak tree. Yes, much more. She would taste of warmth and innocence and a heaven he could only wonder about. Then he would bury himself deep, deep inside until he became a part of her. Then he wouldn't feel the damned cold.

Laughter vibrated around him, a slow, mocking sound and he clamped his hands over his ears. He was a fool to have held back. A fool to hold back now when he wanted her so desperately, and pure or not, Callie wanted him. The seduction would be easy. And then it would be over. Catherine would get her due. The Evil One would have his vengeance.

But Callie?

The last question was what bothered him, what made him hold back when he throbbed for release. It was what drove him from Wisdom House, to the streets of the French Quarter in search of an escape. Any release. He needed a soft, sweet woman to make him forget Callie Wisdom.

Smoke filled the club. A rowdy jazz tune blared, drowning out the voices and the laughter, and the roaring in Alex's ears.

He leaned against the bar and touched shaking hands to his temples. He opened his eyes, yet he still saw her. In his mind's eye, in the smooth swirl of the brandy the bartender poured into a glass at his instruction, in the shiny reflection of the sax that one of the musicians played, in the mirrors above the bar where his own reflection stared back at him, his hair dark and smooth, his eyes hypnotic, his features handsome and perfect. So perfect . . .

"Hey, baby. How about buying me a drink?"

He stared into the mirror at the woman next to him. Silver hair, pale skin . . . *Callie.*

But when Alex turned, he saw long bright-red hair framing milk-white skin accented with heavy blush and eye makeup. A slow grin slid across the full red lips of the woman. She touched his shoulder. She wore a spandex top with a deep vee that left little to the imagination, and it sent desire knifing through him.

He closed his eyes and shook his head, as if he could shake away the woman who filled his thoughts. If only he could.

"Maybe another time then," she said, embarrassment in her voice.

Alex forced his eyes open and nodded. He turned back to the bar and downed the brandy, as if it could cloud his thoughts. He didn't even have that escape anymore. There was no escape, except for one: *Callie.*

He stared into the reflection above the bar and went rigid. Staring back at him from the far corner of the room was a woman with long silver hair, pale skin. Was it her?

He whirled and stared through the smoke to the vision who stood near the door, a tall shapely brunette at her side. But Alex had eyes for only one of the pair.

Callie?

A long shimmering curtain of pale hair plummeted to her waist. She wore faded denims that molded to the roundness of her backside, a black leather halter top leaving a wide expanse of tanned skin for his inspection. But it wasn't so much the way she looked. No, it was the hair. Soft, fragrant hair that reminded him so much—

No.

It wasn't her. It couldn't be. He'd followed her back to her house, seen her slip inside.

But even as reason pounded through his head, he strode forward.

He pushed his way through the crowd until he reached her. The brunette had disappeared, and the woman stood alone. She struck a sexy pose with her breasts arched forward as she leaned back against the wall.

"You dropped this." Alex grasped a plastic lighter near her feet and held it out.

Her luscious pink lips curved in an enticing smile when her gaze met his.

"Thanks." She took the lighter from his outstretched hand, her fingertips brushing his palm.

"None necessary. My pleasure." Before she could pull her hand away, he closed his fingers around hers. At the touch, images rushed at him: his hands on her thighs, his erection buried in her, his body driving hard and fast and furious into hers; this was her fantasy he saw as she stared at him with those large gray eyes, that damnable seductress smile on her face. So she wasn't the complete innocent he'd imagined. Here Callie was, enticing him with her thoughts, making him have fantasies of his own.

His hands trembled for a brief, fleeting moment as reality pushed past the desire. This wasn't her. It couldn't be. He knew that.

But as he stared at her, saw only *her,* he couldn't bring himself to admit it. He forced the doubts aside and pulled her closer, entwining their fingers. Her mind's erotic images became all too vivid, and he grew hot and hard, his lust overpowering his ridiculous uncertainty.

He was what he was. A deceiver. A seducer. A fantasy. This woman's fantasy. His Callie, his sweet, innocent Callie's fantasy.

"Helen!" It was the brunette. She stood on tiptoes, stared past the bar full of people and motioned to the woman in Alex's arms. "Helen! Come on!"

Helen? No, *not* Helen! his body cried. This was Callie. Sweet, soft Callie.

"Just a sec!"

"You can't leave yet," Alex said, making his voice rich, deep. He could feel the heat rushing through her body, settling between her thighs, and he knew she was wet. Ready. "You and I have some unfinished business."

"Helen!" came the brunette's shout as she pointed frantically to the door, the red neon EXIT blazing above. "Come on! We're outta here!"

This was *not* Helen. He pulled her closer, possessiveness racing fiercely through his body. Still, Callie had to choose to stay, had to give herself willingly. "Your friend's waiting. What are you going to do?" His voice was low, too low to be heard above the frenzied chatter and the blues band's music wailing through the bar. But she heard loud and clear. Alex made sure of that, his thoughts whispering through her head so there was no doubt as to his question.

She stared after her friend who rounded the bar, picking her way through a maze of people. Then she glanced at her hand clasped firmly between Alex's large ones. Her gaze slid to his face. "That all depends."

"On what?"

"On you."

"Me, or what I'm going to do to you?"

She gave him a knowing smile. "I like details," she said, but Alex already knew that. He knew the exact way she wanted to be touched, fondled, licked. He leaned forward, murmured a few descriptive phrases into her ear, and had her breathing in short gasps even before his fingers traced the underside of one large breast.

"Damn, girl, get the lead out and get your ass in gear!" the brunette cried as she pushed her way back through the crowd to them. She cast an impatient glance at her watch. "What the hell's keeping you? We're meeting Jimmy and Dean out at the river in a half hour."

"I'll pass."

"But Jimmy expects to see you," the brunette said, casting a long, thorough glance at Alex before dragging her gaze back to her friend. "It was your idea to do the lake tonight. What am I supposed to tell him?"

"Tell him to get lost," Callie said, then leaned closer to Alex dismissively. The brunette gave her one last furious glare, then turned and marched away. "I'll catch a ride home later," the blonde called after her.

At Alex's raised eyebrow, she explained, "Jimmy's an okay time, but boring as hell. Horny all the time, but it's the same old sex, same position, same pinching and squeezing until my ass is black and blue. The guy needs to learn a couple of things when it comes to women. But you," she trailed her finger down the front of his shirt, lingering near the button of his pants. Her voice softened. "Why, I bet you know just about everything there is to know."

"More," he said, a wealth of promise in the word.

She smiled—a slow, sultry curve of her full lips that said she was ready for a little demonstration. "Come on, baby. Let's have a little private party of our own." She threaded her fingers through his and led him from the bar to a small room atop one of the clubs that lined Bourbon Street.

It should have startled him that she'd take him to such a dump. His Callie. His sweet, pure, innocent Callie was too refined to go slumming. But he couldn't see beyond the lust clouding his vision, heating his blood.

"It ain't much," she whispered the moment they were inside, Alex's dark gaze sweeping their surroundings. "We could go somewhere else—"

He pressed his fingertips to her lips, and she kissed them. Desire screamed in his head, sending an echoing shiver through his body. Callie trailed a teasing fingertip down the front of his shirt, flicking buttons as she went. When her hand reached the button of his pants, she cupped him and Alex let out a ragged breath.

The zipper hissed, and then long, silky fingers wrapped around him.

It was heaven. The only heaven he would ever know. The realization sent bitterness swirling through him, but the lust overrode it as it did every emotion: bitterness, hate, guilt for what he was about to do.

He dipped his head, savoring her lips. She tasted of innocence and warmth and all the things Alex had long ago given up. His Callie. His sweet Callie . . .

Another lingering kiss and she pulled away from him to move toward the bed. He watched every move she made, her hips swaying to the drumming rhythm of his heart.

A saxophone wailed from the street below, a slow, sexy melody that made his stomach clench in anticipation. Laughter echoed, carrying on the night breeze that blew through the open set of French doors and skimmed Alex's bare torso like a lover's teasing caress. With trembling hands he tossed his shirt over the back of a lopsided chair and watched her slip out of her jeans, her panties. She stretched out across the bed, her naked body reflecting the pulsing red neon sign of the strip club directly across Bourbon Street.

Alex watched her with hungry eyes as she slid up the mattress, leaning into the pile of pillows propped against the headboard. She smiled and her legs fell open in silent invitation. She was so wet, so ready, and he'd barely touched her. Yet.

Stepping forward, he drank in the sight of her pale hair draped across her shoulders, her breasts peeking through the silver strands, the dark nipples hard pebbles that made his mouth water for a taste. Just one slow, sweet taste to satisfy the lust that raged inside of him.

His body trembled, and he closed his eyes. In his mind's eye, he could still see her. Ready, waiting for him, moonlight casting her pale flesh in jagged shadow. A roar filled his ears, the sound of his own blood surging through his veins. Anticipation sizzled the length of his spine, and his heart pumped faster . . . faster.

Then he was over her, the mattress groaning beneath his weight. He trailed his hands up the insides of her thighs, higher, until she clawed at his shoulders and tried to bring him close.

"Please," she begged, the word pushing past the drumming of Alex's heart. He opened his eyes and stared down.

His body went rigid.

Staring back up at him were scorching brown eyes. *Brown?* His gaze drank in her features, parted crimson lips, the color smeared across her face where he'd kissed her only a moment before. Dishwater blond hair wrapped around his fingers, not the delicate strands that reminded him of moonlight.

"What's the matter?" The blonde grasped his buttocks and tried to pull him inside of her, but he shrugged away. The shock of their contact had him trembling—his body desperate for her and his mind desperate for someone else . . . for the silver-haired innocent he'd been fantasizing about.

Fantasizing, of all things, when he himself was a fantasy! What was he doing? He was *this* woman's fantasy—her body as hot and throbbing as his own. Only, he couldn't bring himself to touch her, despite the lust which urged him on, made his body shake like a junkie desperate for a fix. God, how he needed it—this body, this heat, just for a moment. He would pump hard and fast and deep—

"No!" The word came from somewhere deep inside. He managed to get to his feet, every inch of him ice-cold and craving. . . .

But he craved another.

Go to her! The voice roared inside his head. He wanted to, needed to, but a vision of Callie Wisdom's wide, frightened eyes held him back. And as much as he wanted her, he still couldn't bring himself to take her. He could not damn her, like Catherine had damned him.

She is Catherine.

Yes. He had to remember that. He *had* to.

"Wait—" the blonde called after him as he rose and dressed. He heard the rustle of sheets, the squeak of old mattress springs, but he quickly disappeared outside.

The Quarter was alive, the streets brimming with people. Alex pushed past a couple of drunks barring the doorway downstairs and strode down the sidewalk, his pace fast, almost desperate. He walked as if he could outrun the truth.

"You want her."

The voice came from behind and he stopped, turned to find Caine leaning a few feet away against the side of a brick building.

The man wore a Hawaiian shirt, frayed blue-jean shorts and flip-flops. His long blond hair had been pulled back into a ponytail. A gold hoop earring dangled from one ear. Two days' growth of beard covered his broad jaw. He smelled of the ocean, his skin bronzed from the sun.

"She likes to surf," the Viking told him as if reading the question in his mind. "So I like to surf. You know the drill. Or you did." He pushed away from the wall and moved closer. "You're not playing by the rules anymore."

"I am. This game is just a little harder than the others."

"You want her," Caine said after a long silent moment, as if contemplating Alex's answer.

"I'm built to want her. It's what I am. What you are."

"You *want* her, and it's got nothing to do with what we are."

Alex shook his head, desperate to ignore the truth, that Callie was different. She wasn't supposed to be. She should be like all the others. He should feel the same way. Want her with the same intensity. Take her with the same urgency instead of holding back.

Hell, he should have done it even faster. Unlike the other women, this one offered sweet revenge. This one he should enjoy. This was the seduction he'd dreamt of.

Yet he couldn't.

Just as the thought rushed through his mind, he felt a coldness wrap around him and squeeze. He doubled over with the pain and came up gasping.

"You must do it," Caine said, his face grave.

"I can't. She's . . . different," Alex said, voicing the truth for the first time.

"You have to. Think about Catherine and all that she's done. She's your enemy. Enjoy this revenge."

"The way you enjoyed yours?" Alex eyed Caine as he reminded the Viking of his own past. Of the way he'd slain his enemy that day on a battlefield.

"I did enjoy it."

"But look what it got you." An eternity of service to the Evil One. And all because Caine had killed the man who'd murdered his wife and child. He'd slit the man's throat, felt the sweet rush of revenge as he'd ended his life. Unfortunately, one of the man's comrades had chosen that moment to end Caine's. He'd died on the spot without ever having the chance to ask forgiveness.

He'd been a good man. Fair. Kind. In love with the memory of his wife and child. But he'd gone to Hell for one act. He'd traded a moment of revenge for an eternity of damnation.

Caine embraced the job easily because he'd made his own choice. He'd killed the other man on his own terms. Remorse had come, but only after death. He'd spent the past several hundred years doing the Evil One's bidding and regretting the life he'd taken.

Penance.

"You think too much," Caine told him. "We're here. We *deserve* to be here." Pain flashed in the man's eyes, quickly fading into the pools of fathomless green. "Just do what you are meant to do."

"Is this you talking or the Evil One?"

Caine shrugged. "I do his bidding. So do you. So we must."

In the blink of an eye, the man was gone, and Alex found himself standing alone, the humid night air surrounding him.

He didn't feel its warmth, only cold. So much cold, and when he stepped inside his home moments later, he grew even colder.

Home. He nearly wept at the irony of the word. This manor house had been his home a long time ago, before Catherine.

Anger fired through him and Alex closed his eyes, calling the memories forward. He needed to remember, to see Catherine again, to make himself go to Callie and do what needed to be done. To do what justice called for.

Remember, a voice chanted in his head. *Remember what she was. What she did. Remember. . . .*

"Allow me to be so bold and introduce myself."

Alex's eyes snapped open. He stared at the woman in pale blue silk who stood in his garden. He knew she was a fantasy, a memory, but he allowed himself to be swept away, to recall. Moonlight outlined her figure, filtering through the gauzy folds of her gown to shape each perfect leg. Her dress plunged low, revealing a delicious swell of bosom that made his stomach clench.

The sound of sweet music floated from the open French doors behind him where the elite of nineteenth-century New Orleans gathered. His guests. But he wasn't much of a host tonight. Not when such exquisite beauty called to him.

He stepped forward, leaving the porch behind to take the gloved hand she held up. "I should know the name of one so breathtaking," he murmured, a moment before touching his lips to the back of her hand. "But, I'm afraid . . ."

"I am Catherine Drashierre, and you must be?"

"Alex Daimon," he said. But she already knew. He could see the recognition in her eyes, and he wondered briefly what hidden agenda lurked there. Then she smiled at him, and all speculation ended.

Chapter Ten

"Walk with me," she said, her voice a seductive whisper that shivered up and down his spine. And when she turned, Alex followed.

Walk with me, talk with me, tell me your secrets.
The words slid into his ears, weaving a hypnotic spell. Potent. Irresistible. And though Alex longed to drown out the silent commands, he couldn't. Just as he couldn't keep himself from looking at her, drinking in the picture she made so close to him.

"How long have you been master here?" Starlight kissed her silver hair, giving her an angelic appearance. But in her eyes there was nothing so pure. No, Alex read every lustful thought, felt every sinful command, his body hot, hard, aroused.

Lie with me, touch me, taste me.
The words filtered through his head, making it

very difficult for him to concentrate on what she was actually saying. Some nonsense about tobacco crops. His family business, and yet he couldn't recall the first thing about raising tobacco. Her nearness was giving rise to another more pressing matter.

Alex tugged at his cravat and wondered at the sudden heat that spread through him. The heat had nothing to do with the ninety-degree weather of the sultry Louisiana night, but everything to do with her, with that damnable voice that sounded inside his head.

"I'm a painter, you know." She turned to him, her breasts spilling over the top of her dress, making him ache to reach out and cup them.

"Really? I would have thought a lady of your . . . assets would be lounging away in some man's parlor, playing the role of dutiful wife."

"I may be many things, Monsieur Daimon, but dutiful isn't one of them." Her eyes twinkled with a heat that leapt across the space between them, like hot invisible fingers, to caress his jaw, his eyelids, his lips. The touch sent raw flame shooting to all the wrong places—wrong because he was dead sure she was someone's wife, and Alex made it a point never to cuckold another.

Then again, he'd never been looked at in quite this way. Oh, he'd been pursued by many women— rich women, poor women, fat women, thin women—all had heard of his notorious reputation in the bedroom and were anxious to find out if there

191

was any truth to it, but none like this woman. None who radiated such raw sexuality.

A hot lust incinerated his common sense and made him stand there in the moonlight with this Venus instead of playing the host inside. Undoubtedly this woman had her own reputation, and a legion of ardent pursuers.

She sighed, a soft breathy sound that made his nerves tingle. "This entire place was made for canvas, you know. Everything is so beautiful," she murmured. "So lush."

They stood on the edge of the garden that overlooked acres and acres of neatly planted crops. But she wasn't staring at the land. Instead, those wide, blue eyes stared at him. They tempted him.

Hold me, kiss me, press tightly against me. . . .

"Yes, everything here is very beautiful. Very lush, indeed, *chère*," he said, pulling her full against him, pressing his rock hard arousal into the soft cradle of her hips.

"I'm afraid you presume too much, monsieur." She placed a hand against his chest. "I merely asked you to walk with me, show me your . . . property. Nothing more," she said. Her words were breathy, and full of indignation . . . but her gaze invited more. Much more, and Alex had never been one to ignore an invitation, not when it involved something he wanted so badly.

"You need only give the command, lovely lady, and I shall be the gentleman and let you go." He stood still and waited for her to pull away, to slap him, to run screaming back into the party and tell some jealous husband or overbearing father how Andre Daimon's rebellious rakehell of a son had seduced her. It was a story his father had heard all too often.

She stared at him, and he knew she wouldn't pull away. As much as he knew she wanted to touch him, too. To be touched. Desire filled her eyes; so strong, so primeval it was, he almost cried out.

He dipped his head and claimed her lips.

Yes, sweet Alex. Want me, crave me. . . .

Need had spiraled fast and deep through him, turning his senses into an inferno, but this time, he felt it for what it was. Then, he'd been too smitten by her beauty, her voluptuous charm, to recognize the truth.

"You were made for the delicate stroke of a brush." She'd trailed her silky fingertips over his face, down his throat, her palm coming to rest over his pounding heart. "I would be honored to do your portrait, and . . . whatever else you may require in return for your valuable time as my model."

No! The word screamed through his head, forcing him away from her. Alex stumbled backward, watched her smile as her vision faded to a tiny pinpoint, and he closed his eyes.

Cold wrapped around him, disintegrating the vision and pulling him back to the present. He opened his eyes and stared at his surroundings. He stood inside what had once been his home.

Gone was the music, the laughter. Now there was nothing but an empty shell that echoed only with death and decay.

Alex moved into the study and stared at the fireplace, at the painting of himself still hanging above the chipped marble mantel. His eyes went to the final brush stroke. He still knew where it was, could see the soft blend of color. And he felt the brush as it passed along the canvas, covering the last spot.

That was what had obliterated his freedom once and for all.

Chained his soul for an eternity of service.

Despair filled him. And lust, as always. He fell to his knees, his body still hot and throbbing for the woman who'd damned him.

Still her soft luscious body offered delight and relief and warmth. Blessed warmth . . .

Gathering his anger, Alex consoled himself with the sweet revenge that he would have very soon.

"Come, Callie. See my latest masterpiece."

Callie was dreaming. She stared across the monstrous room at her father who stood at the far end, paintbrush in hand, a colorful canvas before him. He turned toward her and smiled, his eyes twinkling with precious sight.

"It worked, Daddy. I knew it would. I just knew it!" She tried to run to him, the floor cold beneath her bare feet. But with each step, he seemed farther away. The room larger. Longer.

"Come, sweetie. See what I've done." He turned his back to her and resumed his painting, his deep, melodious voice humming a tune she remembered from childhood. It was the same song that had lulled her to sleep night after night as he'd held her,

her head tucked beneath his chin as he'd rocked her to sleep. Ages ago, yet in her mind's eye she could still see him, all warmth and smiles.

"Come, Callie," he said again. "Take a look. It's for your mother. She always loved sunsets. Remember when you were little and we used to take a picnic basket up to Frenchman's Point? We would eat then lounge the evening away, watch the sun go down over Petrie's Bayou. . . ."

His words faded as Callie stepped forward, faster and faster, until she was practically running. For all the good it did her. He drifted farther away, the room became longer. . . .

"Wait for me," she begged. Still he disappeared, leaving only his canvas behind, a wide expanse of polished hardwood floor bridging the distance between her and it. The soft lullaby drifted through Callie's ears for the next few moments, then silence—a complete and utter silence that prickled her skin.

"Daddy?" Her gaze drank in the room. It was empty, the only movement that of white sheers that covered French doors on both sides of the room.

Cool air whooshed through, breaking the silence and making her jump. The sheers billowed, stretched, only to drift back to the floor and settle before the next gust of wind. The strange thing was, Callie felt the breeze blowing through, whispering across her skin, but she couldn't pinpoint the direction it came from.

The sheers blew toward one another, toward the center of the room where she stood, as if the wind blew *into* the room, not through it. The air was desperate to get inside, to get at her.

Come and see my masterpiece. The words were carried on the breeze, but no one spoke them. They came from the canvas, from the colorful images that she couldn't quite make out at such a distance.

Callie stepped forward, and this time her steps brought her closer. The sheer drapes tickled her skin as she walked, the wind assaulting her from every angle. Icy it was, yet not nearly cold enough to calm the blood heating in her veins. Her nerves were alive, as if an electric charge surrounded her, expectancy strumming through her body.

The sheers billowed, their edges passing across her skin like a live wire. The air around her seemed to hum.

She reached the picture that wasn't really a picture. Just a mass of color. And like a child staring at a forbidden object, she found she had to touch.

The paint was thick, damp, beneath her fingertips. She swirled the collage of rich color, loving the texture, the feel.

That's it, love. Feel me. All of me.

She jerked her hand away and inched backward, her ears still tingling from the deep, hypnotic voice so unlike her father's.

No. It couldn't have been a voice. There wasn't anyone in the room with her. It was empty now that Daddy was gone.

Look hard, love. I'm here. Right in front of you. Waiting.

The colors swirled, took shape, altered, as if Callie stared through the kaleidoscope she'd begged her father to win the first time she'd gone to a carnival. Twenty-five cents to toss three balls inside a milk crate and win a five-cent prize. A rip-off, but not to a wide-eyed five-year-old who'd gazed upon the kaleidoscope like an astronomer views a telescope. Callie just knew she could see clear into heaven with that tube. And she had done so.

She'd seen multicolored angels with wings that blossomed at the turn of her wrist. It had been nothing short of heaven.

The same colors were there on the canvas. But she didn't see any angels this time. This kaleidoscope was different. The colors were all shades of one color. Red.

Vivid, erotic, the color of ripe lips, succulent strawberries, nails pressing into taut, muscular flesh at that perfect moment of bliss.

The thought made her shiver, or maybe it was the man's image that appeared in the riot of color. Slowly, his features grew visible, pushing the color back, until a very lifelike image stared at her.

He was perfection, his body a deep tan against the firestorm surrounding him. His torso was bare, revealing swirls of dark silky hair that covered his broad chest, to whirl into tiny funnels and disappear beneath the waistband of his black jeans. They were tight jeans, they hugged his lean thigh muscles just enough to make her mouth go dry even though it was only a picture.

Just canvas and paint . . .

I'm *real*, came the rich deep voice. *Heated skin;*

silky hair; tight, taut, bulging muscle . . . I'm every-thing you dream of in a man, sweet Callie.

But this wasn't a man. It was merely a picture. One-dimensional.

I'm real, the voice assured her. It was *his* voice. Just as his eyes, so dark and all-knowing, stared back at her, challenged her. *Reach out, Callie. Just reach out to me and you'll see that I'm all you've ever wanted. Real, and very, very desperate—*

"You're not real," she stressed. "And there's no way you can talk." She closed her eyes, as if block-ing out the picture would also block out the voice. No luck. The words slipped through her conscience, whispered across her nerves until her heart pounded faster.

Open your eyes, Callie. I'm the reality you fan-tasize about, the lover you only dare touch in your dreams. But it doesn't have to be just in your dreams. I'm as real as you'll let me be. You need only ask.

Her eyelids fluttered open. She found herself standing clear across the room from the canvas, as if common sense had sucked her backward, out of harm's way. Out of *his* way.

But he was just paint and canvas.

Only the canvas grew into life-size proportions right before her eyes. And then Alex Daimon was no longer just canvas and paint, but real. Like a dark angel stepping from the fires of Hell, he left the painting behind to cover the distance to her in several long strides.

Anticipation sizzled through her body. Her blood

raced hot and demanding through her veins, and all at the sight of this one man she'd met two days ago—a man she felt as if she'd known a lifetime.

"This can't be happening." She shook her head. "You—you can't be real. I just saw you in the painting. *In* the painting, for heaven's sake. . . ."

"You wanted me here, in the flesh, and so I'm here." He gave her a smile as tempting as sin. As deadly, too, her conscience whispered.

She shook her head. "But I don't want you here. I want you to leave."

He seemed to consider her request, then stared at her with those dark eyes of his. Those eyes saw much, more than she wanted them to.

"That's not what you really want, Callie. If it were, I'd be gone"—he snapped his fingers—"just like that. *If* that's what you really wanted. I'm only here because deep down, inside, you want me here." He held out his arms and indicated their surroundings. Then his eyes grew darker, more knowing. "And you want me somewhere else, too. Someplace deep and wet and hot—"

"Stop it! I don't want that. I can't want that. I have my father to think of. His time's running out. . . ."

"And our time is just beginning. Think of yourself, Callie. For once in your life, give up the noble causes and think of yourself."

She couldn't help but watch his mouth, the way he formed each word. It was so intimate, as if his lips moved against her skin. . . . A tremor danced up her spine. A wet heat flooded between her legs as if his presence had cracked the dam she'd built around her feelings. She'd always been careful not to get too close, always thinking of others before herself. Always being so dependable, reliable, so completely and utterly boring.

And where had it all gotten her?

On a dead-end street, lonely and afraid of being even more lonely and afraid.

"There's nothing to fear. I'm harmless," he said, giving her a disarming smile.

"And I'm the Queen of Sheba," she murmured. Still she didn't back away when he stepped forward to within a bare inch of her.

Then he dropped to his knees, head bowed, and took her hand. He gave her a sly look. "At your service, my queen."

She couldn't help the sound that bubbled up inside her. It was laughter and anticipation, for as disconcerted as she was, she couldn't deny that he was flesh and blood, and all male.

For some reason, that thought made her truly happy. Maybe because she'd been living in such a dream world for so long, her life was so unreal that she needed something that was. And these warm fingers touching her were so *very* real.

The sound of her laughter brought him to his feet. He appeared shaken for the briefest moment, then he reached out, his fingertip tracing her lips as they curved into a smile.

"Laugh for me again," he asked, and she could have sworn she heard a note of desperation in his voice. "Please. Once more."

She did, because she couldn't deny him anything when he touched her so tenderly, so purposefully. And more than that, she couldn't deny herself. She wanted to see the rapture on his face, and she did the moment the sound again passed her lips.

Head thrown back, eyes closed, he relished the sound and she realized how truly exquisite this man was. He was perfection. Dark perfection—forceful, wild, like a hurricane with so much energy, mystery. How she longed to harness that essence, pull it deep, deep inside herself . . . pull *him* deep, deep inside herself.

Her face flamed, and he opened his eyes as if reading the thoughts racing through her mind. They were dangerous, lewd, erotic thoughts that turned her blood to liquid fire.

"Touch me, Callie. I know you want to."

She did want to. Her fingers itched, yearned to reach out.

Still, she might have refused. Might have tried to shake some sense into her raging hormones. Might have closed her eyes and tried to shut out the sound of her own labored breathing. The sound of his heart echoed as loudly as her own.

She might have done all those things, except as real as he was, he wasn't. She knew that on a deeper level—but for the first time, she welcomed the fantasy. Because she did want him, desperately, she would allow it in her dreams.

"Touch me," he murmured again, and she reached out.

Her fingers played down one muscled bicep, her

touch leaving a vivid trail of blue as if she were fingerpainting. It became the same shade that surrounded them.

Where her fingers touched, she felt a response on her own skin. Down one arm, over the curve of one shoulder, fingertips lingering at the pulse that thrummed frantically at the base of his neck. Touch drifting down his chest, her chest, lower, lower still. . . .

She marveled at the strange sensations, crisp hair beneath her fingertips, smooth, satiny fingers, in turn, stroking her. Yet he didn't move. He stood like a statue beneath her inspection. Only his eyes followed where she touched, and in turn, his gaze touched her. It spoke to her.

You want this. You want my touch—over your skin, sifting through your hair, trailing along your thighs, parting you, feeling your heat . . . your wet, ripe heat—

Glass shattered and Callie's eyes snapped open. The vivid images faded, shoved aside by reality as she sat up straight. Wide-eyed, she stared around the storeroom of her shop and saw Mikey, nothing but a pile of shattered crystal pieces on the floor.

A can of diet soda lay on its side, the liquid covering half her desk, drenching the precious page of the book—taped together as it was—where the incantation was printed. Where it *had* been printed. Soda drenched the page, blurring the letters until they were unreadable.

Panic seized her, but only for a moment. So what

if the words were gone. She knew them by heart, could recite them in her sleep. Not that it did one iota of good.

"Cal, are you all right?"

Callie turned toward the voice coming from the doorway to the office. In it, Alice stood.

The girl gave her a concerned frown, worry lighting her wide brown eyes as her gaze roamed over the mess on the desk before coming to rest on Callie. "I heard some funny sounds. . . . Like a moan or something." Her gaze cut to either side of the room. "Are you alone? It sounded like—"

"I'm alone," Callie cut in, her face burning. Not that she had anything to feel guilty about. Sure, she'd been fondling nothing short of a Greek god in her dreams, but he hadn't been real. Just her very vivid imagination.

If only her skin didn't still tingle, her thighs burn.

One glance at Callie's heated face, and Alice asked, "Are you sure there wasn't someone back—"

"Not a soul," Callie snapped, her tone sharper than she meant it to be. "I'll just clean this mess up." She grabbed for a box of Kleenex.

"I'll help," Alice offered, her worried frown still in place as she eyed Callie's trembling hands. Her eyes lit on the shattered angel figurine. "Oh no. Your mother's figurine."

Callie blinked back sudden tears and stooped to pick up the shattered Mikey. "I must've knocked it over in my . . ." The words died in the lump in her throat. She hadn't even given Mikey—her mother—

a second thought. Her focus had been on the vision of Alex and her own damned feelings.

"Let me," Alice said, helping Callie gather the pieces and toss them into a nearby trash can. When the deed was done, Callie spotted a tiny blue glint near the leg of her desk. One blue sapphire eye winked at her from the floor.

"Cal, are you sure you're all right?"

"Fine." Callie let out a deep sigh, snatched the sapphire from the floor, and dropped it into her pocket. Mikey wasn't completely lost. "I—I must've dozed off and knocked the soda over." She stared down at her lap; the jeans she wore were now stained with diet soda. "I've been so tired. . . ."

The thought ground to a halt when she saw the tiny speck of blue paint on her thigh. Her mind rushed back to the dream, to the blue paint she'd smeared on Alex Daimon's perfect muscles. She bolted from the chair and stumbled for the bathroom.

Alice's voice trailed after her. "Cal, what's wrong? You look like you've seen a ghost. It's only a stain. It'll come out. Just use a little club soda—"

Callie slammed the bathroom door and flew to the mirror. For a split second, she didn't want to look, afraid that her dream might turn into more than a dream after all.

She forced her eyes open and stared at her reflection. There was not a speck of blue anywhere. She fingered the buttons on her blouse, jerked the ends open and searched for any tell-tale paint. Nothing.

Giddy relief bubbled through her. The speck of color on her jeans was just some weird coincidence. It had all been a dream. Just a wild, crazy dream. How could she have thought otherwise? She must have picked up the drop of paint somewhere else. Of course. Maybe at home, in her father's studio.

"Did the stain come out?" Alice asked when Callie joined her at the front of the store.

She nodded. "Completely. The club soda did the trick."

"Thank goodness. The way you hightailed it to the bathroom, I thought you were on fire instead of just covered with a diet soda."

"Thanks for mopping up the spill."

"No problem. Are you finished back there?"

"Uh, yeah. No more ledgers for today. I'm going cross-eyed." She needed to do something real. Something normal for a change. Anything to get her mind off Alex and her dream. "I thought I'd lend a hand up here. Where do I start?"

"With that box of cookie jars," the girl said.

"Cookie jars?" Callie dug out one box and pulled out a white-and-gold cherub with big, round cheeks and a halo that served as a lid. "Did I order these?"

Alice laughed. "Cheesy, but they're still kinda cute, and a guaranteed hot seller. That shop over on Decatur sold tons of those angel canister sets. Who wouldn't want a cookie jar to match? Here—" She handed Callie the price gun. "Get to work."

"Yes, boss." Callie gave her a salute. Then she tackled the crate, unpacking boxes, wading through tissue paper until a dozen ceramic cookie jars stood on display. But no matter how fast she unpacked, how she tried to concentrate, she couldn't push Alex Daimon from her mind.

You have nothing to fear. I'm harmless.

"Oh, no." Alice's voice drew her back to the business at hand—a cookie jar with a broken wing and halo.

"I—I guess we'll have to return this one." Callie prayed her voice sounded normal. Especially when she felt anything but. Hot, edgy—nothing even remotely close to normal.

"I'll take it."

"Another stray? Isn't your apartment already full?"

"I hate to see anything wasted. If you hadn't completely shattered your mother's figurine, I would have saved him, too. A little glue and this little guy'll be as good as new. He can keep me company." Alice leveled a stare at her. "I'm back sitting at home on Saturday nights. I saw Roger last night after all. Things didn't exactly work out." A shadow passed over the girl's face. "I decided not to see him anymore."

"Why?"

"He has that look."

"What look?"

"I don't know. Just that look."

"Not all men are like Jimmy, Alice."

She had obviously hit a sore spot, for the girl blew up. "How would you know? You never let one close enough to find out. Instead, you spend your time daydreaming in the storage room. You're a great one to talk, Cal."

Callie responded in kind: "So I don't date a lot. I've still known a lot of great guys, none of whom were like Jimmy."

"Name one."

"My father."

"Name another."

"Burgess."

Alice shook her head. "Relatives and senior citizens don't count, Cal. I'm talking the available, under-fifty guy with a job and half a conscience. One who doesn't think with his crotch, or talk with his fists."

"This isn't about me, Alice. I'm fine. This is about you. You can't hide away forever. You'll end up old and lonely and—"

"Bruise-free?"

"I was going to say, you'll miss out on a lot. Men do have some good points." She tugged at the top button on her blouse, her skin tingling, the dream of Alex still much too vivid in her mind no matter how she tried to tuck it away.

Touch me, Callie. I know you want to.

She clenched her fingers and focused her attention on Alice. Tears swam in the girl's eyes, and a hand squeezed at Callie's heart.

"Here," she said, handing the girl the broken cookie jar. "It doesn't have a crotch or fists. You're safe."

Her words brought a smile to Alice's face. A tear slipped down the girl's cheek.

"Time," Callie said, brushing a strand of hair back from the young woman's face. "Give yourself time. Then you'll meet a nice man, and you'll find that things can be pretty good with the right person. You might even be glad if he does a little thinking with his crotch." The words were new for Callie, she wasn't used to being so open, but they felt right.

"Maybe." Alice smiled and the faraway look disappeared from her eyes. "You're right. I'm free, and Jimmy can rot in Hell for all I care."

I'm sure he is, Callie added silently, *if there is any real justice in the world.* She hadn't given up hope enough to think that there wasn't. No matter how unfair her own circumstances seemed.

"The past is past." Alice wiped at her eyes with renewed determination. "Over and done with."

If only Callie could say that. Instead, the past was haunting her, surrounding and blinding her like a fog. Not that she wanted to see through it. Not if disaster waited for her. Death.

Nodding to Alice, Callie willed her thoughts aside and concentrated on pricing cookie jars. She spent the next several hours unpacking boxes, pricing items, and paying the store inventory some much needed attention.

It was much later that afternoon, after Callie had decided to close a few hours early, that she returned to the storeroom and sat down at her desk. She'd already walked Alice to her car, despite the girl's ardent protests about leaving Callie alone.

Callie knew it was more that Alice didn't want to be alone, but she said nothing. When Alice got lonely enough, the girl would open her heart to others again. That was important.

Light from the streetlamp outside the store pushed through the shadows, lancing through the cracked door of the storeroom to mix and mingle with the soft glow of the lamp on her desk.

She reached for the smeared page of Catherine's book of spells and stared at the mess of ink that she'd thought would be her salvation. The words were already burned into her memory. Not that it did any good. She could recite them until the Mississippi River dried up—she'd tried already and felt nothing—and it wouldn't do a bit of good. She knew that, even though she forced herself to open her mouth to try again.

The strange string of syllables sailed past her lips and Callie closed her eyes. When the spell worked, *if* it ever worked, she would know. She'd feel it.

She whispered the words again. And again.

No help. No salvation. Nothing.

Callie gave in to a fresh bout of tears. So much for saving her father. He would die. So soon, the end would come. She would have to say good-bye to him, the last person she had left in the world. The only person . . .

Good riddance. The words whispered through her head, so soft, yet so deadly. She clamped her hands over her ears, desperate to shut out Catherine Drashierre's evil voice.

You can't stop it, Callie. I won't let you. And deep down, you don't want to stop it—because I don't want you to stop it. I am you. . . .

209

Callie's stomach churned and she doubled over, the voice pervading her, battling for control. That's what Catherine wanted: control of her body. Callie hadn't wanted to admit that before.

She was *possessed*. The notion was straight out of some horror movie. It couldn't be. It just couldn't!

But as the spasms gripped her, her muscles contracted, and the heat spread through her body, Callie admitted to herself that there was no other explanation for the visions she'd had, the episodes. She wondered if it might not be better to give in, to let Catherine have control. She'd tried to stop the curse, to help her father, and every avenue had been a dead end. There was no help. No fighting her ancestress's power. No escape—

Wrong! Her father's image pushed its way into her head, past the part of her that wanted to give up, the part so very, very tired of fighting.

But it wasn't so much his image that made her stiffen, fight to get to her feet and stumble to the door of the storeroom. No, it was another man's image. Taller, darker, more handsome. Certainly more dangerous. Her guardian angel, it seemed. He was a dark, beautiful, mesmerizing angel come to save her from Catherine and the unreality of her life, just as he'd done at the mausoleum last night—

No. That too had been a figment of her imagination, a product of her possessed mind's hallucinations. She'd met a very attractive man. It was no wonder she fantasized about him. But the line between her dreams and fantasies, her memories and visions of the future, it was blurring. She didn't know what to believe anymore. And her fantasies . . . When she'd been a teenager, she'd had wonderfully romantic daydreams about Matt Dillon, Leif Garrett, and eventually Brad Pitt. After *Interview with the Vampire,* she'd been smitten.

But the dreams she was having now were . . .

Not so different, she told herself. Just more intense, and that was understandable considering the pressure she was under, what with her father's condition deteriorating so rapidly.

Callie leaned against the wall of the storeroom and fixed her gaze on the overhead light. She concentrated, willing her muscles to relax as she forced Catherine away and pictured Alex.

He called to her from the light in that rich, rumbling voice of his that was as stimulating as an actual touch. And it was even more potent, she realized as her body relaxed and a slow fire spread over her skin. It was so mesmerizing.

Callie rubbed her hands over her arms and the strange sensations disappeared. *Good,* she thought, *because I have work to do. I still can save my father. I just have to remain logical. In control, with a clear, competent head.*

And a clear, competent person who wanted something done right would naturally go to a professional. If you have roaches, you call in an exterminator. If your plumbing is screwed up, you call a plumber. If the IRS is breathing down your neck, you call in an accountant, and maybe a good lawyer. And if death is knocking on your door . . .

Well, they had professionals for that, too. She was in New Orleans, after all. Home to generations of voodoo queens. She could certainly find someone more qualified than herself to help her father. She had the incantation. She just needed to know how to use it.

She grabbed the phone book and scanned the appropriate pages. She couldn't just sit in her storeroom all night feeling like she was starring in *The Exorcist*. She had to do something, to help her father and herself.

Help came a few minutes later in the form of a rusty voice on an answering maching that picked up at the number she dialed. It was the only number in the book that gave her any feeling of hope at all.

"Greetings, fellow spiritual beings. This is Margaret. Whatever ails you, bring your troubles to me. If you want love, money, power, I can give you everything. By appointment only, of course. Leave a name and number, and I'll call you with a convenient time. Peace be with you, and may the Goddess answer your requests."

Beep.

Callie took a deep breath, then spoke. "Mrs. Churchwood, my name is Callie Wisdom, and I need your help. It's urgent and I don't have time to wait for an appointment. I hope you don't mind, but I'm coming over now—"

"Decatur street," came a voice on the other end after the short squawk of a telephone being picked up.

"Mrs. Churchwood?"

"The one and only. I'm at Fifty-five fifty-five Decatur. But don't bother coming tonight."

"It's urgent."

"Eight tomorrow morning."

"But I need to see you tonight—"

The woman was adamant. "The preseason starts tonight."

"What?"

"The New Orleans Saints go head to head with Dallas. I never miss a game."

"But this is a matter of life and death."

"So is this. Did you see what happened the last time we played the Cowboys? A massacre. Not this time, though. Not if my victory spell has anything to do with it."

"Please. This can't—"

"Tomorrow morning, and you ought to be thanking the powers that be for that. I'm sure to be in a good mood thanks to tonight's inevitable victory."

"I'll be there," Callie said, wishing she could go tonight but knowing there was no way to change this woman's mind.

"Bring your wallet, *chérie*. I take credit cards and checks, but I prefer cash."

"Thank you."

"Cash," the woman stressed again, "and don't be late." Then the line went dead.

Determination surged through Callie, and she snatched up her purse, the torn page, and the book. Folding the page, she placed it inside the book, then she stuffed that into her purse. She headed for the front door. Her eyes watered and she rubbed them. She'd go home, take several aspirin and try to sleep. Maybe then she'd stop feeling like an extra for a Walking Dead movie.

As she rounded the corner near the register, the bells jingled as someone tried the knob on the front door.

"There's a light in the back," she heard.

"But this sign says they're closed," another voice answered.

"Try anyway."

The bell jingled again, and Callie crouched down behind the counter. She punched the button on the cash register, cringing at the bell that sounded as the drawer opened.

The first voice sounded excited: "Did you hear that? Someone is inside." The bell jingled more, and a loud rapping ensued.

Callie reached up into the register, pulled out a wad of bills to appease Margaret Churchwood, shoved the drawer back into place and crawled back toward the storeroom. She'd slip out the back door and head home. A customer was the last thing she felt like dealing with tonight.

She needed some rest. Otherwise, she knew she'd have another blackout. She felt it, a strange urgency inside her.

It's me, Callie. I'm getting stronger. The day is getting closer—

No! what was left of her courage countered.

Catherine couldn't win. She wouldn't!

But Catherine was the least of Callie's problems.

She realized it the moment she entered the alleyway behind the shop. For when she stepped into the shadows, locking the door behind her, it wasn't Catherine behind her. It wasn't Catherine's deep, intoxicating voice that whispered in her ear.

"I've been waiting for you."

No, the speaker was someone far more dangerous to her senses. Her sanity.

"Alex," she breathed. Then he touched her, and her common sense disintegrated.

Chapter Eleven

"Finally, we meet again." Alex's voice slid into her ears and did funny things to her pulse.

She managed to let go of the doorknob, but she couldn't turn. His chest presented a solid wall at her back. He was too close—so close, in fact, that she wanted to lean back, to melt into him. And melt she would if the sudden wave of heat that shot through her when his hand closed over her shoulder was any indication.

She managed to swallow. "What do you expect if you lurk around the back alley of my shop?"

"To see you, of course."

It was the truth. She knew it, that's why she'd pointed it out, but hearing him confirm her thoughts made it all seem somehow more real. He'd been waiting for her. *Waiting*.

The knowledge frightened her a little. But more than anything it was thrilling, especially since the scent of him—the musky fragrance of heat and sex and masculinity—reminded her of the dream she'd had in the storeroom. She had the sudden incredible urge to turn around, to trace his shoulder, to feel his touch on her own skin—

Stop!

A dream. It had been just a simple—albeit very nice and *very* erotic—dream. But a dream, nonetheless.

Only there was nothing dreamlike about the man whose heated breath prickled the skin at her nape. No, he was very real, and he was having a very real effect on her body.

She shoved a damp tendril of hair from her temple, her own skin fiery beneath her fingertips. Louisiana was definitely too hot in summer.

Too hot even in the dead of winter if Alex Daimon was around, she amended.

"What are you doing here?" she managed after endless seconds of silence.

"I thought we already established that." His cool fingers gently kneaded the knotted muscles in her shoulder and she longed to close her eyes. The sensation was very arousing, and at the same time, oddly soothing, as if he sucked away her frustration, her exhaustion, her worry, with the chill contact of his purposeful fingers. "I came to see you."

"But why?"

"I thought we already established that."

"I—I don't have time for this. I told you about

my father. He needs all of my attention right now. There's no room for a relationship in my life."

His soft chuckle filled her ears and sent ripples of heat down her spine. "Well, then. We're a perfect fit. What I want is a lot less complicated than a relationship, *chère*. Those few kisses the other night weren't enough. Sweet," he murmured, his finger trailing the length of her neck to send a delightful shiver clear to her toes. "Very sweet, but not nearly enough."

"Maybe they were enough for me." They were *too much*, in fact. He overloaded her senses with his very nearness.

"Were they?" he asked.

No! her body screamed, but she managed in the calmest voice she could muster, "Maybe." She stiffened and pulled away, though his body still made her feel like a stick of butter lying too close to a hot frying pan.

Gathering her wits, Callie managed to twist around until she stood facing him. And she wondered as she stared up into those incredibly dark, incredibly hungry eyes, if she hadn't bypassed the pan and slid straight into the fire.

"Maybe yes, or maybe no?"

"I—I'm not sure," she answered honestly.

"Have dinner with me."

"Dinner, huh? For a man who isn't interested in a relationship, that sounds like a date if I've ever heard one."

He smiled. "Not a date. Just a few hours in my

company—for you to make up your mind about later." He paused. "Call it foreplay."

The word conjured all sorts of images, and Callie swallowed. Or tried to. Her throat was suddenly so dry that she couldn't manage the effort. Instead, she wet her lips. The motion was innocent, but was all the more provocative because of it; she saw that in his eyes.

She tried to make light of the situation. "Dinner with a man who lurks in alleys, scaring the daylights out of unsuspecting female shopkeepers? I'd probably be crazy to say yes. You could be the next Jack the Ripper for all I know."

He smiled and murmured, his voice low and teasing, "Jack's not such a bad guy—all-in-all—and I've certainly been called worse."

"Should I be afraid?" she asked, half-laughing. Still, a bit of fear rippled through her.

He trailed a gentle fingertip along her cheek and asked, "I don't know. Of what?"

"Now that's a million-dollar question if I've ever heard one," she snapped. And it was one she didn't have an answer for. There were too many options. Common sense told her she should definitely be afraid of *him*, of a man who made her feel so many things she'd never felt before, a man who stole her concentration when she needed it most.

But another part of her urged her to go with him. While Callie hadn't been around the block very many times—hell, she'd never even made it past the corner—she knew the intensity of the feelings he stirred was rare. There was the powerful lust, but it wasn't just lust she felt for Alex Daimon. There was something else, an emotional link—since that first night he'd come to her in her dreams and comforted her. The link grew stronger when he'd picked her up off the road and taken her to his home. Then he'd somehow kept her father from dying, called him back when most people would have been eager to let the man go. Not Alex.

Yes, she felt more than just the lust. That's what made everything so complicated. Pure, carnal appetite she could have dealt with, resisted, but this . . . this *want,* physically and emotionally, was another story entirely.

She craved this man, longed to taste him, to lose herself with him. At the same time, she wanted simply to hold him in her arms, to be held in return. She didn't feel so lonely, so lost with him. It was a truth that alone encouraged her to take what he so generously offered: an eager ear, a comforting touch . . . earth-shattering sex.

Dinner, reason insisted, killing any and every other thought. She could do just dinner. What harm was there in eating with this man, spending a few hours in his company?

"A million-dollar question, huh?" He raised one dark brow. "Quite a hefty sum, but if you're up to a bet . . ."

She gave him a wary glance. "What exactly did you have in mind?"

"If I admit whether or not I'm Jack the Ripper, you have dinner with me."

"The *next* Jack the Ripper," she corrected. "And

how will I know you're telling the truth?"

He crossed his fingers. "Scout's honor, of course."

"I bet what you know about scouting could fill my mama's thimble."

"Good bet. I've never been a Boy Scout."

"That much I do believe."

"And you don't believe I'm harmless enough to have dinner with?"

"You? Harmless?" She gave him a long glance from the top of his dark head to the tips of his polished black boots. Then she shook her head, a nervous laugh bubbling up in her throat. "I'm not much of a gambling woman, but I'd be willing to lay my money on the fact that you're one very dangerous man, Mr. Daimon—to every woman within a hundred-mile radius." *And certainly to my sanity,* she added silently.

"Alex," he corrected. "And I'm only interested in one particular woman." He smiled again, a devilish twist to his sensuous mouth. "I promise I'll be a good boy. Come with me, Callie." The way he said the words, so soft and sexy and persuasive, she found herself nodding. Her father was already in bed. Burgess was taking care of him. She couldn't do any more with the incantation tonight, and she couldn't see Margaret Churchwood until tomorrow morning. An evening sitting alone in her room at home, or outside in the garden, crying and worrying and fighting her blasted grief wouldn't do her or her father any good. And she was hungry.

The realization startled her. She'd been feeling so

queasy, so completely *strange* thanks to the incessant voice inside her head. But now, for some reason, she felt very normal, and very hungry, as if she could eat a six-foot po' boy, an extra large pizza . . . *him*.

He smiled as if he'd heard the lewd thought. Her face flamed, but she smiled, as well.

"If I say yes, it's just to dinner. Nothing more. I have to be home early. My father waits up for me," she lied.

"Just dinner," he murmured, looking as pleased as if she'd stripped off her clothes and flung herself at him. "And then I'll send you on your way to your papa. Let's go." He laced his fingers through hers, and then they were making their way through the swarm of people who filled the Quarter. Despite the throng of tourists and the heat, Callie felt more relaxed, more at peace than she'd felt in a long, long time.

When the streets grew too crowded, Alex pulled her into a nearby alley.

"Wait a second," she said, pulling against his hand. His proximity made her nervous.

"I'm not Jack the Ripper," he said, smiling over his shoulder. "We can spend a few hours trying to push our way through to Bourbon Street, or we can spend all of ten minutes taking a shortcut."

She hesitated a moment, then let him lead her deeper into the shadows, through a maze of back routes that shot her sense of direction to hell and back. They dodged empty crates, an occasional dumpster, a few drunks, and even a man and woman in a very heated embrace. A throaty moan from the woman affected Callie, began a deep throbbing between her legs. She took a long breath, the alley's humidity filling her lungs and raising her body temperature a couple of degrees.

It was definitely too hot to be outside.

Especially with him.

They'd just rounded a corner into what Callie was sure was a dead-end, but suddenly she was staring down an endless path. She pulled to a stop.

"Do you work down here? You know your way around better than anyone I've ever . . ." Her words ground to a halt as she heard a faint cry coming from a darkened doorway just ahead of them.

My imagination, she thought, until she stepped forward and spotted the small shadow crouched against the sagging doorframe. "It's a little girl," Callie said, but Alex had already passed her to hunker in front of the child.

His soothing deep voice crooned, "There, there, it's all right, sweetheart."

The light from a nearby back door pushed through the darkness, and a thin sliver of light fell across the little girl's frightened face.

"My God, she's bleeding," Callie gasped as she saw the fresh cut on the girl's forehead.

Alex reached to cup the child's chin and take a better look, but a fraction before his long, lean fingers could make contact, his hand started to tremble.

Callie saw surprise in his dark gaze, then fury

223

before his expression shuttered, locking her out of his thoughts. He let his hand fall away, his entire body quaking.

"What's wrong?"

"I . . ." He shook his head, as if he could cast away the trembling, as if he could escape whatever unseen thing had brought about the strange reaction. "We have to get out of here," he finally said.

"But we can't just leave this child like this."

Alex faced her. "Trust me. She's better off. Come on, Callie. Somebody else will find her, somebody who can help her."

"*We* can help her," she snapped. "Or at least I can. Go ahead if you want. I won't leave her." Visions of the strangled women Guidry was investigating danced in her head and Callie pushed past Alex, dropping to her knees in front of the little girl. Her fingertips went to the cut on the child's forehead.

The little girl immediately shrank back.

"Don't be afraid. I'm not going to hurt you," Callie crooned, then tried again. This time her fingertips touched soft flesh. She examined the cut. "What happened to you?"

The girl shook her head and trembled. "I ain't s'posed to talk to strangers. My mommy told me not to."

"Well, now. That sounds like good advice." She smiled. "My name's Callie." She held out her hand to the little girl. "And yours is?"

The little girl looked uncertain for the space of a heartbeat, then she whispered, "Emily."

224

"Good to meet you, Emily." Callie's fingers closed around her small ones and she gave the girl's hand a warm squeeze. "It's awful dark out. I bet your mommy said not to be out after dark, too."

The child nodded, tears spilling over as she said, "And—and she said not to mess up my dress. This is my special-occasion dress. Mama made it just for our trip to New Orleans." The little girl stared down at the torn hem of her purple dress. "This is my first time. Mama didn't want me to come with her, but I begged, so she made me this dress and told me to stay close. But I didn't. I let go of her hand, and then I couldn't find her. I got scared, and I started to run. That's when I fell."

"That's what happened to your head?"

The little girl nodded. "She said not to run, but I did anyway. I was just trying to find her. I turned around and she wasn't there anymore." More tears flowed free and the little girl's bottom lip started to tremble.

"There, there, we'll find her."

"Callie." Alex's deep voice came from behind her. She heard impatience and something else. Regret? What did he regret? That she'd made him stop for an extra five minutes? "Please. We need to get out of here—"

"So go on, if you're in such a hurry." Her words came out short and clipped, her anger fueled by his impatience. Her voice softened considerably, however, when she chanced a glance at him and saw a stricken expression on his face, vulnerability, fear. Suddenly she wanted to wrap her arms around him and chase the haunted look from his eyes. She would have done just that, but the child's soft whimpering demanded her immediate attention.

"Emily," she said, turning back to the girl. "You calm down now, honey. We'll find your mommy." She dusted some dirt from the nasty scrape on her head. Reaching in her pocket, she dabbed a tissue at the tiny trail of blood dripping down the girl's cheek. On closer inspection, Callie noticed a scraped knee and a bruised knuckle.

The little girl swiped at her eyes. "You'll find my mommy?"

"Yes, we will, but first you tell me how you ended up back here."

"The lights. A whole street full of them." Emily wiped at more tears. "I just wanted to see them for a second. Mommy said no. Said we didn't have time. But I was just looking. I meant to go right back, but when I tried, I couldn't find Mommy anymore. It got real dark, and then I couldn't even see the lights. . . ."

"It's all right, honey." Callie wiped away more of the girl's tears and gave her a smile. "Do you know where you were the last time you saw your mommy?"

The little girl shook her head fiercely. "I don't know. I was bad. I didn't listen. She said to hold her hand, but I let go. . . ." The words faded into a sniffle.

"It's going to be all right," Callie assured her. Grasping both small hands in hers, she said, "Look at me, Emily. Just look into my eyes and I'm going to help you find your mommy." All Callie's past fears of using her power evaporated. This was something she knew, something she understood: helping a lost child. And it was something she had to do. She ignored Alex's gaze that burned into her as she stared hard and deep into Emily's eyes. Soon she left the alley behind, traveling through the girl's memory until she emerged onto a brightly lit street. She stared up at the woman who held her hand and said, "Stay close, Em, honey."

Callie stared around, seeing the street, the lights, the people, through a child's wonder. Her eyes lit on a street sign, then her gaze swung back to more familiar surroundings.

"Callie." Alex's voice pulled her back to the dark alley, and she glanced up.

"A block over," she said. "Her mother was a block over, near Independence Hall." She stood up, still holding one of Emily's hands. "Let's go."

Alex said nothing. Instead, he simply followed Callie, his gaze dark and unreadable.

She found his silence unsettling. Maybe he didn't like kids. It seemed the most obvious explanation for his behavior, but Callie sensed there was more. Once she had Emily safe and sound and back with her mother, she intended to find out the real reason.

Minutes later Callie emerged from the alley, Emily's hand tightly in hers, and pushed through a maze of people until she stood on the very same corner she'd seen through Emily's eyes. Not five minutes passed before she heard a shout.

"Thank God!" The woman flew at them, and

Callie immediately recognized the blond mop of hair, the concerned eyes. This was the same woman who had stared down and said, "Stay close, Em, honey."

"Emily, I've been looking everywhere for you!" She snatched the little girl from Callie's arms. "I didn't know what—" Her words died as her wary gaze shot to Callie.

"We found her in an alley, looking at the lights." Callie extended her hand. "She panicked and fell when she realized she was lost."

"I messed up my dress," Emily cried. "I'm sorry, Mommy. I know I wasn't supposed to—"

"Sshhh, baby. It's all right." Emily's mother's expression finally softened and relief crept through her features. "Thank you," she said to Callie. "Thank you so much." Then, after giving her a meaningful look, she led her child away.

"You don't like children, do you?" Callie asked several moments later. Emily and her mother had disappeared into the crowd. Callie turned and studied Alex's profile as he stared out across the madhouse the Quarter had become, his eyes dark and emotionless. Cold.

No, not cold, she amended. There was something in the dark depths that kept them from that. It appeared as he stared at her, was something more than desire. It was a brightness that flickered in the brown-gold depths. She could see something she couldn't quite name.

"On the contrary," he said. "I used to adore children."

"*Used* to?"

"I haven't been around them for a long, long time."

"Why not?" From the flash of pain across his features, she knew she was prodding a wound, but she couldn't stop herself. She wanted—no, needed—to know why. She wanted to find a reason to keep from walking away from him, away from anyone who could abandon a child in need.

"You ask a lot of questions," he snapped.

"I want to know. Why not?"

He shot her an angry glare, and for a moment she thought he'd be the one to turn and walk away. Finally, after a long silent spell, he muttered, "I'm not around children because I don't like to be around them, anymore."

"But why?"

He turned on her and there was raw fury in his gaze. "I had a younger sister who died. Now whenever I see a child, it reminds me of her. Is that enough for you?"

"I'm sorry," she whispered, guilt battling the relief spreading through her. "But I'm also glad you're not a heartless jerk."

At her words, his gaze seemed to soften. He shook his head and turned back to stare across the street. "I'm not good with kids anymore. They don't like me. But it's for the best."

"And why is that?"

"They just don't. Kids sense things. They know what I am. That is," he rushed on as if he'd said something he hadn't meant to, "They know what sort of man I am."

"And what sort of man are you?"

"One who isn't good with kids."

Quiet settled between them, disrupted only by the chatter of passersby.

After a long, silent moment, Callie asked, "Would you really have left Emily in that alley?"

"No, I suppose not." The way he answered, tired and sad, despite the way he had remained cold and aloof while she'd helped Emily, Callie believed him. She couldn't erase the memory of him, concern in his eyes, his hand reaching out when they'd first spotted the child.

Minutes later, they were walking into Petrie's, a nineteenth-century townhouse turned restaurant near the corner of St. Charles and Bourbon.

"A table for two," Alex told the maitre d'.

The man looked them up and down with a thorough eye. "We have a dress code here, sir. Suit and tie only."

"I'll remember that the next time. If you could find us something now, I'd really appreciate it—"

"Do you have a reservation?" the restaurant employee cut in, impatience in his voice.

"No."

"Sorry, sir, but we seat on a reservation basis only. No reservation, no seat." The man's tone was short and clipped. "This is a very exclusive restaurant. Please phone ahead the next time you would like to join us, and we'll try to accommodate you." He waved them away and went back to the reservation log on the stand in front of him.

"Maybe we can go someplace else," Callie offered. "There's Michael's down the street. I bet they're not too full—"

"We're already *here*," Alex told her before turning back to the maitre d'. He closed the reservation book with a swift flick of his wrist, drawing the man's surprised attention. "Please find us a table." Steel edged each word of his quiet command, and Alex stared at the other man for a long moment. Power radiated from his body and Callie felt herself inching back, both afraid of a confrontation and fully expecting one, especially when she saw a large, suited man, obviously security, step up behind the maitre d' and grumble, "This guy giving you trouble, Harry?"

"Uh, no," the maitre d' finally murmured. "Just a lost reservation. One moment, sir," he told Alex, his tone suddenly respectful. "I'll find you something."

As they waited, Callie clutched her purse and stared through the marble-floored foyer into the rest of the restaurant.

It was the sort of dining establishment designed for couples. Small round tables barely large enough for two people filled the first floor; the second story at the top of the carved oak staircase was reserved for even more discreet dining. Or so Callie had heard. In the back, French doors opened onto a stone courtyard, a fountain in its center bubbling with water, surrounded by dozens of blazing torches casting flickering shadows in all directions.

The only other light came from small votives on each table. Couples laughed and smiled and leaned closer to each other, their hushed whispers mingling with the soft jazz tunes played by a well-dressed trio near the open patio. The room seemed to beckon Callie inside, the ambience seducing her like a lover's touch.

Suddenly she wasn't so sure she'd agreed to just dinner. Panic filled her for a split second, and she turned to Alex, ready to excuse herself and get out while she still had a rational thought in her head.

The moment her gaze lit on the slight tremble of his shoulders, the strange expression on his face, her panic gave way to concern. She reached out, compelled to touch him and ease the guilt she could see on his face.

"Alex, what's wrong?"

Alex felt Callie's touch on his arm, her fingertips burning into him with their blessed heat—a heat that stoked the fire already raging inside him. But oddly enough, the fire didn't consume him. In those few moments they spent waiting to be seated, it was something much worse that threatened.

"Is it Emily?" Callie asked.

It wasn't Emily. The girl had merely been a reminder: of what he was now, what he'd been so long ago.

"I . . . I'll be back," he said. And before she could respond, he left her standing in the doorway of Petrie's, staring after him as he darted into the restaurant toward the courtyard.

The trembling in his hands grew worse. A wave of cold froze his blood, making his entire body quake in response.

"Sir? Are you all right, sir?" A voice called after him as he pushed his way through to the courtyard, gulping for fresh air.

He closed his eyes as his trembling grew worse. Control. He had to get his control back. But control was a distant memory being shoved aside by a prominent image from the past.

"*Alex. Come and play, Alex!*" a child's voice squealed. "*Come and play. The water's so warm.*"

He reached up and clamped his hands over his ears, his gaze searching Petrie's courtyard for a wild moment before he saw the men's restroom across the way. He rushed toward it.

A split second later, he burst into the room. The door slammed open against the wall with all the force of the anger and fear and dread crippling his body.

The voice in his head was louder. More distinct. More real.

"*Please come and play, Alex. Just for a few minutes. Just come to the water's edge. I promise not to splash and get your new boots wet. I promise!*"

"What in the blue blazes is going on?" came the startled voice of the restroom attendant. The words died the moment Alex stared into the man's dark eyes. The attendant backed up a step.

"Go on and take care of your business, mister." He motioned Alex to the stalls. "It's all yours." He watched Alex with cautious, fearful eyes that betrayed he knew what Alex was, that he could sense the evil.

Some men could. There were certainly those who spent their lives hunting down the Evil One and his minions, trying to destroy them. And yet they merely tried; they would never succeed. *Never.* Alex knew firsthand. He'd come up against too many priests, evangelists, and the like. None had been able to end his misery.

He pushed past the man and reached the privacy of a bathroom stall just as his legs gave way. He went down on his knees, memories raining down with the force of a Gulf Coast storm during hurricane season. Fast, furious, and devastating. He barely had time to close his eyes, or to brace himself before the vision filled his head.

Chapter Twelve

Alex walked through time, through a scene from his past. Only this time he wasn't the fool he'd been, blinded by love and lust. No, now he knew the truth. The dread. The terrible aching helplessness as he watched his beloved baby sister Veronique, and faced the realization that he'd allowed her to die. He'd killed her.

"Alex, come and play." Veronique flew at him, her five-year-old arms outstretched, ready to fling around his neck the moment he knelt down on the soft grass that banked Jackson Creek.

"Not now, love. Maybe after we finish lunch." He glanced at the picnic basket atop the lace table-cloth carried from the main house. Then at Catherine, her graceful form stretched out on the ground, her white lawn dress a stark contrast to the blanket of green grass beneath her. Her blue eyes were light and promising, her lips slightly parted, glistening wet and inviting in the hot afternoon sun.

"Pooh," Veronique said, squirming out of his embrace. "You said this was a picnic. Picnics are s'posed to be fun. You always swim with me, Alex. 'member last week?"

"We have company this time, *chère*."

She stared past him to Catherine and the bright spark in her eyes dimmed. "I hate company." She turned and marched toward the creek, her lower lip jutted out to indicate her displeasure. "I don't need you, anyway. I've got Delilah." She whistled, and a huge basset hound came ambling around the trunk of a nearby oak. "Come on 'lilah. We're going swimming."

"I think she's a little jealous," Alex remarked as he lowered himself down next to Catherine. Her hand quickly covered his, and their fingers entertwined.

"It will pass," she said. "Once she realizes that I'm here to stay."

"Are you?" he asked.

"Aren't I?" she returned, her voice low and seductive, her tongue trailing along her bottom lip. A jolt of heat went through him to settle uncomfortably in his sex.

"At least for today," he murmured, leaning closer, his lips near her ear. "And tonight."

She laughed, a throaty sound that sent another wave of heat through him.

Catherine trailed a fingertip along the curve of

one muscled bicep hidden beneath his white silk shirt. "Maybe you could pose for me again after dinner? I just have a few more things to perfect and then—"

"Alex!" Veronique squealed, drowning Catherine's words. "Look at 'lilah! She fetched the ball like you taught her last week!"

Alex glanced up to see his little sister splashing in the creek, and Delilah jumping and wagging her tail. A red ball peeked through the dog's huge jowls.

"Master Daimon? Sir, your mother needs to speak with you." A shadow moved over him, and Alex glanced up to see one of his family servants.

"Now? We're right in the middle of a picnic."

"Now, sir. She's just arrived home. When the staff informed her that you had, er, company, she demanded to see you."

Alex winked at Catherine. "Keep an eye on Veronique and Delilah. The child's liable to drown the poor animal."

She smiled and waved him away. Quickly he was striding across the grounds toward his family mansion, nestled as it was in a cluster of oak trees, Spanish moss dangling from them like huge silver spiderwebs. His mother had called him inside to berate him. "I'll not have a woman like that keeping company with my son," she was saying when they heard Delilah's first bark.

Alex was halfway back across the grounds when he heard Veronique's cries. As he reached the creek, he saw her small head bob, her hands reaching out, flailing in the direction of Catherine, who stood on the creek bank watching.

Watching?

Then his sister disappeared completely, and her cries disappeared.

Alex dove into the water after her, knowledge of her death knifing through him even before he pulled Veronique's limp body from the shallow water. He begged and pleaded to the heavens, cried for God to save her. But why would God do anything when the Devil's minion stood on the bank not a foot away, so pristine and perfect in her fine lawn dress, and invited?

He hadn't known what Catherine was, then. He'd known only a bitter helplessness as he'd tried desperately to revive his baby sister, his efforts to no effect. He was too late.

Too late.

"I—I couldn't do anything, Alex. I tried to reach her in time. I tried."

He looked up to see Catherine on her knees beside him now. Tears streamed down the woman's cheeks, but he saw this time that the remorse didn't touch her eyes. Nothing had ever seemed to touch those eyes. No hint of feeling. No softness. He realized the truth now.

She hadn't gone in after Veronique, hadn't even waded out to try. She'd done nothing. She'd let the child die because Veronique had seen her as what she was. As Alex had not. *Evil.*

"I—I panicked," Catherine said, her voice breaking on the last word, as if she felt she needed to explain. "Froze."

He closed his eyes, gathering his sister's limp body close and simply holding her. As if he could hold her with him and keep her soul from floating away.

But she'd already gone.

Come and play with me, Alex.

Yes! his mind screamed. That's what I should have said. What I should have done.

Instead, he'd left her alone with a woman who'd stood by and watched her drown, a cold, unfeeling demoness who couldn't have helped his sister even if she'd wanted to. Not that she had, of course. Veronique had seen through Catherine, sensed an evil Alex had been too blind to see.

Why hadn't Catherine reached out?

Because she hadn't wanted to. Veronique had feared Catherine, and disliked her; she'd seen the evil in her, and so Catherine had wanted the child out of the way. She hadn't wanted to reach out— and even if she had, Alex now knew, she couldn't have. Catherine could no more have grabbed Veronique than Alex had been able to comfort Emily. Children were pure, untainted, and his and Catherine's kind could not touch them.

For a moment when he'd seen Emily's tears, he'd forgotten; he'd felt only a gut instinct to help her. He'd wanted to rescue this child as he'd been unable to save his sister.

But the Evil One hadn't let him forget what he was.

Alex opened his eyes and stared down at his hands, at their shaking. He couldn't forget, couldn't escape. The Evil One was reminding him of Catherine and what she'd done to him. Of what she'd taken: his precious Veronique and his power.

Yes, he'd been the one responsible for his sister's death. He'd been blind. Too blinded by lust to see the truth. He'd believed Catherine's lies, her excuses.

And what was the truth now?

That Callie hadn't hesitated. She'd reached out to Emily without a second thought. She'd helped that little girl when Alex hadn't been able to. She wasn't like Catherine. She wasn't—

"Mister Daimon, sir, are you all right?" The restroom attendant's voice cut through Alex's reverie. A tap on the door followed.

Alex forced himself together and stepped out of the stall, his gaze riveting on the attendant. The man smiled at him, ice blue eyes staring hard and deep and through Alex.

"What are *you* doing here?"

"Like it?" the Evil One asked, twirling. The white jacket of the attendant's uniform was a stark contrast to the man's dark skin. "Thought I'd try out a new look. What do you think?"

"Does it matter what I think?"

"Actually, not a bit. Just being polite, my boy." The Prince of Darkness's eyes turned colder and the temperature in the room dropped several degrees.

"Having a little trouble?" he asked. His gaze locked on Alex's trembling hands.

"As if you don't know."

"You should listen to your friend Caine and quit stalling. Make love to her, Alex." The command was simple, short and sweet. The Evil One stared at him for a long drawn-out moment and Alex felt frozen and burned at the very same time. His blood pounded in his veins.

"She's a pretty piece, Alex, and it's been so long since your last assignment."

"No more than a few days."

"Too long for you, my boy, and too long for me. I'm tired of waiting. Do my bidding or suffer the consequences."

"Consequences?"

"I can't touch your precious piece—not spoil her anyhow. But I can put an end to that pretty face of hers." He raised a hand and Alex watched as the short, manicured nails of the attendant grew sharp and pointed. "I've always enjoyed carving." He laughed then, a sound that grated in Alex's ears, was sandpaper on his raw nerves. "And I can always use a new subject."

No! The word ripped through Alex's thoughts and his trembling subsided as anger gripped him. "She's mine," he said instead.

"Only so long as you do what I say."

Alex nodded. He couldn't say no and risk Callie's physical well-being. And from now on, he couldn't risk not being with her.

"I think we understand each other, my boy," the Devil said.

At that moment, a man pushed into the restroom. The Evil One gave Alex a wink, picked up a tray of mints and said to the new arrival, "Good dinner, sir?"

"Get out of my way, man. Too many martinis."

As Alex turned and walked away, he heard the Evil One's soft reply in his head.

"Your last martinis."

Alex walked back to just outside the French doors and stared into the restaurant. Callie sat at a small table in the far corner. Every few seconds, she glanced around her—looking for him, he knew.

He touched a finger to his lips, then trailed his fingertip down the doorway. Her eyes went wide and she shifted, her tongue coming out unconsciously to trail across her bottom lip. Alex focused on the simple gesture, let it feed the lust setting his blood on fire.

So he could do what he had to do.

So he could make her truly his, even if for only the short blessed time until the deed was done.

Then the Evil One would come for her—no, for Catherine.

He had to remember to hate Callie for the monster inside of her. He had to! Vengeance was all he had left. He'd lost everything. The book. His sister. Himself.

Payback was all he had left.

He knew that, but as Alex eased into the seat next to Callie, the table so small that his thigh brushed hers as he sat down, Catherine and revenge were the farthest things from his mind.

He saw only the woman in front of him.

Felt only her.

Wanted only her.

Callie. Sweet, sweet, luscious Callie.

"Are you all right—" she started to say, but a tuxedo-clad waiter arrived before she could finish.

"What can I get for you this evening?" the waiter asked.

"Could we change tables?" She tugged at the top button of her blouse. "Maybe sit closer to the doors? It's awful crowded in here. And hot."

The waiter nodded, and Alex helped Callie up, his fingertips caressing the soft skin near her elbow as he steered her after the waiter to a small corner near the open French doors. A miniscule breeze blew through, and Callie breathed a heavy sigh of relief.

"It's not exactly cooler," Alex said.

"No, but it isn't so closed in. It's much better." She smiled.

"Now, what can I get you?" the waiter asked after both Alex and Callie had been seated.

Callie stared at the menu, then at Alex who was busy staring at her, his menu untouched. He ordered a bottle of wine—fine wine, she was certain—but continued to stare.

"I'll have the jumbo shrimp platter," she said, "a side salad . . . ooh, and bring me a shrimp cocktail, too."

"Nothing for me," Alex finished. When Callie

243

gave him an incredulous look, he added, "As much as you ordered, you're going to need someone to help you finish it off."

"Cheapskate."

"I'm not being cheap. Just practical, *chère.*"

Callie wondered why he wasn't eating. Alex Daimon certainly wasn't a cheapskate. Not dressed in a silk Armani shirt, designer jeans—deliciously tight designer jeans and black snakeskin boots. There was nothing cheap about him.

Alex leaned forward on the table, his forearm resting so close to her, her skin prickled. She searched for something to distract her from his physical presence. As if anything could.

She licked her lips, incredibly conscious of his: the way they'd felt against hers, the way they'd tasted. . . .

"You look a little flushed."

"This weather," she replied, tugging at the top button of her blouse. But it wasn't so much the weather. The air conditioner was running in the main section of the restaurant, filtering out to beat back the heat that pushed in through the open doors. No, the heat Callie felt had little to do with Mother Nature, and everything to do with the man sitting next to her.

"I'm sorry I kept at you about Emily," she said, eager to fill the sudden silence.

He didn't flinch at her mention of the child, as if the episode in the alley had never happened. It was as if the man she'd seen so out of control had been simply a figment of her imagination.

"Let's not dwell on the past. The present is much more interesting." One finger traced the stem of his wine glass and she could've sworn she felt Alex's touch on the curve of her neck. Soft, purposeful, and oh so delicious . . .

"That was quite a disappearing act you pulled at my house when my father revived," she said, desperate for a distraction from the unnerving sensation.

"There you go about the past again. If you'd wanted me to stay, *chère,* all you had to do was ask."

"I didn't say I did, but . . . Even if I had, one minute you were there, the next you were gone! Burgess didn't even see you leave." She gave him a wary smile.

"Your butler had other things on his mind."

Callie's good humor evaporated as she thought of her father. Her eyes filled with tears and her vision blurred. All at once, she felt Alex's fingers close around her own and a comforting warmth stole through her.

"Don't, Callie. Not tonight. Put all the pain, all the worry out of your mind. Just for tonight."

She nodded, because there was nothing else she could do. And because she wanted to push it all away. Just for a little while. She'd been suffering, crying, unhappy for so long. For the next hour or so, she wanted to be normal. A normal woman with a normal man, having a normal dinner and conversation and . . .

And what?

Nothing, a voice whispered. Here at this table was where her association with Alex Daimon would end. At least, until she found a way out of the mess her life had become.

Yet, for now, she could pretend that nothing else existed. She could smile and flirt and be happy. Just for a little while.

She blinked back the moisture in her eyes and forced a smile. "You're right. I need to think about something else."

"How about me?" he asked.

She found herself saying something she never would have before. "You've definitely caught my interest."

"The real test is whether or not I can keep it."

"Can you?" she asked breathlessly.

"I'm sure I can think of some way." Alex loosened his grip and slid his fingers up her arm, their tips brushing the sensitive inside of her wrist.

"So tell me about yourself," she managed after a long, breathless moment while her body tried to control the sudden mind-rushing sensations that assailed it. "I—You know everything about me, and I know nothing about you. Do you work? Or did you win the lottery?"

He laughed. "The lottery?"

"From the way you're dressed, you obviously have money. So which is it? Work or luck?"

"Which would you guess?"

"From the way you treated that maitre' d, I'd say you're used to being in control. I imagine you work. A very prestigious, very high-paying, high-profile kind of job where you get to order everyone around." She took a sip of the wine the waiter had quietly poured for her.

"Is that what I did? Order him around?"

"Not so much order. It's the way you handled yourself, the way you spoke." Callie took another drink, her mouth suddenly dry. Warmth crept through her, fogging her senses with each delicious taste of the wine. "You're obviously used to being in charge."

"Once. A long time ago." He shook his head, as if shaking off a bad thought. "But not anymore. Now, I simply do what I'm told like everyone else."

"Really?" At his nod, Callie added, "So who has the pleasure of telling you what to do, Alex Daimon?"

"What?"

"What company do you work for?"

"I help in the family business," he answered, before tossing down the entire contents of his own wine glass. "Tobacco."

"Export, import, what?"

"We grow it."

"Where?"

He gave her an impatient stare. "You certainly ask a lot of questions."

She took his impatience in stride. And the wine was making her forgiving. "We already established that outside. And I don't usually eat dinner with strange men, so naturally I'm curious."

"Am I still strange?" he asked.

"The strangest," she answered. Her lips curved

into a lazy smile. "So, where does your family grow tobacco? I don't think there's been a farm in this area for ages. The Beauregards over off of River Road still have the original sugar mill used at their plantation in the early 1800s, but the thing hasn't been used in ages."

"Northern Louisiana," he offered. "We have a big spread north of here."

"So what are you doing here in New Orleans, and why are you staying at that rundown place on the other side of the cemetery—"

"Here we are," the waiter announced, cutting off her question as he arrived with a huge platter of food.

"Did I order all of this?" she asked after the waiter had spread out the delicacies in front of her, refilled their wine glasses, then disappeared.

"Unless you've got a twin I don't know about," he said with a laugh.

She gave him her warmest smile. "I plead temporary insanity."

"You can plead as much as you want, *chère*." The seductive words did more than a touch ever could. "—but you don't have to. I'll gladly give you anything you want."

She gave him a pointed stare. The wine freed her from her inhibitions and made her bolder than she might have otherwise been. "You do that on purpose."

"What?"

"Try to shock me."

"The truth is so shocking?"

"There you go again."

"I speak what's on my mind. *You* are on my mind."

"Why?"

"Because one kiss wasn't enough."

"There were two kisses. One at your place, and one at—"

"So your thoughts aren't so different from mine. You've been in my head since that first night."

"You *haven't* been on my mind."

"Liar," he said softly. She would have been angry at the presumption, except the way he said the word, almost as if he whispered a term of endearment, sent desire knifing through her.

"The food's getting cold," he reminded her after a moment. Callie fixed her attention on her plate. She reached for a shrimp with relish, as if putting extra effort into the act could distract her from the dangerous thoughts racing through her mind.

Callie's thoughts were dangerous. Alex could see them mirrored in her eyes, then his gaze dropped to her mouth and he found himself mesmerized. Her full lips curved as she smiled at him, the gesture both innocent and provocative at the same time. The she reached over and picked up another of the shrimp that adorned her chilled cocktail glass. Her lips closed around the succulent morsel. He all but found release right then and there.

She reached for another, this time pausing to dip the seafood into cocktail sauce before aiming for her mouth. He watched, entranced, as she laved off the sauce, then took a big, juicy bite.

"Oops," she murmured, a dollop of red sauce falling to stain the white tablecloth. "I'm not usually such a messy eater."

"I have that effect on women," he murmured, bringing another smile to her mouth.

"It's not you, I'm afraid. It's the wine." It glistened on her lips, a tiny drop working its way down her chin, and he couldn't stop himself from leaning closer, reaching out one tanned finger to gather the drop, skimming her full bottom lip with his knuckle.

"And I thought it was my devastating charm driving you senseless." He pulled his hand back and touched his knuckle to his lips. He tasted her—salty skin, sweet wine, and ripe woman.

"Is senseless the way you want me?"

"I want you any way I can get you, *chère*."

She gave him a small grin. "You sound like you're after my heart."

"Your heart, or maybe another part of you." He couldn't stop his eyes from drifting to the tabletop, from wondering if she tasted as good all over. He wondered if she was as bittersweet in the soft, hot spot between her legs.

His arousal strained against the fabric of his jeans as she ate another shrimp, and another. Those senses he'd been given when he was cursed, heightened as they were, were driving him mad. He could smell her, taste her, could taste the shrimp on her lips, the wine. He'd been to the brink of this insanity time and time again, but the drop had never been so steep, and he'd never been so high up, so anxious to fall. Strange, but at this moment it seemed new; it was as if he waited to explore uncharted territory.

Him? A man who'd had more women throughout the past century than he could possibly count, much less remember?

Yes. With Callie, every taste, every smell, every experience felt brand-new. He was the virgin and she his tutor, showing him each new sensation, new feeling.

Feeling?

The notion astounded him. He hadn't felt anything save lust in such a long, long time. It was terrifying. She frightened him, this woman, this girl, this virgin. He must not ruin her.

It's *Catherine!* he reminded himself. Or soon will be.

Emotion warred inside of him, but the battle was quickly over. His lust was the victor. Alex reached a hand beneath the tablecloth and found the skin of her thigh burning through the material of her skirt.

Callie stiffened, like a rag doll through which someone had just shoved a spiked rod. Her hand quickly covered his—to push him away or maybe to pull him closer. He didn't wait to see which. He worked his fingers higher, gathering her skirt beneath his fingertips, until his flesh made contact with hers. She gave a surprised little gasp.

The emotions raging on her face were too confusing for him to read. Strange, considering he'd had no trouble sifting through anyone's thoughts until now.

Until Callie.

"No," she breathed, but he could see in her eyes that she didn't mean it. She didn't know what she meant. Confusion flashed across her features, and her bottom lip trembled, full and inviting. He moved his hand higher, Callie's heat pulling him up her thigh despite her hand holding him at bay.

Then he touched her there, and her indecision fled. Desire blazed in her eyes and her mouth opened, just a slight, sensuous bit. It was enough for him to know that she liked, and wanted, what he was doing. She would never admit it, though.

Suddenly he wanted her to do just that. He had no need to have her accept what he was offering verbally; as long as her mind and her body agreed, the rules of Heaven didn't require she say the words. But he wanted her to. He *needed* her to.

"No?" He curled his fingers, drawing away from the heat of her for a short moment. She gasped. "Such a shame, *chère*. I thought you wanted me to touch you."

"I . . ." Her voice shook, the word trembling on her parted lips. "I—I do."

"Are you sure?"

Obviously torn she nodded, and Alex almost reached out. But part of him needed to hear more, to hear every soft syllable as she acquiesced to the need that burned between them.

"I can't hear you, Callie," he whispered.

"Please." She paused for a deep breath of air. "Please . . . touch me."

He trailed one finger against the crotch of her silk panties and she gasped, the napkin clutched in her hand. His finger traced tiny circles, closer to their lacy edge, until he slipped the tip of one finger inside and felt her.

Hot. Wet. Delicious.

A small cry caught in Callie's throat, and her head fell back. Her hand softened atop his and her whole body shivered. He could see her surrender in her features, the soft trembling of her full bottom lip as he inched higher, deeper, her legs parting for his finger.

"Please," she whispered again, and he wasn't sure if she meant for him to stop, or to continue.

Not that she had a choice. Nor did he. He couldn't stop, couldn't pull away if the legions of Hell had been calling him back.

But they wouldn't, of course. They wanted this. As did he. God help him, he wanted Callie—soft and vulnerable and utterly helpless beneath him.

"Will there be anything else, sir?" The waiter's voice disrupted Alex's thoughts. He glanced up.

Callie stiffened, as if reality had called back her sanity, returning her to the restaurant, to the dozen or so curious gazes glancing their way. She turned beet red, shoving him away, her legs closing abruptly.

With every ounce of strength he had, Alex pulled back. But it wasn't easy. His body shook. Control was almost impossible to attain. Sensation ruled.

253

He wanted to reach out, pull her onto his lap, onto his throbbing cock and bury himself deep inside her. He would fill her, push in to the hilt, raise flames to destroy this restaurant so they could focus on their lovemaking alone. He would become a beast, a raging, carnal beast. Then he wouldn't have to think.

Not about vengeance.

Or salvation.

He would focus only on the whirlwind of feelings cycloning around him, hurtling him toward satisfaction—those most precious few moments of satisfaction he could ever know.

"I—I have to go." Callie bolted to her feet, her chair tumbling backwards. "It's getting so late—"

"But you haven't finished your dinner." Alex was on his feet, but she'd already righted her chair. She snatched up her purse, keeping her gaze anywhere but on him.

"I—I've had enough." The wine's relaxing effect seemed to have worn off. Awkwardly, she clutched her purse. "Uh, thank you. Everything was"—she cleared her throat—"uh, very nice."

"It could have been so much nicer."

She looked at him then—because she couldn't help herself, he knew. He didn't know much else about what was racing through Callie Wisdom's mind, but he knew that. Her emotions were in her eyes.

"I doubt that," she said, a last feeble chance at protecting herself.

He went for the kill. "I can prove it." He stared

hard and deep into the smoky gray-green of her eyes. "Give me a chance."

She couldn't seem to make her lips form a reply. Alex reached out, tracing their softness, wishing with all his being he could tell her not to be afraid, not to fear what was inside of her, these feelings, this thing they had between them. But he couldn't, because he knew she *should* be afraid. More afraid than she'd ever been in her life. Alex didn't just want her body. It was her soul he was after.

She shook her head, the gesture quick and frantic. "I—I don't think so. It's so late and I'm really busy . . . with my father and all." The waiter took that opportunity to hand Alex the check. The man shrugged, and Alex almost decapitated him on the spot. While he was busy flicking several bills onto the table, Callie used the momentary distraction to escape.

Alex wasn't sure what drove him after her.

The need to soothe her fears?

Or the very painful arousal throbbing in his pants. It was a pain he knew only she could ease.

He didn't bother to discover the answer, just pushed his way out into the street, his gaze frantically searching the crowd. He had to find Callie, had to have her. He had to!

Chapter Thirteen

Callie walked faster, dodging past people as she hurried down Bourbon Street. She didn't chance a glance behind her, but she knew he followed. She could feel him. The sensation drove her all the faster. She had to get away.

She wouldn't be responsible for what happened. She'd lose herself, just as she had in the restaurant. She hadn't meant for things to go so far between them, but when he'd touched her . . . And then when he *hadn't* . . .

For a split second, the world had stopped. She'd waited, and then she'd begged!

She closed her eyes as guilt and humiliation washed over her. What sort of person was she to let a man—no, to actually *invite* him to—do such things to her when a restaurant full of people surrounded them? With her father alone and dying at home?

She blinked, clearing her head of the final effects of the wine. If only she could blame it on the alcohol. But she could have had three bottles of wine instead of three glasses, and she would have still felt what Alex Daimon had done to her—what she'd *begged* him to do to her.

Which was why she had to get away. Now. If she spent any more time with Alex, she would lose the battle with her raging lust. Even now a small part of her urged her to stop, to return and throw herself into his arms and let all her troubles slip away for a few blessed, carnal moments.

Maybe if she slept with him, she could push him out of her system. Maybe this was simply years' worth of self-repression. One tawdry encounter and her lust might be sated, and then she could get back to business.

Yes, but once wouldn't be nearly enough. Sleeping with him would only make her want him more. She knew it deep in her gut, just as surely as she knew if she stopped now, she would never find the strength to flee him again, to return to her lonely life and her futile efforts to save her father.

The enormity of that realization made her heart pound almost out of her chest. She hardly knew this man. He was a stranger. So how could she feel so inexplicably connected, *consumed*—as if there were other forces at work drawing them together?

Crazy!

That's what she told herself, and she kept moving.

She rounded a corner, her senses on alert. Her gaze darted frantically from side to side. She needed an escape. Someplace to hide . . .

The thought ground to a halt when she spotted an open doorway. Blue neon flashed above it, intermittently casting shadows across a multitude of faces as a line of people pushed in and out of the small club beyond. He'd never be able to find her, if she managed to get inside.

Callie braced herself and shoved her way through. The darkness inside swallowed her as she pushed deeper into the throng.

That's a good girl. Run, Callie. Run!

The soft words sounded in her head, and Callie came to a dead stop. Her hands tingled. Heat gripped her for a split second, then someone crashed up against her backside.

"Hey! Watch it," came a disgruntled female voice behind her. "Keep the line moving."

Callie shook away the disturbing sensations and moved forward. Had Catherine been speaking to her, encouraging her flight, or had the words come from her usually dormant common sense? She hadn't recognized the voice.

Music filled her ears and drowned out the pounding of blood in her temples. Steeling herself, Callie worked her way through the crowd, past groping hands and invitations to dance. The last thing she wanted to do was dance. She was running for her life, her sanity.

At last she reached the far wall, leaned against it, seemingly so far removed from the club's entrance, she wondered if she'd even be able to find her way out. Rather than frightening, the thought comforted her. Relief seeped through Callie and she closed her eyes. She would find a table, order something to calm her nerves and wait a half-hour. That should put Alex Daimon far away from the Quarter by then. Surely he would think she'd gone home.

Don't underestimate him. This time the voice was familiar; it whispered inside Callie's head and she stiffened. *He's dangerous, Callie. He'll ruin you if you let him too close.*

"Go away," Callie practically wept, but the voice was relentless.

I'll never go away. I'm a part of you now, Callie. I can help you. I can help us. I can keep Alex from harming us if you simply give me the chance. Let me help. Give me control.

Callie shook her head frantically and a wave of heat washed through her, like someone had closed her into an oven. Her stomach churned and she doubled over, her breaths coming in short, frantic gasps.

Stupid, girl. You can't fight me. I'm here inside of you and you're already so tired. Tired of fighting for your father, tired of fending off Alex, tired of trying to change fate. Rest now, and let me ease the burden. Just give your troubles to me. Give your soul to me.

"No," Callie whispered, desperate to fight, to somehow counteract the truth that Catherine

Drashierre had unquestionably managed to creep inside of her, wanted complete possession of her.

Never, she promised herself. She was still in control, and she was staying in control. This seemed like something out of a movie, unbelievable, but she had no choice but to believe. Callie could not run from this as she had her own power. Going to Texas, fleeing, would not help her now, and she could do nothing but stay and fight. Which was what she would do.

She'd let the situation overwhelm her once before but it would never happen again. This time, it wasn't her happiness but her father's life hanging in the balance. If she failed, he would have no hope.

"I need some air," she gasped to herself, wishing she'd never fled here. This club was too small. There were too many people. If she could just get some fresh air . . .

Fresh air won't get rid of me, Callie. Nothing can do that. I'm a part of you now.

"No. You won't take control. I won't let you."

A chuckle exploded inside her head, only to die down as the voice hissed, *Stop fooling yourself. There is nothing you can do. Stop fighting me, Callie; you can't win. You can't—*

The words died as Callie felt a touch on her shoulder.

"I thought you were calling it a night."

Alex's deep voice pushed through the noise and chaos of the club, and Callie's eyes snapped open. He'd found her. Callie's nausea, like Catherine's voice, disappeared, and she managed a deep, calming breath. Still, she knew her composure wouldn't last.

"I—I was a little thirsty," she mumbled, her body already feeling the inevitable effects of his presence.

What was the sense in fighting what she knew would happen? She'd tried to run, to escape both him and herself, but it hadn't worked. Alex had won. Her damned, desperate hormones would never let her leave him again. They raged as his gold-flecked gaze washed away her will.

"Well, since we're here," he said nonchalantly, reaching out to grasp her hand, his fingertips sending delicious tremors through her body, "Maybe you'd like to dance before . . ."

"Before what?"

He stared at her a long moment, then replied, "Your drink, of course."

But she knew he'd meant much more. *Before I take you to bed. Before I slide deep inside you and love you. Before I . . .*

Crude words filtered through her head, but want coiled in her stomach, spiraling outward, pushing the last remnants of her doubt and fear aside, until nothing kept Callie from twining her fingers with his and following Alex out onto the crowded dance floor. For a split second, she thought of the numerous offers inviting her to dance, some from good-looking men, some from not-so-good-looking men. She'd turned them all down, content to hide away, to keep her focus.

But she couldn't refuse Alex. She didn't want to. Blue neon lights swirled overhead, casting dancing shapes across his handsome features. All around them, bodies gyrated to the slow, erotic rhythm of the music that slid into Callie's ears, weaving a hypnotic spell that sapped her last bit of will.

Her purse slipped to the floor at her feet, and she let Alex pull her forward, until his body stood a fraction from hers. He was so close she could feel the heat of his skin.

She closed her eyes, letting the warmth and the music and luscious smell of Alex consume her senses. She swayed, feeling the fabric of her clothes slide over her skin with each movement. In her mind, she imagined Alex's touch replacing that fabric, his fingertips scorching, setting her ablaze. . . .

She felt the solid length of him press against her then, the iron rod of his arousal pressing into the soft flesh of her belly. Adrenaline flooded her body and her every nerve stood at attention.

"Open your eyes, Callie." The soft command lifted her heavy eyelids when her own will couldn't manage. "I want you to look at me. Let me see everything you're thinking . . . feeling." And with the words, he grasped her other hand, now holding both captive.

She stared into Alex's eyes, letting their dark fire consume her. For a heart-stopping moment, their gazes fused, locked, and she felt him touch her *inside*, his heart reaching out to hers—*crying* out, it seemed.

The feelings disintegrated as an image hit her. Her power, it was working of its own accord, feeding her visions. . . .

I bet you could teach me a few things. The words rang in Callie's head and she saw a woman, dishwater-blond hair draped over a stained pillowcase, melon-like breasts glistening with sweat and reflecting pink light filtering from a window.

"Callie?" Alex's voice cut into her thoughts, but it couldn't bring her back from where his gaze had pulled her. A dark, humid room, window open to New Orleans' night sounds, and the naked woman spread out across the bare mattress.

Come on. I'm ready for you. The blonde's legs were spread wide. The scent of sex burned Callie's nostrils, and she clamped her eyes shut, trying to obliterate the picture.

"Callie? What's wrong?" His hands went to her shoulders.

She shook her head frantically. "N—nothing." She jerked free of him. "We can't do this," she murmured, snatching her purse up from the floor. Alex reached for her again, but she shrugged loose, moving to the side to let a dancing couple move between them. She whispered the words, more for herself than Alex, though she knew he heard them. "I can't do this." Then she turned and beat a hasty retreat from the club.

He didn't follow her, and she was glad—or at least she told herself she was. She didn't know what she'd seen, but it had been a part of Alex's past and not a very pretty one.

It shouldn't bother her. She'd told him, and herself, she didn't want a relationship. What did it matter who he'd been with?

It doesn't, she thought frantically.

Also, came another realization: Alex wasn't the clean and pretty stuff her dreams had conjured. He'd had a life before her, apparently a lurid one. This was the precious reality she'd been begging for—complete with less than perfect people. And with it came other unpleasantness. Sex wasn't as simple as one man being attracted to one woman and acting on that attraction. Sex meant Risk. Not everyone had an unsullied past like her own, and there were life-threatening diseases out there. Or she could wind up pregnant. . . .

Where had these starkly real truths been when she'd been begging for him to take her in that restaurant?

Lost, right along with her common sense. Alex did that to her, made her forget her common sense, her responsibilities, her father—everything save the slippery heat between her legs.

She refused to acknowledge the strange sense of loss inside of her that grew as she fled. Instead, she buried the feeling beneath dozens of reasons why her attraction to Alex wasn't healthy, or reasonable; she steeled herself against the regret that lingered by clutching her purse and hailing a cab.

"St. Charles and Dumaine," she said as she crawled into the backseat. She had to get back to her car, then home—exactly where she should have been rather than out, falling victim to Alex Daimon's expert seduction.

But she'd been a willing victim. Didn't that make her wrong, sullied somehow?

The wail of sirens cut through the night. Callie glanced out the cab's front windshield. Outside, red and blue lights whirled, dispelling the darkness where several police cars were gathering in front of a dilapidated brownstone. A uniformed officer stood out in the center lane waving traffic past. A coroner's van was parked at the curb.

Callie didn't think much of the scene at first. New Orleans was a city. Crime was rampant. There were gang killings, drive-by shootings, Mafia hits, not to mention the usual domestic fights that more often than not, resulted in injury or death. Then she spotted the familiar blue regulation Ford that Detective Guidry drove.

They'd found the missing woman.

"Stop," she told the cab driver.

He shook his head. "I got to drive through, miss."

"Let me out."

"But the cop's waving me through."

"I don't care," Callie insisted, reaching up to grasp his shoulder. "Let me out."

He put on the brakes and she climbed out, despite the angry honks from the cars behind them and the police officer who frowned and emphatically motioned them forward.

Callie tossed a five-dollar bill through the cab window into its driver's lap and headed for the sidewalk.

"I'm sorry, ma'am, but you'll have to steer clear of this area," a police officer told her as she tried to walk past.

"I need to see Detective Guidry," she replied. She stared toward the doorway of the brownstone and glimpsed the man's face. He stood engrossed in conversation with two other officers.

"Sorry, but you can see he's busy. Now, if you'll step back."

"Guidry!" she shouted. The detective turned from the doorway and searched the crowd. His gaze finally found her, and she waved.

"Keep that area clear," he shouted to the officer in front of Callie, then he turned back to his conversation.

"Dammit, Guidry! You can ignore me, but I'm not going away," Callie called.

"Not surprised to see *you* here, Miss Wisdom," a voice rang out. The reporter Callie had seen at the other crime scene rushed at her, microphone in hand. "Do the police have any leads? What about your input into the case—"

"Walters! I'll have your ass thrown in jail if you don't get the hell away from here." Guidry appeared from nowhere, and several other officers stepped forward to push the newsman back.

"Guidry, I need to talk to you," Callie said, refusing to budge when an officer came to move her. "Come on; or else I'll have to do my talking with the *Picayune*."

The detective glared at her, then muttered, "Let her through. What the hell are you doing here anyway?" he demanded.

"You found that girl, didn't you?" He didn't have to say a word. The truth was obvious in the way he shifted from one foot to the other, the anxious light in his eyes, the grim set of his mouth.

The girl was dead. Callie's chest tightened and her stomach shifted. She hadn't been able to help, and it had cost this girl her life. Worse, she couldn't stop future killings. And there *would* be more. She knew that just as surely as she knew anything.

"I'm sorry," she said. "But you have to double your efforts to find this guy. He won't stop."

Guidry gave her an odd look. "Things have changed, Callie. We don't think it's the same killer anymore. The MO's are completely different."

Callie shook her head, somehow knowing the policemen was wrong. "It's him."

"Look, we gave it a try and we didn't come up with anything. I appreciate what you tried to do, but I've got a whole helluva lot of shit coming down on me right now. I can't ignore the facts. The DNA evidence is giving us completely different evidence for every killer. Unless it's a gang—"

"But I saw the same man with those last two bodies," Callie interrupted. When Guidry shook his head and turned away, she grasped his arm. "I'm telling you, it's the same guy. Each woman had the incision marks, didn't they?"

"Go home, Miss Wisdom."

"Let me see the body," Callie insisted. She stared past the yellow police tape to the dark stairwell leading to the second floor.

" 'Fraid I can't."

"Listen to your gut, Guidry. You know the killings are all related. The incisions—"

The cop turned on her. "They could have been made by anything, and they're all in different spots. It's inconclusive as evidence. The D.A. already—"

"You've got how many dead women? All of whom were reported missing first. The killer kept them alive for a little while, had his fun, then got rid of them. That, alone, might be enough to link their deaths—"

"Give it up, Miss Wisdom. Go home."

"Did this body have the cuts?"

"Her wrists were clean."

"But they were somewhere else? So he's changing to throw you off track. You know it's the same guy. That's why you brought me in at the beginning. You had a hunch—"

"I had an attack of temporary insanity. I thought I would blow this case wide open, nab a serial killer and guarantee a promotion and get back some of the respect I . . ." He paused, then said instead, "I was wrong, and so were you. The FBI sent someone down from their Serial Killer Crime Unit to do a profile on each of these murders. The agent came up with different profiles for every one."

"But the cuts—"

"Are coincidental. The first body had them because she was suicidal, tried to do herself in. The second scratched herself while struggling with the killer. We determined that, and also found a different blood type—the killer's—which didn't match any other blood type found at the other crime scenes. I'm through speculating, and I don't have time for you. I can't hope for some hocus-pocus any longer and keep spouting the same crap to my superiors. Every newspaper in town has been having a field day with the New Orleans Police Department for my bringing in a psychic. I'm this close"—he held up two fingers—"to being pulled off the street and stuck behind a desk in Records. I know you think you know what you're talking about. Hell, I even still believe in you, Callie, but my ass is in a sling. We've got six bodies, now, Miss Wisdom. *Six* have been found—with different profiles and DNA descriptions for each killer."

"It's one man, Detective. I swear to you. I felt it."

"Didn't you hear a word I said? We've got genetic blueprints of six killers and each is different."

"I know what I felt . . . and that man is your culprit." She gesticulated madly. "I know what I saw."

"You didn't *see* anything. That's the problem. I need a description. Specific details. Not some nonsense about a shadow man and bloody fingerprints on a wall."

"It's the same man," she repeated with trembling lips. When Guidry merely shook his head, she added, "Okay. Let me see her. If I can't give you anything concrete this time, then you can keep looking for six different suspects."

"Callie, I don't have time—"

"Okay. I'll talk to Walters and tell him the truth: that it's the same guy, and that the New Orleans Police Department, not to mention the FBI, has been ignoring a vital link between the murders. They brought in a psychic, then ignored her. I think the citizens of this town will be a little upset that the police chief is busy spending all of their taxpayer dollars to chase the wrong leads."

Guidry gave her a cold look. "You're a psychic. A cosmic cuckoo—at least according to a lot of people. I doubt we'll be crucified for not listening to some nut—even if I did call you in."

Callie sighed, the truth of that statement sinking in. "You're probably right." Silence stretched between them. Was she the only one being forced to examine the supernatural in her life? Maybe the rest of the world should be given a wake-up call. And all she needed was a few concerned citizens to make her threat to Guidry dangerous. "I guess if you're willing to take that chance . . ."

"I could have you thrown in jail for obstruction of justice," Guidry snarled after a long, contemplative moment. "Then you wouldn't get a chance to stir up any trouble."

"I would still get a phone call, and you can bet I won't call my lawyer."

"I don't like threats."

"Neither do I. Besides, it's not a threat. Just the truth. I want to help, Detective Guidry." When he simply glared at her, she added, her voice soft and desperate, "Please. I *need* to help."

With her words, his anger gave way to weary frustration. He nodded. "All right, but if I let you in and you still come up empty-handed, from now on you keep your nose out of my business and your mouth shut."

"Deal."

"Barker!" he shouted. A uniformed officer appeared at his side. "Take Miss Wisdom up to see the body before the coroner bags it."

"The girl was killed right here in her own house," Barker said as he led Callie past the police barricade at the front door. Guidry followed.

Callie was surprised. This wasn't the kidnapped girl from the other night; this was another victim. She found herself wondering if the girl she'd seen was dead. Most likely. "Was there a break-in?" she found herself asking.

The young officer shook his head. "No sign of anything like that. I'd say she knew her killer."

"How did it happen?"

"Slit her throat—ear to ear."

Callie threw a glance over her shoulder at Guidry. The detective kept his eyes averted. "No wonder there were no incision marks on her wrists. If he was draining blood . . ." Callie let the thought trail off, following the officer up the staircase of the ancient building. The stairs were barely supported by a black iron banister, rusted in several spots. The second floor was no better, its rotting hardwood floor creaking with every movement.

"In there," Barker said, pointing to a doorway blocked off by yellow tape.

Callie ducked beneath the tape and into the bedroom. A police photographer stood inside, snapping photos from different angles. Two other men dusted the windowsill for fingerprints. An investigator walked back and forth, reading particulars into a microcassette recorder. The body lay, covered, upon the bed inside.

"Let's get this over with," Guidry snapped. Barker nodded, stepped forward into the room and yanked the sheet down.

Callie's blood turned to ice, and her heart stopped beating as she stared at the woman's face. Dishwater blond hair spilled across the dingy pillowcase.

Suddenly Callie knew—even before she grasped the woman's cold hands and stared into her sightless eyes—who she would see. Her murderer would be the very same man she'd danced with not a half-hour before.

The man she'd seen . . . touched . . . wanted.

The blackness flashed, sharp and consuming, as Callie felt her entire body tremble with her power. She gripped the corpse's cold hands harder, holding on for dear life as the familiar black shadow appeared. She could not see the face.

"You're back? Please! Whatever you want, I'll give you. Just don't hurt me. Please! Don't hurt me!" The blonde's tears came then, fast and furious and searing against Callie's cheeks as the woman begged and pleaded for her life.

The shadow's inhuman chuckle grated in her ears.

"I don't want you to spread your legs, darling. So what else have you got?" A blade flashed a brilliant silver, catching the gleam of the shadow's eyes, and Callie saw them this time.

Clear, intense, consuming—she knew those eyes.

Please! the blonde begged.

The shadow moved into focus, his features taking on distinct qualities, and Callie watched as Alex whirled, turning away.

Please! the woman begged again.

"Miss Wisdom?" The sound of her name obliterated the image, called Callie back. She blinked.

"Miss Wisdom?" the voice asked. "Do you see anything? Do you see the killer?"

She nodded slowly—so slowly it hurt her neck. Her eyes burned. "Your killer *is* the same man."

Guidry gave her a doubtful look. "We've been over this before. It can't be the same sonofabitch."

"But it is." She tilted her head and stared up at him. "I saw him this time."

"You can give a detailed description?"

The words hurt as they formed on her lips. "I'm afraid I can do better than that," she whispered. "I can tell you where to find him."

Chapter Fourteen

"You're sure this is it?" Guidry frowned, squinting through the windshield of his car at the mansion that loomed in front of them.

It looked like something straight out of a Stephen King novel. One of the Greek pillars that supported the porch was deteriorated, half of the post eaten away by years of neglect. Rotted vines slithered up the front of the house like a swarm of dark brown snakes. Windows, their glass a forgotten memory, stared back at Callie like the empty black sockets of a skull. Huge oak trees, their branches withered arms, embraced the area, blocking out the shafts of moonlight. The place was dark, gloomy, lifeless.

"The lieutenant is gonna deep-fry my ass for sure," Guidry muttered, glancing behind him as if he were sizing up his chances of turning away the handful of police cars that had arrived as backup. The officers stayed in their cars awaiting Guidry's signal.

He seemed reluctant to give it.

"I know what you're thinking. I thought the same thing when I first set eyes on it."

"The only things living in this place are rats and cockroaches."

"That's how it looks on the outside. Inside it's completely different. I saw it myself."

"The night before last? When this guy picked you up off the road and brought you home with him after you passed out? And why was it that you fainted again?"

"The heat, maybe. Or exhaustion. I haven't been sleeping much lately."

"Sleep-deprived." He shook his head. "That's great. Just friggin' great. Desk duty, here I come."

The disgust in his voice sent a burst of indignation through Callie. "Look, I thought it was strange that he's been showing up nearly every time I turned around. He's been to my store twice. When I passed out, he just happened to be driving by." She blew out a deep breath. "It all makes sense now." At least, *why* he was following her made sense.

Because of who he was.

What he was.

A *killer*.

Worse, she was the one person, the only person still alive and breathing, who could identify him. Guidry had told her they'd found the other girl— dead—yesterday. Mrs. Bodine's daughter. Callie tried not to let herself be swept away by guilt, tried not to think of the other time she'd failed, the little girl. . . .

"You've turned into a good-looking woman," the detective said, interrupting her thoughts. "Maybe this guy—whoever he is—just liked what he saw and didn't believe in beating around the bush. What's to say he's a killer or that he's targeted you? Maybe he's just a little obsessive and has the hots for you."

Callie leveled a frown at him. "You don't believe me."

"I'm just saying that you could be wrong. There's always a possibility."

"I saw this guy when I touched the latest victim. He is the killer." She turned away and stared at the decrepit old house. "I should have seen it before."

"Why didn't you? If it's the same guy, as you claim, why didn't you see him the last time?"

"I did. Sort of. And deep down, I knew something wasn't quite right that first moment this guy walked into my shop. I just didn't know what it was. Until tonight."

"Until you touched him and saw the woman," he repeated. She'd explained what had happened at the club. At her nod, he asked, "How many glasses of wine did you say you'd had at dinner?"

"What's with all this skepticism? You got me involved, remember?" she reminded him. "I wasn't exactly jumping to volunteer."

He ran a hand over his face and she noted the tired lines around his eyes. "I thought it was the right thing. Hell, it *was* the right thing. It was the only thing. I had no leads. When I heard you'd moved back here, I pulled you in and . . . I'm still coming up empty."

"Not this time. Go inside and see for yourself. The outside is just to keep people away." She shook her head. "God, it all makes so much sense now. He probably brings his victims somewhere around here. That concrete room I saw, it's probably somewhere nearby. This whole place is a front for his killings."

"Maybe," Guidry muttered. He studied the house as if searching for answers. "Let's just say you're right. Explain one thing to me. Why would he risk everything by getting close to you? Your involvement with this case has been all over the newspapers, thanks to that pissant Walters. This guy would have to be either a masochist or just plain stupid to get anywhere near you."

"Or maybe he's really smart."

"Meaning?"

"Meaning, he knows I'm right. That I can sense him. That I'm telling you guys the truth. What if he was getting worried that you might start to believe me?"

"So he gets close to you, gets rid of you, and keeps his kill-fest going?"

'It was either that or Alex Daimon truly did like her, was attracted to her. Wanted her. Wanted to touched her, kiss her, love her . . .

Reality check. This was a killer, for heaven's sake. A cold-blooded murderer. How could she be having such thoughts for a man with so little regard for human life? A man who surely wanted to kill her just as he'd killed each of the victims bloodying his past.

Because she was a red-blooded female with needs like any other! she found herself answering. As abnormal as her life was, what she was feeling was completely normal. She longed for companionship. For sex. For love.

For normalcy.

Yet Alex Daimon was anything but normal.

"I'm right," Callie told Guidry. "Trust me on this. I'm absolutely sure."

The detective shook his head. "The only thing I'm sure of is that if you're feeding me a load of bullshit, my ass will be history once the lieutenant gets wind that I let you lead me around on this wild goose chase."

"Go inside," she whispered, her gaze going back to the house. "See for yourself."

He let out a heavy sigh, studied the house a second longer, then picked up his mike and summoned his backup.

He opened the car door. "Unemployment line, here I come," he muttered as he climbed from his seat. "Stay in the car," he ordered before slamming the door. He gave a signal to the other officers to circle the perimeter.

A few hand motions from another man who came up beside Guidry, and a team of men filed out of a SWAT van that had pulled into the drive. Like blue-black ants, the officers swarmed around the house.

At the road, back behind several police cars, Callie could see a Channel 21 News van. Walters was also here, ready and waiting for the police to screw up so he could broadcast it to the good citizens of New Orleans—and, in the process, crucify her.

A phony. A loony. A freak.

All her life she'd been called those things by skeptics such as Walters. And there were many times she'd wished it was true. But none had been as painful as being called a killer. She saw the headline clearly in her mind:

PSYCHIC KILLS CHILD
Led police astray,
freed murderer to kill again.

For a split second, she recalled the police station where she'd been called to identify the Milbeau County child killer. She'd been brought to Louisa Jenkins, the blond-haired six-year-old who had nearly been the lunatic's sixteenth victim. She *had* been a victim. She'd been physically and emotionally abused before her escape, and she'd also gotten a good look at the killer.

"*I can't! Please don't make me look!*" Callie heard Louisa's voice.

The girl, still traumatized after her experience, had been too young and upset to be a credible witness. That was why Callie—who'd seen the killer through the eyes of his victims—had also been present for the lineup.

Callie had stared at each man and tried to think, but it had been impossible with Louisa clinging to her hand. Callie had been consumed not by the faces in front of her, but by the little girl's pain and fear that had flowed through her fingertips.

The emotions had been so intense, so crippling, that instead of seeing, Callie had merely *felt*. She'd been unable to concentrate, unable to see. She'd chosen the wrong man.

One of the suspects, Jackson Mae, had walked out of that police station a free man. That very afternoon, he'd followed Louisa home and snatched her off her front porch. He'd been intent on eliminating any witnesses, and he succeeded.

He killed Louisa and went after another victim, and another, before he finally slipped and the police managed to catch him. But he'd taken three more lives, and all because Callie hadn't been paying attention. She might have identified him if she'd just kept her attention focused rather than the feelings rushing through her—Louisa's anguish. Those feelings had overrun her reasoning, and so she'd failed.

She'd let Louisa down by failing to do what she needed, to keep her mind on the lineup rather than the terror of the little girl. Callie had let Jackson Mae walk free and given him the chance to kill again.

She'd been just as guilty as the man himself.

That's when she'd vowed never to use her *sight* again, and she'd stuck by that vow. Until Guidry had played on her sympathy and pulled her into this latest series of murders.

But the past was repeating itself. Once again, she'd been so caught up in feelings—her own this time rather than the victim's—that she'd failed to see the truth. She'd been consumed by lust and long-ing, and she'd completely neglected the fact that Alex Daimon was the killer. And Mrs. Bodine's sec-ond child had died. And now so had this dishwater blonde.

The realization turned her stomach and hardened her resolve. No more. She knew the truth now, she recognized it, and she wouldn't let any more victims fall into his hands. Her gaze darted between the many police officers as they secured every angle of the house. Their guns were drawn. Ready.

There was only one person who would be de-stroyed tonight.

Alex Daimon.

Callie closed her eyes, dread settling in her stom-ach. And sadness. And fear for Alex.

She shook away the absurd thoughts. A cold-blooded killer: that's what he was. He'd used, ma-nipulated her. She was undoubtedly the next victim on his list, once he was through playing his deadly game of seduction. He was trying to keep her from helping the police, from discovering his identity by manipulating her. He would kill her.

But she wouldn't wind up his victim—anyone's victim—ever. And she wouldn't let another inno-cent life be taken.

Her gaze went to Guidry. The detective stood at the plantation manor front door, his gun aimed, his stance rigid. He signaled to the men around him, then aimed his foot. A forceful kick and what was left of the old door crashed open, then toppled from its rusty hinges. Guidry and his men disappeared inside.

You're wrong, Callie.

Alex's voice slipped into her thoughts. She jerked around, her gaze sweeping the empty interior of the car. A sudden breeze disturbed the humid stillness of the summer night. The air whispered over her skin, cooling and heating her at the same time.

I'm not a killer. I am many things, but not that. I'm here to help you. From the beginning, I only wanted to help you. You're wrong about me. So very wrong.

The voice was sad, but she didn't believe it.

Trust me, Callie. You don't have to be afraid, to distrust me.

"Yes, I do," she insisted, shaking her head and swatting at her arms, as if she could push the breeze away as easily as a man's hands.

I would never hurt you, Callie. I don't know what you think you saw, but I only want to love you.

She shook her head. "Leave me alone. Please. Just leave me alone."

As quick as it had stirred, the breeze settled.

I only want to love you, came the slow, deep, mesmerizing voice.

Her nerves prickled and heat flowered in her belly. Desire rushed through her, filling her with an ache that made her nipples throb and her thighs tingle.

He's a killer, she reminded herself. And these were incongruous thoughts.

I'm not a killer, the voice insisted.

"Get out of my head, dammit!"

"Miss Wisdom?"

Callie glanced up into the puzzled face of Detective Guidry. He leaned into the open window on the driver's side. "What the hell's going on?"

"I . . . nothing." She shook her head. "I—I think I dozed off. I must have been talking in my sleep." As if she could tell him she was hearing voices. Worse yet, that she'd been talking back to the voice. He'd definitely think her a nutcase.

She gave another glance at his hard face, and she knew he already thought much worse than that. "What's wrong?" she asked.

"The place is empty, that's what's wrong. Sonofabitch."

"He probably hasn't come home yet. Just wait for him."

"You don't understand. The place is literally empty. It was abandoned a long time ago from the looks of things. There's dust everywhere and not a piece of furniture in sight."

Her gaze went to the manor's front door where police were filing out, disappointment and anger alternating on their faces.

Empty?

Denial rushed through her, and she shook her head. "That can't be. I was here. Did you look in the library? Did you see the piano? The painting? The bookshelves?"

"I'm telling you, there's nothing but a bare room with mice and dust all over the place," he said, then he turned to several officers and signaled them back into their vehicles.

As Callie tried to digest the news, he opened the car door and climbed into the driver's seat.

"But the bedroom upstairs—" she started, only to have him frown at her.

"Just give it a rest," he growled. He shoved the key into the ignition. "Not another word. Please."

"No," she said. She opened the passenger door and climbed from her seat before he could put the car in reverse. "I'm telling you, this place is occupied." Her legs ate up the ground as she rushed toward the front door.

A car door slammed behind her and Guidry called out, "Callie, wait—"

"I know how it looks on the outside," she said as she mounted the front steps and rushed through the black hole of the house's front door. "You have to look inside. In the library. I was standing right—" The words jumbled together and stalled in her throat as she burst into the library.

Dust coated the floor. Cobwebs draped the corners, the threads catching rays of moonlight that spilled through the busted-out windows. Floorboards creaked as a mouse scampered along the far wall.

"No," she breathed as her gaze shot to the now-vacant wall above the mantel. There was no picture, nothing but a gaping hole that revealed the inside of a soot-streaked chimney. "No!"

She fought back the truth, but it was there staring back at her. The room was as lifeless as the outside of the house.

Phony. Loony. Freak.

The words whispered through her head and made her knees tremble.

"You were tired," Guidry consoled as he came up behind her. His hand gripped her shoulder. "It's understandable you might get a little confused."

"You don't think I'm confused. You think I made this up."

"I think you might be nodding off and dreaming. I had a cousin who did that. He didn't get enough sleep, and he started imagining he saw this giant St. Bernard that kept talking to him. Turns out he was falling asleep for short periods and dreaming about the damned animal."

A St. Bernard? she thought indignantly. "I didn't imagine this, or dream it." *Or did I?* She didn't want to believe Guidry, yet she couldn't deny the truth. The house *was* empty.

Her gaze swept the room again as questions raced through her mind. Had she really imagined her time here? The house? And what about Alex? Had he been a figment of her imagination? A creation of her deprived hormones? A dream? Was the stress of her father's situation finally wearing her down and causing hallucinations? Were all the weird things she'd been feeling simply sleep deprivation?

She stared at the mantel, remembering the picture, remembering Alex. The way he'd stared at her, touched her, kissed her—

"Come on. This isn't doing anybody any good." Guidry urged her backward, away from the library and the proof of her deteriorating sanity.

"I'm sorry," she murmured, still trying to grasp the truth. A hallucination.

"You did your best. Let's just forget it." He steered her toward the front door. "I'll drop you at your car."

"Yes." She shook her head, still dazed and confused. A hallucination . . . "I mean, no. My car's at the shop. You can drop me—"

"Say cheese!" The flash of a camera followed the statement, and Callie blinked at the blinding light.

"Somebody get this guy out of here!" Guidry called as he moved outside.

"Another wrong tip?" Walters asked, thrusting a handheld recorder out as he followed. He fended off an officer who rushed up and tried to push him out of the way. "Come on, Guidry. Just tell the people what's going on. We deserve to know the truth."

"The truth is that we're obligated to check out all possible leads." Guidry pushed the man's tape recorder aside and tried to usher Callie away from the pushy reporter.

"Based on *solid* evidence," Walters gibed as two officers grabbed his arms and pulled him back. "This lady's a psychic. And look what happened—"

"She's empathic," Guidry corrected, cutting him off. "Not psychic. And she's just serving as a consultant to help weed out the false leads we've been receiving. We're not basing the whole case on one person's opinion." Guidry steered Callie down the front steps, toward his waiting Ford.

"Don't you think tax money could be better

spent—Ouch!" Walters struggled against the two policemen restraining him. "I have rights, you know."

"Christ, this is getting out of control," Guidry complained as he climbed behind the steering wheel and stared through the windshield. "That guy just doesn't give up." His words faded as the shrill ring of a cell phone filled the air. He answered it: "Guidry here." He went silent as he listened. "Yeah. She's here."

Callie knew even before his gaze met hers that something was wrong. She saw it in the stern set of his jaw, the way his teeth clenched and his knuckles turned white.

"It's another body, isn't it?" Callie asked when the call ended and he punched the OFF button.

"I'm afraid not." He shook his head, and sympathy flashed in his gaze. "It's your father."

"I'm so sorry, Ms. Wisdom. I wish I had better news."

Callie stood in the hospital room and stared through a hot rush of tears at Dr. Moire—a specialist the ER doctor had called in after examining her father and speaking with Dr. Broussard.

Moire, a fortyish man with graying black hair and wire-rimmed glasses, patted her shoulder in an awkward gesture that did nothing to ease the dread welling inside her. Or the pain. Or the heartache.

Denial thundered through her head as she stared down at her father, his face nearly matching the white hospital sheets he lay on. His eyes were closed, his body limp and lifeless. The only movement was that of his chest as it pumped up and down to the steady beat of a nearby respirator.

A *respirator*.

She'd known his condition was serious. She'd watched his life slowly seeping away. She'd even felt his cold chest the past night when he'd been limp. Dead.

Before Alex Daimon had touched him.

She shook the thought away. She'd been mistaken. No way had he actually been dead and then alive, all because of Alex's touch. That was impossible.

She focused on her current situation. She still had time. Not much, but time nonetheless.

". . . condition has remained steady for the past few hours, despite the onset of coma," Dr. Moire was saying.

"He was awake when I left the house this morning," Callie murmured. Sick, but awake and talking to Burgess. The sight had actually sent a rush of hope through her after the previous night's scare.

That hope had faded.

This wasn't merely a loss of consciousness. Her father was no longer breathing on his own. His heart was weak. His kidneys and liver had all but shut down.

Dr. Moire spoke. "Your butler—a Mr. Burgess, I do believe his name was—said that he seemed fine most of the day. A little tired and sluggish and ill, of course, but still conscious. Your man went to fix dinner and when he returned, he found your father unresponsive. The onset of a coma is always a tragic thing. Of course, with MS we usually have a little forewarning."

"You really think he's suffering from multiple sclerosis?"

"I think MS is *one* of the illnesses, because the sudden onset of coma isn't very common. See, with MS, the patient suffers a gradual deterioration. He becomes disoriented, even psychotic to a certain extent. Muscle tone becomes severely lax, which affects organ function. Then the coma sets in. This usually takes several weeks, but sometimes can take as long as a month or two. This particular case is grossly atypical, which is why, after going over his chart, I've yet to rule out a secondary illness."

Atypical. That described her father's condition to a T. It wasn't typical of any illness currently known to the medical community, because it wasn't an illness. It was a curse.

And it was killing him.

She touched his forehead. He was cold and clammy and still. So very still. Another bout of tears burned her eyes, but Callie refused to cry. She'd wasted too much time already on her tears.

And her hormones.

A vision of Alex sitting across from her, his mouth glistening with wine, popped into her head for a brief, heart-stopping moment, but she pushed it back out. She'd wasted too much time already lusting over this man she couldn't want.

A man she *shouldn't* want.

The man might even be a figment of her imagination.

Again, she wondered if Guidry was right. He'd tried again to convince her of her mistake while he drove her to her shop to pick up her rental car so that she could hurry to the hospital. He said she'd actually been so exhausted, she'd slipped into slumber and *dreamed* Alex and the house.

Was it possible?

Did it matter? Either way, she'd spent her precious time and attention on something other than her father, and it was going to stop right now.

"Thank you for everything, doctor," she said.

"Don't thank me until I've actually done something. I've ordered a series of tests to rule out several different illnesses. Once we have results back from those, we can determine an effective way to treat your father." Even as he said the words, she saw the doubt in his eyes. The compassion.

He was trying, but he knew as well as she did that his treatments would do no good. Her father was gravely ill and in all likelihood, it was too late to reverse his condition.

"You've done all you can, and I appreciate it."

Callie leaned down and kissed her father on the cheek. His skin was cool against her lips. The scent of fresh paint and happiness that had always clung to him was missing; it had been overwhelmed by the sharp smell of disinfectant and death.

She clamped her eyes shut and fought back the tears, but one slipped free anyway. The hot droplet wound a path down her cheek and plopped onto her father's jaw. He flinched ever so slightly that she wondered if she had imagined it.

Maybe.

Then again, maybe not. He was still with her. Still breathing, albeit with help. Hope rushed through her, along with a rush of urgency.

"Hang on," she whispered with a renewed sense of determination. "I'm going to fix everything. I *am*." And with that, Callie turned and walked out of the hospital room.

She *was* going to fix things, and she wasn't waiting for tomorrow morning. Time was running out, and Callie had waited long enough.

Margaret Churchwood, voodoo queen extraordinaire and Callie's one-and-only shot at deciphering the hows and whys surrounding her father's curse, was getting a visitor tonight—whether she liked it or not.

Chapter Fifteen

Margaret Churchwood did *not* like visitors in the middle of the night; Callie knew it from the string of curses coming from inside the immaculate townhouse.

She stepped back and let her gaze sweep the front of the two-story brick structure located on the pristine St. Charles Avenue, in the heart of New Orleans' garden district. The streetlight illuminated the perfectly landscaped bushes that lined the front walkway leading from the sidewalk to the door. White daisies glowed from the flower boxes in front of the downstairs windows. A bright porch light cast a yellow warmth on the WELCOME doormat on the front stoop.

The house appeared neat and immaculate and so *normal* that again Callie checked the address she'd scribbled down from the phone book. She'd expected a lot of things when she'd spotted Margaret's ad in the yellow pages, but normal wasn't one of them.

She'd seen many of the boarded-up, dilapidated voodoo houses down in the French Quarter, not to mention the string of neon-lit psychic shops that lined Bourbon Street. A person could buy a love potion or converse with the Other Side, then pick up a souvenir T-shirt or postcard on the way out.

Callie stared at the address she'd scribbled down from Margaret's ad, with its gypsy-looking woman with flowing black hair, piercing dark eyes, and hoop earrings big enough to double as circus props. Her attention shifted back to the house. There wasn't a neon light or a souvenir T-shirt in sight, no sign offering anything like a séance or a palm reading. There was nothing but a well-kept yard.

Maybe she'd made a mistake.

The maybe changed into a definite *yes* when a sixty-something woman wearing a pink housecoat and matching slippers pulled open the front door. Her snow-white hair had been wrapped around green sponge rollers. A white cold-cream mustache glowed on her upper lip.

No love beads or gris-gris bags hung around her neck. She looked nothing like the exotic depiction in the ad.

"I'm sorry. I must have the wrong—" The words ground to a halt as she noted the woman's New Orleans Saints button pinned to the housecoat. She remembered Margaret's euphoria about tonight's game, and her gaze narrowed. "Margaret Churchwood?"

"Yes?"

"The Margaret Churchwood from the yellow pages? The Margaret Churchwood in the ad with—"

"That's my ad, all right." The old woman chuckled, the sound warm and comforting, like the smell of apple cider on a cold, wintery day. "I know, I know," she added when Callie simply stared at her in disbelief. "I don't look like the dad-burned picture, but who would after four kids and six grandchildren?" She smiled, and the cold-cream mustache twisted up at the ends. "That was taken in my younger days. I had a figure back then. And more hair. And not so many wrinkles." She shook her head. "I've tried everything. Vitamin E cream. Retinol. Garlic and cucumber—that's what this is." She dabbed at the corner of her mouth and took a taste.

So much for the cold-cream theory.

"Not bad if I were a tossed salad, but I seriously doubt it's tightening my skin, no matter what *Woman's Day* claims." Her gaze narrowed. "So what are you doing on my doorstep in the middle of the night? This is a reputable neighborhood. People work for a living, you know."

"I'm Callie Wisdom. I called earlier tonight about meeting with you in the morning." She pulled Catherine Drashierre's faded leather book from her bag. "I need you to take a look at this. I know it's late, but I couldn't wait."

"You'll have to. I was just closing my eyes. I need

my beauty rest—not to mention I still haven't recovered from the Saints' terrible loss tonight." She stroked her pin. "I swear, if we could just keep a good quarterback." She shook her head. "Come back tomorrow, child, and I'll be happy to help." She started to close the door, but Callie gripped the frame.

"Please! I have to see you tonight. It's urgent."

"That's what you all say. 'I need this man to love me *right now*.' Or 'I need to speak with my long-gone Granddaddy Joe *right now*.' Child"—she shook her head—"everything in life doesn't have to be *right now*. Slow down, take a deep breath. That's what's wrong with you kids today. Not a one of you has any patience."

"This isn't about patience. It's a matter of life and death. My father's life." She blinked back a wave of tears and leveled a desperate stare at the woman. "And his death."

". . . so that leaves me with this," Callie finished fifteen minutes later, indicating the book that sat in the middle of the small round table in Margaret's back room.

After hearing Callie out, the woman had ushered her around the outside of the front of the house to the side alley. A few moments later, she'd flipped on the light in a small room attached to the back of the house.

The room Callie was led into, its walls draped in red to match the velvet-draped table, was a complete contradiction to the stylish townhouse's exterior. It lived entirely up to Callie's expectations of typical witch-woman decor. From the crystal ball that sat on a shelf in the far corner, to the stacks of Tarot cards, to the power beads dangling from the ceiling, the room all but screamed "Welcome to the Other Side."

Margaret had traded her pink bathrobe for a royal purple drape. Her cucumber-cream mustache had been licked away. She'd even popped large round hoops into her earlobes and slathered on some bright red lipstick. She looked every bit the gypsy she claimed in the ad, give or take twenty years. She also looked every bit the psychic. But Callie needed more than looks; she needed an answer before it was too late.

She trembled. A crazy reaction, she knew. It was at least ninety degrees in the small room, maybe even hotter given the enormous amount of red velvet swathing the walls. She should be burning up.

But the coldness came from inside her. It was the fear and terror that lived and breathed in her soul.

Fear for her father.

Fear for the past.

The future.

Her possession.

She squelched the thought. *Maybe* she was being possessed. Maybe she was merely hallucinating. Either way, it didn't change the here-and-now, or the all-important fact that her father needed her.

And you *need* me, the now familiar female voice whispered in her head. *I can help. I can ease your load. Just put your trust in me, Callie. Let me take control. Just give in. Say yes and you can rest. You can't do this alone. You're not strong enough, but I am. Let me prove it. Give in to me now and save yourself the heartache. It won't matter in the end, anyway. I'll still be here. I'll always be here. Now and forever.*

". . . all right?" Margaret's voice finally pushed into Callie's head and drew her attention.

She summoned her courage and tried to squelch the shaking of her hands. Fear kept her from slumping in her chair and weeping. Instead, she stiffened.

She was determined, despite the voice.

Frightened because of it.

Whatever promises the voice now made, Callie knew that giving in wasn't the answer. Callie wouldn't merely be giving up her troubles. She'd be handing over her soul.

"I—I'm fine. I mean, I'm not. I need help. My father needs help."

"You look very pale. Tired. Something's draining your strength."

"I'm not getting much sleep. I've been too worried."

The woman eyed Callie as if she didn't quite believe the explanation, as if she sensed that Callie battled more than the exhaustion.

She knows I'm here, the female voice whispered. *She knows, and she won't help you.*

"She will," Callie ground out.

"What did you say, child?"

"You will—help me, that is. Won't you? Please."

Another long, searching look came before the

woman's gaze finally shifted to the book. She reached out and touched the worn leather the way one would touch a hotcake: tentatively at first. As her fingers inched across the worn leather, her caution seemed to slip away. The frown creasing her chubby face didn't disappear, though. She pulled the book toward her and flipped to the torn-out page.

"I know that's the spell," Callie said. "I *know* it."

"And how's that?"

"I feel it." At Margaret's curious stare, Callie added, "It's a power I have; I can feel things."

The woman nodded. "I knew there was something about you. Something different." The woman continued to eye her as if trying to come to some conclusion. "So, you're empathic?"

Callie nodded.

"That explains it then," she said, but she didn't look like a woman who'd just had everything explained. She still looked puzzled. Wary.

Because she knows I'm here. Inside of you. Taking control of you.

"No," Callie breathed, closing her eyes and gathering her strength.

"What did you say, dear?"

"I said I don't know." She opened her eyes. "I don't know what I'm doing wrong. Maybe I'm not saying it correctly. Mispronouncing words or reading the phrases wrong or something. I just know that the incantation isn't working."

"You're sure this is it?" Margaret eyed the page

before lifting her gaze to Callie's. "Maybe you're wrong."

"Am I?"

Margaret's gaze returned to the page. For the first time, Callie noted the crystal that dangled from a gold chain suspended around her neck. The woman trailed her fingertips over the page before touching the crystal and closing her eyes.

"No, you're right," the psychic finally said.

"Then why can't I make it work? I'm saying the right words."

"That's the problem. *You* are saying the words. This is a personal book of magic. A grimoire. This book was put together by a very powerful witch or warlock. These spells are very individual. They were created by a specific power, and they must be used by that same power."

"So what you're saying is that only the book's owner can recite the spell and make it work."

"Exactly."

Dread welled inside Callie. "But that can't be. This book is old. Too old."

"Yes. Judging by the way it's bound and the wear of the leather, I would say it dates back to the early nineteenth century." Margaret turned the volume over in her hands. "Maybe even earlier. Of course, I'm no expert on books. Séances are my specialty. And love potions."

"I don't need a love potion. I need to save my father." Callie leaned forward in her chair. "Surely, there's some other way. The owner of this book is long since dead and buried. There has to be some other way."

Margaret looked thoughtful as she studied the book. She turned the pages and trailed her fingertips over the words. "Well, if you were a powerful witch, you might be able to . . . But you're not, so I'm afraid you're out of luck."

"But that's not fair."

"That's life, child. I'm afraid this book is useless."

And you, too, are useless, the female voice inside Callie whispered. *You can't save your father. Or yourself.*

Leave me alone, Callie silently begged. *Please.*

I'll never leave. I'm here to stay, so you might as well accept it. Accept me.

"I won't. I can't. I have to help my father." As the words left her mouth, Callie saw the odd look on Margaret's face, and she realized she'd voiced her thoughts aloud.

"I think you should leave now," the woman blurted, shoving the book back toward Callie. She pushed away from the table and rose from her chair. "I don't like this."

Callie pleaded, "Listen, you're my last hope."

"I'm just an old woman." A frightened woman, her gaze showed. "I can't help you." She shook her head again, her mouth drawn tight, her gaze everywhere, anywhere, but on Callie. It was as if Medusa herself sat across from her, threatening to turn her to stone at a glance.

The woman was scared because she did know about Catherine.

The realization came at the same time that Callie felt a wave of heat sweep her. Her hands trembled and she gripped her chair to keep from teetering over. Her vision blurred and the voice whispered again through her head.

Why are you wasting your time with this old woman? I can help you, Callie. I can ease the burden if you'll just let me. I can help you as no other can. I have the power to make everything better. All you have to give me is your trust. Your agreement. Your soul . . .

"No," Callie ground out. She blinked frantically, drawing air in and out of her lungs as she fought the blackness that threatened.

"Go!" Margaret's voice pushed past the roar in her ears and drew her back to the present, to her frantic grip on the red velvet tablecloth.

"I . . ." Callie swallowed, searching for her voice as she fought for control. "I can't. Not until I figure out a way to help my father. I can't give up. You have to help me. Surely there's something. . . ." Her words trailed off as the woman backed away.

One of Margaret's hands gripped the crystal that hung around her neck. "I mean it," she said. "Get out of here." She motioned toward the back door she'd led Callie in through.

"Please!" Callie struggled for her wallet. "I'll pay you extra. If you'll just give me a few more min—"

"Go!" The woman shook her head again as she

301

pulled open a door partially hidden behind one of the red velvet drapes. "Now!"

"But—"

"Just take the book and go." And with that, Margaret Churchwood disappeared. "And God help you," her voice floated back.

But God couldn't help Callie. No one could. Margaret had been her last hope, and she was gone.

Callie heard the woman's footsteps echo and fade. Somewhere in the house a door slammed. The click of a dead bolt followed.

Callie barely resisted the urge to go after her. To beg and plead more.

It won't matter. She won't help you. She can't. She fears me, and so should you. There are none alive with the power to best me!

Where the voice had earlier seemed helpful and coaxing, it was again cruel, sending a burst of fear through Callie. She snatched up the book and left the house, trying to outrun the voice, the threat.

She climbed inside her car, tossed the book on the dashboard, closed the locks and simply sat. Her fingers clamped around the steering wheel, and she held on as desperation bubbled over in a burst of blinding tears.

Her entire situation was hopeless. However she fought, Catherine was inside of her, and her father was dying. There was no hope for either of them. The voice was right. This was it. The end of the line. It was time to accept the inevitable.

The trembling started again, in her fingertips, working its way through her body, creeping and consuming, and this time she didn't fight it off. She couldn't. She was tired. Defeated.

That's it. Give in. Save yourself more trouble. I'll win in the end anyway, Callie. No matter how hard you fight, it won't be enough to stop me. I'll win. I've always won. Relax. Accept it. Accept me.

She had no choice. She was too worn and exhausted. Too lost in despair. The cold started in the pit of her stomach. It worked its way outward, like icy tentacles sliding along her nerve endings, cutting off the feeling until she was all but paralyzed. Her breathing slowed. Her heart crept to a snail's pace, barely beating.

Only her tears continued to rush, the moisture sliding down her cheeks, spilling onto her lap.

If only things were different. If only she could change fate and thwart death. . . .

The thought trailed off as a vehicle passed by and a flash of headlights filled the interior of her car. The worn leather cover of Catherine's book caught the glare and the sight stopped Callie's heart in her chest.

The realization of what lay in front of her was enough to knock the air from her lungs. She gasped and willed her trembling fingers to move, to grip the book and take a closer look to be sure.

But she knew, even before she fought back the trembling and picked it up. She trailed her fingertips over the cover, feeling the slight bumps and grooves, so faint she hadn't noticed them before. The book was so old and worn and faded that she hadn't even realized there was anything on the cover. But it was there. She felt it now.

She wiped frantically at her eyes, blinking back the moisture as she flipped on the inside light and held the worn leather volume at an angle. The light reflected, catching the worn etching on the cover, and there was no mistaking the familiar symbol staring back at her.

A crest.

His crest. It was the same emblem she'd seen on the man in the portrait above Alex Daimon's mantel. The same as she'd seen embroidered on Alex's shirt.

Alex.

But was he a figment of her sleep-deprived imagination, or a real man? Was he a murderer?

She didn't know. She knew only that Alex was the owner of the book.

More than that, he was her last chance to save her father.

She needed him.

Alex knew it the instant she walked into his abandoned manor. He felt her fear and her desperation and her desire.

Yes, she needed him. In more ways than one.

He let her move closer, into the library where his spirit dwelled. Then he couldn't help himself; he moved closer to her, circling her, drinking in the sight—long blond hair flowing past her shoulders, a face streaked with silent tears, eyes glistening with a desperation that tore at his soul.

Her scent filled his nostrils, teasing his senses,

tantalizing him until the ache for her became sharp and distinct and nearly unbearable. Her heat reached out to him like the teasing touch of a woman's fingers—soft and beckoning and stirring.

She stopped in the library and stared up at the mantel where his picture had once hung, as if she could will it back.

"I know you're here," she finally breathed, her chest rising with the effort. Her nipples, taut and aroused by his presence, strained against the thin cotton of her shirt.

Alex couldn't help himself. He reached out. He knew his touch was little more than a stirring of air, a whisper of wind across one ripe tip, but she still felt it. He saw the way her nipple quivered and hardened even more, stretching out to him, begging for more.

"I can feel you," she breathed.

"Do you?" he murmured.

She whirled, searching for the voice on the air, for him, but she couldn't see him. Her gaze darted wildly, her chest heaving with the sudden burst of panic that coursed through her.

There was excitement, too.

He circled her, touching and teasing, making her body jerk and her eyes darken with a need Alex recognized all too well. But there was also fear.

Her forced the realization away. He cared for nothing—for no one—save the need burning him up from the inside out. He had denied himself for far too long. He was cold, so very cold, and he needed some warming.

So did she, he realized as he noted the goose-bumps dancing up and down her arms.

Summoning his magic, he restored the room to its past splendor. As his gaze swept past, the dark walls gleamed. Light flickered from the overhead chandelier. A fire danced in the stone hearth.

Callie stepped closer to the flames, her gaze locked on the mantel, on the picture that now hung in its rightful place.

Alex followed, a silent, invisible force moving behind her, surrounding her. He touched a strand of hair and stroked the soft curve of her shoulder through her blouse. The touches were like whispers of wind, and her body quivered at the contact. Still, she stared up at the picture.

"Please," she whispered, and while the desire pumping through her wasn't enough to draw him fully into this world, her cry for help reached out and yanked him forward.

A tingling swept through him as he allowed his essence to morph into a physical body, one that ached even more than his cursed spirit.

"I've been thinking about you." His voice drew her around; she whirled, seemingly startled to find him standing so near behind her.

"I . . ." She swallowed and searched for her voice. He noted the trembling of her mouth, and he reached out. He stroked the soft plumpness of her bottom lip, felt the quiver against his fingertips, the heat. The delicious soul-saving heat.

But Alex knew he no longer had a soul.

He was a spoiler of women. A deceiver. An incubus.

Callie Wisdom was but another to add to his long list of conquests. She was Catherine, she was vengeance—despite the fear swimming in her greener-than-green eyes. This was the woman responsible for robbing him of his very existence, enslaving him for an eternity, and Alex wasn't the forgiving sort.

"I need to talk to you," she said.

"I need to do much more to you, *chère*." And before she could say another word, Alex pulled her close and captured her lips with his own.

He took her mouth with a savage intensity. Sweeping his tongue along the fullness of her bottom lip, he thrust deep to savor the soft interior of her mouth. Like a dying man, he drank from her, drawing heat from the fountain of life that bubbled inside of her.

But it wasn't enough. He needed more.

He wanted to touch her, taste her, consume her, *curse* her.

Moving his hands down the curve of her spine, he found the soft swell of her buttocks. He cupped her bottom and moved her hips in a circular motion against his rock-hard arousal. A gasp slipped past her lips, the sound feeding his already ravenous appetite.

More, more, more.

"No," she managed on a moan as she tore her mouth from his and struggled for air. "Please, don't. I need to talk to you. I need—"

Alex stifled the rest of her thought with another

deep kiss. He grasped the edge of her shirt, urged the material up until his hands found the throbbing tips of her breasts. Her nipples, hard and distended, rasped against his palms. He tore his lips from hers and urged her backwards. He dipped his head down to devour one luscious nipple.

She arched against him for a long, heart-pounding moment before she finally seemed to gain control.

"No," she gasped, bucking against him.

The sudden motion caught him off guard, and he stumbled backward, his boot coming up against the fireplace grate. A fiery log jumped and sparks flew. An orange lick caught Alex's trousers and the material lit. Alex slapped at the sudden burst of fire.

The scent of burnt flesh filled the air, followed by a frightened cry.

It wasn't the heat or his own pain that brought him up short. It was the soft, concerned hand that reached for his, the touch so tender, so comforting that it brought tears to his eyes.

Tears for a man, a condemned spirit, who'd felt nothing save lust and the need for vengeance over the past one hundred years?

His gaze found hers, and he saw the fear and worry bright in her green eyes.

Green, not blue.

There was nothing of Catherine in this woman who stood before him. No hatred or selfishness or pure evil. Callie was good and kind and selfless.

"I'm so sorry. I didn't mean to hurt you. I really didn't—" Her apology seemed to catch in her throat as her gaze dropped to the blackened skin of his hand. "You're hurt. You're really hurt! We need to call an ambulance. We need . . ." Her words faded; an incredulous expression swept her face as she watched the charred skin fade and smooth back to normal.

Her head snapped up, and her gaze collided with his. "Who are you?"

"A killer." At his words, her eyes widened. "That's what you think, isn't it? What a part of you thinks."

"Maybe," she admitted. Then she reached out and touched his hand. "I'm not so sure. Show me."

As much as he wanted to refuse, he couldn't. She stirred him as no other woman ever had. Callie Wisdom wasn't just any woman. She was his. She was the one he'd spent a lifetime looking for. The one who'd haunted his dreams night after night.

Callie, not Catherine.

He realized then that it had been Callie he'd wanted his whole life. This was his better half, his soulmate. But she could never be his—not as he'd once dreamed.

The truth made him want her all the more—her body and her soul—and he turned away as a trembling gripped him. "Leave," he growled. "Now. Before I lose what little control I have left." He wouldn't touch her, take her. He wouldn't curse her. He couldn't.

Regardless of what punishment awaited him.

Regardless of the punishment that he was suffering now.

He doubled over at a sudden sharp pain that knifed through him. Lust, his cursed lust, was overwhelming. Grinding his teeth, he fought back his need and concentrated on breathing. In and out. In and out.

"I need to know," Callie pressed, her voice as soft and as desperate as the touch that followed. Her fingers tightened on his shoulder as she urged him to face her. "Please."

Suddenly, he *wanted* her to know. He wanted to show her his innocence, to prove to her he wasn't a monster.

But you are.

But he wasn't the cold-blooded killer she suspected him of being.

"You didn't do it," she gasped. She was seeing him leave the woman, seeing him go to find her.

He hadn't taken the blonde. He'd turned away, run.

"You didn't do it," Callie gasped as he opened his eyes. She stared up at him, her gaze incredulous. "You really didn't. You're not the killer."

"No," he admitted. He reached for her hand again and drew her close. His fingers went to her face, his hands cupping her cheeks. "I'm much worse, sweet Callie. As you shall see for yourself."

Chapter Sixteen

"I love you."

The soft words echoed in Alex's ears as he stared at the woman who stood before him. Her long blond hair streamed down around her pale shoulders, framing her heart-shaped face. Her blue gaze held his, her eyes wide and beguiling and pleading.

"I love you." She repeated the words he'd waited so long to hear. Yet the truth didn't fill him with the expected rush of warmth or relief.

It was the night: the tenth anniversary of his father's death. The night Alex inherited the guardianship of the Divine Power.

Ten years. He still couldn't believe how slowly that time had passed. Each day felt like a week. Each week like a year.

"One day you will find your mate, Alex. The per-

*fect woman who will complete your soul. You'll
know her when you see her, when you touch her.
When she touches you, you will feel her as you have
felt no other, and she will be the one. The only
one."* Those had been his father's words.

Catherine touched his face, her hands stroking his
cheek and a surge of heat went through Alex like
nothing he'd ever felt before. Her touch did that to
him. It made him shiver and ache and want.

*". . . You'll feel her as you have felt no other and
she will be the one. The only one."*

He caught her hand and pressed it to his lips,
relishing the feel of smooth, warm flesh. He'd been
alone for so long—for a lifetime—and he relished
the contact.

The heat.

He pulled her close and pressed his lips to hers.
They parted for him as they always did and let him
tease and taste and tantalize. But a kiss wasn't
enough. It was never enough. He wanted more. He
wanted her with a fierceness he'd never before felt.

". . . You will feel her as you have felt no other."

Again the words echoed through his head.

". . . She will be the one. The only one."

"Christ, I want you," he murmured, overwhelmed by Catherine's closeness and the ache that
gripped his entire body.

"And I want you. Right now." She pressed her
lips to his for a wild, deep melding of souls that
sent his senses reeling.

"Now," he breathed into her mouth. He devoured her, drinking and tasting. His hands roamed

her body, drawing in the heat, the nearness, letting it ease the cold loneliness he'd felt for so long. Too long.

"But first I need to know that you feel the same way . . . which is why you must show me, Alex."

"Show you what?" he asked. But he knew. He saw it in Catherine's eyes as he gazed down at her. She'd heard the rumors that circulated throughout the parish about him. About all the Daimon men.

Witches. Sorcerers.

But they weren't evil. Yes, Alex had power. It was his heritage. His legacy. But he'd practiced magic only to help others. To help the poor and cure the sick and keep the land plentiful. He used the Divine Power for good, both the spells he'd inherited and those he'd added himself, and safeguarded it from others who sought to do ill.

No, Alex wasn't evil, but he walked a fine line near it. He'd come face to face with many who sought the Divine Power, and he'd defeated them all. *That* was his legacy. His duty.

His curse.

That's how it had felt more times than he could count, because his power isolated him from others. Responsibility surrounded him, responsibility from which there was no escape.

But this woman was his cure.

With Catherine in his arms, her body pressed against his, touching him, there was no doubt in his mind.

"If you love me, you will reveal all. There can be no secrets between us. Otherwise, we shall never share the pure, rare bond that your parents did. We shall never have complete and utter trust."

Catherine was right. She deserved to know the true man. She deserved to see that he was much more than a man.

"Show me, Alex. I have confessed my heart and bared my soul, just as your mother surely did with your father. Did he not do the same?"

Alex nodded. "He loved her."

"Then, if you love me, you will do the same. So that our love will be as strong. As lasting. As perfect as theirs."

Her words stirred a longing inside of him unlike anything he'd ever felt. His past rushed at him, a lifetime of being alone. Of being different. Of living on the outside and looking in on everyone else's happiness. Of watching his parents and envying the bond that they shared and the love they'd found.

He wanted the same. He wanted it so fiercely that he could think of nothing save the warmth of Catherine's touch.

Alex closed his eyes and concentrated on the beat of his heart. The sound filled his head. The pulse moved along his nerve endings until his entire body was alive. He felt the change came upon him. His body trembled and tingled as a wave of heat washed him from head to toe. Then it was done.

He'd merely changed his clothes in typical sorcerer fashion. He hadn't moved a muscle, but used his mind. His will. It was a parlor trick for a sorcerer as powerful as he.

But to Catherine . . . sweet, innocent, Catherine . . . She was sure to be frightened at the transformation.

The woman he found staring back at him was anything but afraid. A fire lit her eyes. Excitement glowed in her cheeks.

"Yes," she breathed.

The reaction struck him as odd, but then she touched him, her hand stroking over his where he held the Divine Power, his book of magic, his source of power, and heat surged through him, driving away all but need.

"This is it, isn't it? This is your grimoire?"

He nodded. "This is my magic. My legacy."

"And mine now," she added, her gaze steady with his as she drew the book from his hands. He knew he should stop her, but he couldn't seem to find the will to do anything but breathe and feel her softness, her warmth, *her*.

The thought faded as she pulled away. His sanity returned. The caution that had been his constant companion since he'd been given charge of the powerful book welled up inside him and sent a burst of alarm through him.

"No," he began, reaching for the book, but she turned away and stepped out of reach.

"I won't hurt it," she said, her voice edged with a cruelty he'd never seen before. She dodged his hand again as if they were playing a friendly game of cat and mouse. Slipping from his grasp, she hurried away and put a red velvet settee between them. "No, I would never hurt this." She stroked the cover before opening the volume and flipping through the pages.

"It is nothing to be toyed with," Alex told her, making another grab for the book. His fingers grazed her arm and electricity bolted through him, staggering him for a few long breathless moments while she managed to evade him again.

"That book is sacred," he went on. "Powerful. Much more than you can possibly imagine."

She laughed then, a cold, harsh sound that sent a shiver from his head to his toes. It killed the futile hope that they were simply playing. Something was wrong. Very wrong.

"I too am powerful." Turning, she faced him then, a smile on her face that didn't change the iciness of her eyes. "Much more than you can possibly imagine. Then again, perhaps you *can* imagine. You've felt my touch, after all."

"What are you talking about?"

But he knew, even before she shook her head, her laughter cutting him to the quick. "Come now. The warmth," she reminded him. "The forbidden promise. One touch, and you're putty in my hands. One touch and you're mine." She laughed as understanding hit him like a slap in the face. "That's right, darling. You aren't the only one with magic."

"You're a sorceress!"

"You're catching on, Alex."

"Your magic wouldn't work on me," he scoffed. He wasn't merely *a* sorcerer; he was *the* sorcerer. A descendant of the very first.

"It worked because you wanted it to work. Poor

Alex. You were so lonely, so eager to find love that it overwhelmed everything else." She batted her eyes at him. "Not to mention, I am rather irresistible in my own right. I've gotten quite good at love spells. But love doesn't make the world go 'round. Love fades, just as beauty fades and death approaches. For some." She shook her head. "But not for me. Never for me. Not now. Thanks to you."

"You can't use that spell. Only I can use it. I am the guardian of the book."

"You *were* the guardian. I hold the book because you gave it to me. You handed it over willingly so that I could look, and now it's mine. I made a deal to discover how to destroy you, and now the power is mine." She clutched the bound leather tighter, closed her eyes and started to chant a spell he recognized all too well.

Words of life.

And words of death. *His* death.

"Don't—" The words died in a strangled sound as pain exploded through him.

He felt a sharp knife plunge into his chest, Catherine's, felt the twisting and grinding until his breath rushed away and fingers plucked his soul from his chest. Then his surroundings swirled into a pinpoint of light that grew farther and farther away until a cold breath snuffed it out completely.

The lust surrounded him then; it crept inside to fill the space where his soul had once been.

It was his legacy now.

His curse.

* * *

Callie opened her eyes to see the man standing before her, his head bowed, his eyes closed. She had seen it all, the destruction of this man. But he wasn't a man. Alex was a spirit. A tormented spirit.

"So now you know. I am cursed with an ever-burning lust. I am driven to pursue women, to haunt their dreams and seduce their bodies and show them ecstasy."

"Is that a punishment?" she asked with some petty annoyance, but even as she asked the question, she already knew the truth. To a man who'd spent a lifetime searching for love—for one, true, absolute love—an endless string of nameless, faceless women and short-lived release *would* be torture.

"Yes," he said as if reading her mind.

He had read her mind, she told herself. Remember, he is more than a man. He is a spirit, an *incubus*.

She told herself that, yet with his hands closed tightly around hers, so strong and warm and real, she couldn't see Alex as anything but the man he'd once been.

Troubled and alone. So very, very alone.

"I am here to curse you," he went on. "To take your virginity and hand you over to the Evil One himself. He can't touch one as pure as you. But I can. I can take your virginity and spoil you. That's why I came to you. To seduce you. It's what I do. What I am."

"So why haven't you done it?" She knew. Deep

in her heart, she knew the truth. She wasn't just any woman to him. She'd felt it in the tender way he touched her, saw it in the compassion that glimmered in his gaze—but she needed to hear it, as well. "Why?"

"I meant to." He shook his head and turned away, as if trying to hide the truth from her as he'd tried to hide it from himself. "I had every intention. Dammit, I *wanted* to."

"But?"

"I can't." He faced her then and she saw the emotion in his gaze. It was not lust or greed or hatred, but something even more intense, something that sent a rush of joy through her. "When I look at you, I should see Catherine, but I don't. I see you, Callie. I see your goodness and kindness. I see you sitting beside your father and crying for him. I see you helping him around the house because of his failing sight. I see your determination to help him regardless of the cost. Giving up your life in Houston to come home, even when this place has meant nothing but sad memories for you. I see your fear when you touch one of those murder victims and feel their pain. You aren't cold or heartless as Catherine was. You're a beautiful woman, from the inside out." He turned away again and stared at the flames in the fireplace. "That's all I ever wanted. A good woman. One to share my life with, but I was too blinded by lust to see the truth."

"It wasn't lust that blinded you. It was loneliness."

"What are you talking about?"

Callie spoke quietly but forcefully: "I know what it's like to be isolated, to be different, to want with everything in your heart to be normal. You wanted that one true love. That was no crime."

"I ignored my duty. I was the most powerful sorcerer in the world. I was guardian of the Divine Power. That was my job. My heritage. I sacrificed it all for a cold, calculating woman."

"You made a mistake. We all do. In that respect, you aren't so different from everyone else. Maybe you should have sensed Catherine's true nature, but you didn't. You couldn't have because she blinded you."

"But I was more powerful. My magic—"

"It wasn't about the magic. It was about feelings. About being a man. Not about being a sorcerer or a guardian, but a man. And men make mistakes. You have to forgive yourself."

"Forgiveness?" He stared at her, an incredulous look on his face. "It's too late for forgiveness. I have no soul. No conscience. Don't you understand why I'm here? The Evil One sent me to take your virginity, so that he can step in and get to Catherine. He wants to have her, so he sent me to spoil you."

He moved closer and Callie felt herself pinned up against the mantel. He said, "I came to take your innocence so that the Devil can step in and steal your soul. You shouldn't be standing here talking about forgiveness. You should be running away from me, Callie." He whirled her around and shoved her toward the door. "You should run for your life, for eternity, while you still have a chance."

Callie took a deep breath. "*You* are *my* only chance. You can recite the incantation."

He gave a sad shake of his head. "I can't. I am no longer the guardian of the book. Catherine touched it, embraced it, and that was the last I saw of it. She owns it now. I can do nothing for you."

Callie's eyes burned at his words. She sniffled, wiping at the hot tears forming as the enormity of what he was saying sank in. "Then there is no chance." Strangely, saying the words didn't bring the rush of helplessness she expected.

It was because of Alex. Because he was standing just a few feet away, his gaze holding hers, his strength fueling hers; for some reason, his very presence made her feel hope.

Suddenly her next move seemed clear.

She stepped toward him. "So, the fact of the matter is: either you will win or she will win."

He looked sad. "Either way, you will lose."

"Maybe." She met his gaze. "But maybe not."

She turned away and stared at the surrounding room. The flickering fireplace, the deeply paneled walls, the overflowing bookshelves: It was all an illusion.

Oddly enough, this room, this moment, this man, were the only things in her life that felt truly real.

She turned and leveled a stare at him. "I apparently can't save my father, or even myself, but I can save this moment, right here, right now, with you."

"You don't know what you're saying."

"I know that I want you. That I've wanted you from that first moment when you walked into my store. Even before then." She swallowed against the sudden lump in her throat. "When you walked into my mind. My dreams. You saved me then, Alex. You didn't condemn me as you'd been commanded. You gave me strength and hope."

"It isn't real. The desire you feel is merely because of who I am. What I am. It's part of my being. You want me because of the evil magic that flows through me; it makes me irresistible."

"You're right." At his sharp glance, she added, "I do want you, but not because of your magic. I want you because you're kind and compassionate. You helped me when no one else would. Just as you wanted to help that child in the alley that time. You couldn't and now I think I know why, but you wanted to. I saw it in your eyes. Just as I saw it night after night in my dreams when you came to me."

"I haunted your dreams to weaken you. I crawled into your subconscious to make you desire me."

"I don't believe that."

At her words, a gleam of satisfaction seemed to light his eyes, then it faded in a dark wave of anger. "Are you crazy, woman? I'm evil. I work for the Devil, for Chrissake!"

"You're not evil, Alex. If so, you wouldn't be standing here talking to me right now. You would have already seduced me and handed me over to the Evil One." She was stating the truth. She saw it in the glimmer of regret that swam in his dark gaze, sensed it in the tension that filled his muscles. "You're not evil," she repeated. "Right now, right at this moment, you're just like me—lonely and scared."

"I am not scared. You're powerless against me. I could crush you with just the force of my will."

"Not of me, but scared of yourself."

Recognition lit his gaze. He frowned, obviously fighting the truth churning inside him. "You don't know anything. You don't know me, Callie. I can have any woman I want. I'm far from lonely."

"Yes, you are." She knew it—because she'd spent her life being lonely, as well, isolated from those around her because of who she was. Because of what she was. She'd longed for friends, for a boyfriend, for normalcy just as Alex had. She'd hoped for her very own happily ever after.

Part of her still did.

But that wasn't her fate any more than it had been his.

His eyes burned into her, gleaming with a hurt that seared her very soul. She couldn't help herself. She stepped toward him and reached out, trailing her fingertips along his jaw. "You're lonely, all right. But you don't have to be."

He flinched at first, but then he closed his eyes, as if relishing her touch. "You shouldn't touch me," he warned.

"I like touching you."

He drank in the sensation for a few moments before he tore himself away. "I can't let this happen. I won't. I won't let him have you."

"And why is that? Why do you care, Alex?"

"I don't," he snapped. "I shouldn't."

"You do. I know it."

Or was this wishful thinking? she asked herself. Was this an illusion she was building because she wanted him to care, to be her friend, her ally, her lover?

The last thought brought an image of tangled sheets and sweaty bodies, and the blood hummed through her veins. Her fingers itched to reach out to him once more. To feel the coarse stubble of Alex's jaw, the silky smoothness of his lips.

As if he read the thoughts racing through her head, he turned away, putting his back to her.

"You do," she insisted. "I feel it because that's what *I* can do," she said, coming up behind him. "That's what I am. I feel things. I feel you, Alex. Warm and hard and full of desire. You need me."

"I need every woman."

She sighed. "Do you truly believe that's all it is?"

Silence closed around them for a long moment before he shook his head. "It's more. It shouldn't be. There is no hope for me. Or you."

"Then there's just this moment." And with that statement came the realization that she wouldn't, couldn't walk away from him. She wanted him and he wanted her, and suddenly that's all that mattered.

Alex stirred not only her passion, but her compassion. He fueled her strength. He made her feel happy and excited and wary all at the same time.

He made her feel like a normal, attractive woman despite their abnormal situation.

"You really must go." His deep voice drew her gaze, and she stared up into his golden brown eyes. They caught flickers of candlelight and their flecks glowed brighter, hotter. Light danced across the room, playing over the ridges and swells of his muscular torso. His arms flexed and she could feel the tension radiating from his body. "I can't help you."

"Don't help me. Touch me."

"You don't know what you're asking."

But she did. As she gazed into his eyes, she saw his hunger—painful, intense and all-consuming—and she knew he battled a force she couldn't begin to understand.

The realization should have frightened her, but it didn't. She'd spent her lifetime being afraid—of who she was and what she was, of losing her mother and her father, of being possessed by Catherine and losing her life.

The fear hadn't helped. She'd lost so much anyway. She would lose again. To Catherine or the Evil One. It mattered not. The outcome would be the same. Defeat.

But for once, Callie wanted to win. She wanted to get what *she* wanted. She wanted to have one moment of triumph.

However brief.

She touched Alex's neck, trailed her fingertips down until they rested over his chest.

"Don't—" The word faded into a groan as her palm settled over his heart. He closed his fingers

325

over hers. "You shouldn't." His grip tightened just enough to let her feel the power inside him. "I don't know how long I can control it."

"So let go."

"I can't!" He shook his head and whirled away from her. "Don't you see? If I take you, you will be spoiled. My master can step in then. He's waiting to step in. He wants Catherine."

"Then let him have her."

"But he'll have you."

"In the end, Catherine or the Evil One will have me. Either way I lose. But at this moment, I can win, Alex. We both can. We can share each other and think of nothing else. Not the past or the future. Just now. Right now. I want to have this moment with you." She touched his shoulder and drew him around to face her.

"Don't you see? There's nothing left. This is the end of the line. I can't help my father. You can't help him. I can't help myself. Catherine's inside. Even now, I can feel her battling for control, she's trying to stop this, but she doesn't have it. Not yet."

"Not yet," he agreed. "The possession isn't complete until the anniversary of her death. It will be tonight. At the stroke of midnight. I'm sure of it."

As the news settled in, dread washed through Callie, but she refused to crumble or cry. The time for tears had passed. She had little time left, and she intended to make the most of it.

"We'd better stop wasting time. Right now, I'm still me and you're still you."

"I'm not—"

She touched her fingertips to his lips. "At this moment, you are. You're Alex Daimon. You have a conscience. You feel guilt and remorse and regret. You are a man, and just a man. And I'm just a woman. Not Catherine. Not yet."

He shook his head again and stared down at her for a long, silent moment.

"Please," she breathed. She watched the emotion play across his face as she waited for his reply. Regret warred with lust. Good battled evil.

In the end, he said nothing. He simply dipped his head and captured her lips in a fierce kiss.

Then then there was nothing—no worries over death and destruction—nothing save the heat exploding through her body and the hot, hungry man at her fingertips.

Chapter Seventeen

Alex stroked the interior of her mouth, nibbled at her bottom lip until Callie melted against the hard contours of his body.

His body felt so good pressed to her. Better than she'd anticipated. Hotter. More desperate.

The kiss seemed to last forever until Alex led her up the staircase. In a large bedroom he lifted her onto a huge four-poster bed. The bedsprings groaned as Alex eased her down and followed. Rising up, he stared down at her.

The room was dark save the soft flicker of a fire in a nearby hearth and the faint stream of moonlight through the sheer curtains covering a nearby window. Alex's face was a mask of shadows and for a brief, heart-stopping moment, the enormity of what she was doing plunged into her. She was about to give herself to a man. And not just a man. A demon lover. Evil incarnate.

But then he touched her, his fingers so warm and strong and real, and he didn't feel evil at all. Just purposeful as he caressed one nipple through the thin fabric of her shirt. Her worry faded in a wave of desire.

"You are so beautiful." He slid her shirt up to bare both breasts. Then he pushed her panties and jeans down, tugged them free and tossed them to the side. So quickly, she lay naked beneath him, her body flushed and needy.

Lowering his head, he drew one nipple into his mouth. She tangled her fingers in the slick silk of his shirt, gripping tightly. He suckled her breast like a hungry child, and the pressure built inside her. She arched against him and he sucked harder. Her breast swelled and throbbed.

It was too much, too sweet, too hot. A long, low moan passed her lips, and she dug her nails into the mattress, arching further, wanting even more. Alex obliged. He licked a path across her skin and delivered the same delicious torture to her other breast.

As she let go of his shirt and slid her arms up his neck to cup his head, her fingers grazing his jaw, he pulled away. He stared down at her, his eyes bright, catching flickers of firelight from the hearth.

"Don't stop. Please," she said.

"Don't touch me, Callie. I want to take my time, pleasure you, make each moment of this special, but I won't be able to if you touch me. What I feel inside—what I am—is . . . fierce." She sensed the emotion inside him as he battled some invisible force.

She should have been frightened, but she wasn't. Instead, her heart ached for all he must have endured for so long. For the future he'd lost. The hopes and dreams and life.

"These past years have been about me," he went on. "About sating my lust. Satisfying my cravings. But this isn't about lust. This is about love."

The word sent a rush of warmth through Callie that had nothing to do with the intimate way he touched her and everything to do with the emotion gleaming in his eyes.

His fingers played across her cheek, his palm cradling the soft flesh. Tenderness rushed through him as his words echoed in her ears.

"You are my love. Once I thought it was Catherine, but it was you. It was always you, sweet Callie. You are the one. The only one. Let me prove that to you. Let me love you."

She nodded and let him push her arms down beside her where she gripped the sheets as he again dipped his head.

He suckled her long and hard and deep, wringing a moan from her before moving lower, nibbling his way down her stomach, to the triangle of hair at the apex of her thighs.

His fingers slid into the slick folds there and she gasped, gripping the sheets tighter to keep from touching him. She wanted him to love her—with all her heart, she wanted to love and to be loved. If only for the time they had.

Tremors seized her body when she felt the first warm rush of his breath against the inside of her quivering thigh. Then his lips touched her skin in a soft, tender kiss before moving to the part of her that ached the fiercest.

His tongue parted her, and she gasped. He eased his hands under her buttocks, holding her to him, his shoulders urging her legs farther apart until she lay completely open and vulnerable.

It was incredible. She'd never known it could be like this.

"I am the first," he murmured against her moist heat. His deep, husky voice sent a vibration that danced along her nerve endings and settled in the tips of her breasts. "I am the last, and the only one. You are mine, Callie."

He devoured her then, every thrust of his tongue, every caress of his lips, every stroke of his fingers, a blatant act of possession to brand her, and the branding was damningly sweet.

The pressure within her mounted, pushing her more and more toward a threshold she'd yet to cross.

"Let go," he murmured against her. "Just feel what I'm doing . . . let go."

She arched her neck, her lips parted, and a moan erupted from some deep, primal part of her that she'd never known existed. The world exploded in a flash and brilliant light split open the darkness and blinded her. It consumed her.

Only several frantic heartbeats later when the light had faded and she'd calmed to a slight shudder, did he pull away. He shed his clothes and joined her, his slick body pressing against hers. He gathered her in his powerful arms. She knew as she felt the tension that still banked his hard, powerful body, that he'd yet to find his own release.

He wanted to, and she wanted it for him.

She wrapped her arms around his shoulders and captured his lips in a fierce, demanding kiss. She wanted more, she wanted him. Surrounding her. Inside of her.

Sliding her hands around his waist, she stroked the small of his back, smoothed her hands down and caressed his buttocks. His pulsing length pressed into her stomach, sending shivers racing through her. He was rock-hard and deliciously warm.

She opened her legs and arched her body, squirming against the tip of his manhood that slipped to the moist entrance between her legs. He pushed forward just a fraction, the friction sending a wave of electricity through her followed by a slight burning.

She gasped, and the sound seemed to reverberate awareness through her. He tensed, pausing.

Callie refused to be put off. She wanted this. She wanted him. She rocked her hips, begging for more.

"Wait," he rasped, but she pulled him toward her. "We really shouldn't—"

"We should," she breathed, then she gripped his buttocks and arched upward.

Pain knifed through her as she impaled herself on his rigid length. The one motion seemed to break his control. His hesistation disappeared and determination took its place. Hunger.

He gripped her hips and thrust.

She didn't shrink away. The pain subsided into a throbbing pressure that increased as he buried himself fully inside her.

She clutched at his back, urging him faster as he started to move, began pumping into her over and over again, driving her back toward that peak he'd brought her to before.

All too soon, she felt her body clamp around him. Pleasure washed over her like a giant tidal wave, crashing down, tossing her to and fro. She trembled and convulsed around him, her climax consuming her, stealing her breath and filling her with joy unlike any she'd ever felt. It was a feeling that went far beyond the physical.

Alex's followed, as he thrust one final time. He arched his back, his head thrown back, eyes clamped tight.

As she stared up at him and watched him find his release, she knew she'd never seen a man more beautiful, never felt a sensation as exquisite as Alex Daimon spilling himself deep, deep inside of her.

He wrapped his arms around her and rolled onto his back, bringing her to lie atop him, their bodies still locked tightly together.

Callie closed her eyes and gave in to the exhaustive slumber that pulled at her bones. She'd never felt so warm, so protected, so complete.

* * *

Alex stared up at the ceiling and listened to Callie's even breaths. He felt her heart pulse against him, her body warm and soft, and tears burned his eyes.

Tears, of all things! He hadn't cried since that fateful day. He hadn't been able to. But now the moisture flowed freely.

They were tears of joy, because what they'd shared far surpassed anything he'd ever felt before.

Tears of gratitude, because she'd given him the only true glimpse of Heaven he'd ever known.

And tears of sorrow, because he knew what waited for them now that the deed was done.

Just as the thought hit him, Alex felt the iciness snake around his ankle and inch upward, like fingers twining around him, driving out the warmth Callie had given him, sucking him back to the cold.

The sensation crept higher, higher, until he could no longer feel Callie's body pressed to his own, her soul-saving heat around him, her heart pounding against his. He felt nothing, and soon he saw nothing.

Blackness swirled around him.

Roaring filled his ears and soon he heard nothing—nothing save the familiar, chilling voice that rasped, "My turn now."

Chapter Eighteen

Callie didn't want to wake up.

She wanted to bask in the warmth and comfort and strength of Alex a few more precious moments.

It was too late.

She knew even before she opened her eyes that she was alone. Gone was the steady rasp of his breathing. The rhythmic thud of his heart. The steady stroke of his fingers along the length of her spine.

Gone.

She opened her eyes and glanced around the bedroom. Moonlight streamed through a gaping hole that had once been a set of French doors, and there was no mistaking the condition of her surroundings. She lay on an old soiled mattress, the bed frame partially askew thanks to a broken poster. Cobwebs gleamed in the corners.

The mansion was old again, just as Guidry and his men had seen it earlier that evening. For a brief, disappointing moment, Callie wondered if the past few hours with Alex had been merely a dream—a vivid, erotic, wonderful dream.

Her heart clenched at the thought. Maybe. Maybe not. She didn't know . . .

Her train of thought stalled as she reached for her clothes, which lay discarded on the dust-covered floor. Staring back at her were footprints. *Two* sets of footprints. His and hers.

Relief flooded her, along with a fierce rush of regret. Their time together, however sweet, had been much too brief. She wanted more. She wanted a normal life with the man she loved. A *man*, not a soulless demon without a conscience. The Alex who'd touched her and kissed her and loved her had been pure flesh and blood.

Temporarily.

Again, her gaze swept the room, searching. Hoping. She couldn't imagine even the next five minutes without him, yet at the same time, she'd known their time together would end and she'd chosen to love him anyway. She'd chosen to be loved.

Despair dogged her as she fought back tears and left the room. Wood creaked as she descended the winding staircase. The front door stood open like a giant mouth. It was the entrance to the outside world, the beginning of the end.

Her father's and her own.

That's right, the familiar female voice whispered inside her head. *You managed to fight me off, but that time is nearly passed. Soon there won't be anything that you can do. I will be at my strongest and your soul and your body will be mine forever!*

Even as denial raged inside her, Callie knew her ancestress spoke the truth. Midnight would come and there wouldn't be anything she could do about it, just as her efforts to save her father had been useless.

Maybe so.

There's no maybe *about it. You'll die, Callie. Your spirit, your character, who you are deep inside will be snuffed out forever, just like your worthless father.*

"Maybe," Callie growled. "But not yet."

Tears stung her eyes, but she blinked them back. Time was too precious to waste on grieving. She needed to make every last moment count, just as she'd told Alex. While she couldn't save her father's life, she could make his passing easier. She could sit by his side and comfort him, pray for him, and make sure he knew she was there. She could be sure he knew that she loved him and he wasn't alone.

She picked up the faded book of magic that lay in the library and threw it, opened, into the pile of ashes that filled the fireplace. While Catherine might, indeed, win, Callie had no intention of giving her any advantages. Rummaging in her purse, she pulled out a pack of matches and lit one.

Just as the flame ignited, her hand started to tremble.

Don't do it. You'll be sorry if you do. I swear, you'll be sorry!

"The only one who'll be sorry is you, because you'll be on your own, with only your own limited magic to see you through another lifetime," Callie breathed, spitting out each word out as she fought back Catherine and forced her hand toward the fireplace. Closer, closer . . .

No!

The wail pierced her ears as she let go of the match and let it fall atop the open book. Orange danced across the page and licked at the edges. The old paper quickly ignited and started to burn.

Callie fought back her own deafening scream as she forced herself to turn, to move away from the book, fearful that Catherine would take her strength and force her to retrieve the book before it was fully incinerated.

She picked up her steps and made quick work crossing the library. A heart-pounding moment later, she descended the front steps, her hands still trembling, her stomach churning, her knees quivering.

Losing hurt, but she didn't care. She wouldn't let Catherine win entirely. She couldn't—

"I thought I might find you here."

At the sound of Guidry's voice, the churning inside of her stopped. The trembling ceased and strength rushed back to her knees. As if a switch had been flipped, she felt like herself again.

She stared at the detective who leaned against the hood of his car, and panic seized her. Guidry's presence could mean only one thing: bad news.

"What is it? Is it my father? Did he . . . ?" The question faded as Guidry shook his head.

"It's the killer. He struck again."

"Another body?"

"Not exactly." He shifted from one foot to the other, then wiped a hand over his face and eyed her. "Not yet."

"He's abducted someone else, which means there'll *be* another body." Another swipe of his hand and he shook his head, and Callie knew in a terrifying instant there was more to it.

There was more than just another abduction. Another body. Another surefire murder.

"He's got your friend Alice."

The statement hit her like a slap in the face, and she simply stood there for a long, breathless moment. "Alice?" she finally croaked.

He nodded. "But I've got a lead on them. Someone saw them. I need you to talk to the witness, though. To touch him. You might be able to add more details to what he's already telling us if you can see what he saw."

"What time is it?"

"Late. Why?"

Because Catherine would seize control soon, even if she had settled down for now. Destroying her book of spells wasn't going to stop her. She was still taking over, still fighting for another body, another chance at life.

Because her father had only a tiny amount of time left before the curse claimed him completely. Because Callie wanted to say good-bye and spend her last few moments simply holding his hand.

But Alice was missing. And she was still alive as far as anyone knew. And while Callie and her father had no chance, Alice did.

"What's wrong?"

"Nothing. Let's go."

The blackness surrounded Alex, as suffocating as always. It was always absolute as he drifted in nothingness, awaiting his next assignment.

His next punishment.

But there was something different this time. Where he always felt the cold inside, he didn't anymore. He felt it on the outside, holding him prisoner like a giant fist that kept squeezing and squeezing, as if trying to force the life out of him.

Life, though his had ended long ago.

Yet where there was a soul, there was life. Hope. Love.

"You aren't evil, Alex." Callie's words echoed through his head, and where he'd denied them before, he could no longer ignore their truth.

There was no mistaking the warmth that filled him. The love. The goodness.

In a crystalline moment, he knew that the Devil hadn't stolen his soul; he'd merely been holding it captive because Alex, himself, had allowed it.

The Divine Power had been his legacy. His power. His world for so long. When the book had been stolen from him, he'd felt as if he'd lost everything. His past. His present. His future. His livelihood. His *soul,* or so the Evil One—the master deceiver and manipulator—had claimed.

Alex had been as eager to punish himself as the Evil One had been. He'd been a willing victim, easily overpowered by his burning lust and hatred, ruled by it all the while resenting his situation and his captor and the woman he held responsible for everything.

But then Callie had come along and stirred other emotions with her kindness and compassion—feelings far more powerful than the bitterness that had lived and breathed inside of him for so long.

With the realization came a break in the darkness. It was a pinpoint of light that seemed so far away, so tiny, it might have been his imagination.

"You're not evil, Alex." Her words echoed again, and this time he didn't deny the truth.

He focused his mind on it, fixed his gaze on the light despite the fact that the dark void edged in, trying to snuff out the light.

The pinpoint grew brighter, though, larger as he moved closer. Closer, until he found himself standing in his old mansion staring at the book aflame in the fireplace.

Fire danced across its pages, turning his precious incantations into charred ash. The old sense of duty he'd once felt surged to life inside of him, and he reached for the book. Not that he had to retrieve it. He knew every incantation by heart. The Divine Power lived and breathed inside of him.

Yet old habits died hard. He reached in anyway.

Heat licked at his fingertips, and he jerked back.

Incredulously, he stared down at his blistered skin. Pain streaked up his arm, a steady throb that echoed through his body. There was something different about him. This flesh and blood body felt somehow . . . more real.

"Congratulations, Alex."

At the sound of Caine's voice, Alex turned. The Viking was standing in the middle of the room. The usual teasing smile curved his face, but it didn't quite touch his eyes. For a brief moment, Alex glimpsed a wistfulness, a deep-seated envy.

"You made it back."

"I don't understand. . . ." But he did. As the realization that he was now living, breathing flesh settled in, so did the truth.

He'd not only found his soul, but his humanity, as well. His forgiveness.

Callie's love had healed his bitterness, and Alex had finally found the strength and the courage to forgive himself. And that's what being a human was all about. Making mistakes and finding forgiveness. Finding a better path.

"I'm happy for you." As the man said the words, Alex heard a touch of the wistfulness he'd seen earlier. He knew the man wasn't nearly as happy with his punishment as he pretended.

"You shouldn't feel happiness," Alex joked meaningfully. "You don't feel anything. You're soulless, remember? That's what we are."

"Of course. I *would* be happy for you," the Viking corrected, "if I weren't such a heartless bastard."

"You aren't heartless." Otherwise he wouldn't be the Evil One's prisoner.

As Alex thought that, he realized that Caine was a prisoner of himself, not the Evil One. Caine was a prisoner of his pain, of his past, of whatever had happened to drive him to self-destruction.

Alex knew—because he'd been in the same predicament until Callie's love had snatched him out of his self-made pit.

She'd given him the will to forgive. To live.

As if Caine read his thoughts, his charming smile faded into a grave expression, and Alex knew then that the worst had happened.

"*He* has her," the Viking said, and he told Alex where. Then he faded into the darkness.

"Where are we going?" Callie asked when she noticed the direction Guidry had taken. "I thought you said the witness was at the police station."

"Not exactly," Guidry said as he steered the car a few feet and took a sharp left into the cemetery that separated Callie's family's estate from the Daimon mansion.

Trees crowded around the car, their branches reaching for them like knobby old fingers. Bark scraped against metal, the sound like nails on a chalkboard—high-pitched and unnerving.

"So the witness is out here?" Callie tried to comprehend what was going on.

"Not exactly."

"We're going to the abduction site?"

"Not exactly." The detective's voice crackled on

the last statement, the pitch slightly lower, deeper, and much more frightening.

Callie knew even before she chanced a glance at his face and saw the light gleaming in his usually dark eyes that something wasn't right. That *he* wasn't right. A coldness seeped across the seat, snaked around her, and squeezed.

"You're not Guidry, are you?" she asked, voicing her fear aloud.

She was rewarded by a cold, vicious smile. The man slapped a palm against the steering wheel. "Exactly!"

When he turned to her, his usually cool brown eyes blazed a bright, vivid red, and Callie knew the man sitting an arm's length from her wasn't a man at all, but something much more frightening.

"Exactly," he said again. He winked, then his fist crashed into her face and everything went black.

Her head hurt.

Callie touched her temples and felt the lump near her eye as her stomach churned and her ears rang. She forced her eyes open, stirred at the sound of doors slamming, boots crunching, concrete scraping.

A heartbeat later, blazing pain shot through her as she found herself dumped on a cold, concrete floor.

Open your eyes.

She willed herself to ignore the stabbing pain. Her eyelids fluttered and she blinked, desperate to focus on the darkness surrounding her.

A faint whimpering sound pierced the ringing in her ears, drawing her back to consciousness. Another blink and she found herself staring at Alice who sat crouched in the corner, her legs and arms tied, her mouth taped. Fear filled the girl's wide eyes, the sight jerking Callie fully awake.

"Ah, you've decided to join the land of the living again." The deep voice came from the opposite corner, and Callie turned to see Guidry there. "Well, sort of the land of the living. I am living and breathing right now, thanks to your detective friend. His body's not bad, but I prefer those I possess to be in better shape." He touched the slight bulge at his middle. "I'm not much into the beer-belly look."

Callie knew when she saw the gleam in Guidry's eyes; this was the Evil One. He'd come for her. He'd come for more than just her, she realized as her gaze flitted back to Alice.

"Guidry's the killer?" she asked as she fixed on the man once again. "You've been using him?"

"Actually, he's a new acquisition. I will use him, but this will be his first." He smiled. "Actually, the whole plan was quite ingenious on my part. I used several different people, possessing them for a short time to do my dirty work and then leaving them with little remembrance. As far as they know, they had bizarre dreams." He winked. "Haven't you ever heard the expression 'The Devil made me do it?' It definitely applies in this case."

"Different people," Callie echoed. "That explains the different DNA."

"A simple ploy to keep the police annoyed." He rubbed his hands together, and she noted the long, gleaming nails that now flashed in the moonlight. "It was the perfect crime, or rather, crimes."

"But why?"

"Well, I do enjoy being bad. That's part of it. Not to mention, I wanted you to use your *sight*. It weakens you and I'm all about preying on weakness. I wanted Alex to seduce you, and so I created a way to make you even more susceptible. Of course, I never counted on him being so difficult." He frowned. "But it matters not now. The deed is done." He rubbed his hands together. "And you are mine. Catherine is mine. If I—or rather Guidry—kills you with her soul trapped in your body, you both die. Two souls for the price of one." He stepped toward her with a smile. "Time for a little collecting."

"No!" Callie's frantic voice drew Alex through the darkness toward the caretaker's shack that lay deep in the heart of the cemetery.

He burst into the building just in time to see the Evil One—in the guise of the police detective—pin Callie to the wall and raise his hand, his nails gleaming like ivory knives.

"No!" Alex came up short as the Prince of Darkness turned a brilliant white stare on him and pulled Callie up in front of himself.

"I see you managed to free yourself," the Evil One said.

"Callie freed me," Alex snapped. "And now I'm going to free her."

"Oh, really?" The Evil One shook his head. "How quickly we forget. Perhaps I need to remind you how deadly I can be." He lightly drew one razor-sharp nail across Callie's neck, and a thin red line of blood appeared. She trembled.

"Stop—"

"Hush now, or I might lose my concentration and go a little deeper. I'm just tracing a path this time. You wouldn't want me to cut into this precious piece without a little forethought, now would you?"

"Don't touch her."

"Ah, but I shall. I shall touch her, taste her, kill her. I'm going to rip your heart out, sweet," he murmured into Callie's ear. "And there's nothing anyone can do."

Wide, frightened eyes stared back at Alex. But the fear wasn't for herself. He could see it was for him. She wanted him to stand back, to stay away. How amazing this woman was, how pure. The love in his heart grew even stronger, giving him courage and strength when the Evil One's words might have beaten him down.

"I'm going to take your soul," the Evil One was saying to Callie. "And Catherine's." A long, serpentlike tongue flicked out to lick the shell of Callie's ear. "You hear that, bitch? You thought you got away from me, but you were wrong. You're not smarter than me. Or more powerful. Or prettier. Soon I'll have you admit it, and then I'll send you to Hell where you should have been long ago." As if he'd just remembered Alex's presence, he motioned toward him. "Go away, Alex, and let me have my fun."

"No. Callie doesn't deserve this. She's innocent."

"Innocent?" The Dark One laughed, a loud piercing sound. "Not anymore, thanks to you, my boy. And second, do you really think I care?" His mouth drew into a tight line. "Go away, now, Alex, before you spoil my good mood." The King Devil turned back to Callie and lifted a fingertip to the frantic beat of pulse at the base of her neck.

Alex reacted on pure instinct. He caught the Evil One's wrist. Pain streaked through Alex's burned hand, but he ignored it. "I won't let you do it."

"And just how do you intend to stop me?" His one-time master glanced at Alex's chest, and Alex felt a hand tighten around his heart. "You don't have a heart," the Evil One reminded him.

But he did. He had Callie's. It beat inside of him, just as her breaths echoed through his head. She was inside of him, a part of him, because she was *the one*. Because he loved her.

"That won't work anymore," he said. "I don't believe you."

"Then believe this. She will die." Another swipe of the Evil One's nail and blood beaded and dripped further down Callie's throat. "You know I can do it. As long as I occupy flesh and blood, I can do the evil that men do. I am that evil." Callie whimpered. "And I want a soul."

"Then take me. My soul for Callie's."

"I don't see the added benefit. That's one for one."

"Callie is just a person, but I was once a sorcerer. I still am." Alex drew in a deep breath and recited one of his incantations. Light exploded in the small room, illuminating the dark, dank walls for a brilliant moment.

"Nice trick."

"I can do more. I have the ability to do much more. To give life. To take it away. You can't do that. You know you can't."

The Evil One seemed to fill with indignation. "I can do anything."

"No." Alex realized that now, and perhaps he'd always known it, but he'd felt that he owed penance and so he'd endured his punishment. "You can't take life. Not unless you occupy a physical form. You aren't all powerful. You're limited." He sneered, then, hoping to tempt the Devil into taking his offer. "I would give you my soul and my power—"

"No," Callie gasped as she managed to tear free of the hand holding her. "No!"

"Quiet!" The Evil One clamped his hand around her mouth again and drew her tight against him. "Continue."

"Wait!" It was Guidry's voice that filled his ears as the man staggered backwards, hands outstretched. "Don't shoot! You wouldn't shoot a defenseless man, would you?"

"You're not a man." Alex raised the gun, his finger going to the trigger. This was a trick. The Evil

One still possessed the detective. The bright gleam still filled the man's eyes. "I know who you are. What you are."

"You won't do it." It was the Evil One's voice again. Guidry smiled: a cold, calculated expression. He stepped toward Alex, his hands raised, nails gleaming in the dim light. "Give me the gun."

"No."

"Give me the gun or pull the trigger, Alex. Condemn an innocent man to Hell. Go ahead. Do it." Another step and the Evil One reached out, his hand closing around the gun barrel. "Pull the trigger, boy. I dare you."

He wanted to. He would have, but the Evil One was right. He couldn't bring himself to condemn an innocent man. Killing the Evil One meant killing Guidry.

"Do it," the Prince of Lies said again, but it wasn't the jeering taunt of a moment before. The red light in the man's eyes had faded; his irises had cooled to a pleading, desperate brown. Guidry. The detective had somehow struggled into control. "You have to do this," he pleaded. "I can feel his fear. This will trap him below, this will send him to Hell. Take me. Do it now, please. He's going to use me if you don't . . . all my career, all the good I've done will be for nothing. . . . All those people he's killed will go unavenged. . . . I'll try to keep him—" The man's eyes suddenly began to burn again, glowed red once more. A leering smile swept across his face. His hand clenched around the gun barrel.

Alex fired. The Evil One staggered backward, disbelief on his face.

Alex swayed, gasping for air. The gun dropped from his hands as he fought to regain his composure.

"You bastard!" the Evil One spat. "You shot me. You actually shot me!" Blood spurted from his mouth and he slumped to the floor. His chest heaved as the truth seemed to hit him.

"You should have left his body sooner," Alex said. "Now you're stuck, and there's no hope. You're going back to Hell right now."

The detective's body slumped and closed its eyes. "My only consolation," it hissed. Then the body went limp.

Relief flooded Alex. He was aware of a quick movement, and then he turned to Callie, who stood a few feet away. However, it wasn't wide, innocent green eyes that stared back at him. Instead, he stared into familiar ice-blue eyes and he realized that he was too late. The possession seemed complete.

"Leave her, Catherine."

Soul-chilling laughter bubbled from her lips. "You must be joking! I've waited over a hundred years for this, Alex. For her and for you. I won't sell you out this time. You'll die and be out of my way once and for all. Just like your precious little sister," Catherine vowed, a malicious gleam lighting her eyes.

"You *did* kill her." He'd known. He'd known it in his gut all along, but he'd never voiced the feeling. He'd been so desperate for love, then. He'd been so convinced that Catherine was different than she'd seemed.

"Had you any doubt? That little bitch saw through me. She saw that I wanted more from you than just your love." Catherine laughed, a chilling, awful sound. "Your love," she scoffed. "As if I ever wanted that."

Guidry's gun gleamed in her hand as she stepped toward him. "I should have killed you instead of letting the Evil One claim you. He merely took you prisoner, hoping to weaken you and claim your soul once your punishment was complete. I never thought you'd be able to free yourself. My mistake." She raised the gun, her grip faltering once as Alex glimpsed a flash of green before the ice-blue shuttered her gaze once again.

"I love you, Callie," Alex said. Her love had been strong enough to save him. To pull him from a Hell where he'd spent over a century. Perhaps his love could save her and show her that she had the strength to resist, to fight back no matter what the odds. "I love you," he said again, his voice stronger, fueled with the blessed emotion inside of him. No lust or bloodthirsty vengeance drove him now. Just desperation and compassion and sincerity—the very essence of life.

Love.

Catherine froze, her gun in midair, dangerously close to close to Alex. Just a slight shift to the right and she'd have perfect aim; he would lose the humanity he'd managed to find. Then again, he had no desire for humanity without Callie.

"I love you, Callie Wisdom. No matter what happens. Please don't leave me. Not now that I've found you. Now that we have a chance. *Please!*"

She started to tremble. The gun crashed to the floor.

Alex stepped forward just as she collapsed. He gathered her close, feeling her heartbeat, wondering if that heart now belonged to Catherine or the woman he'd fallen in love with.

When she opened her eyes, he saw the truth shining brightly up at him; a liquid green gaze met his, and he knew Callie had defeated Catherine. She'd fought her way back to life, to love.

To him.

Now they could go save her father.

Epilogue

Callie opened her eyes to the early morning sunshine and stared at the man stretched out next to her. She watched the steady rise and fall of his chest and wondered how she could have ever been so lucky. Her life had taken a complete turn over the past few months. She'd gone from hopeless and isolated to hopeful and loved.

Sunlight streamed through the open French doors. A faint ripple of wind licked at the sheer white curtains. Callie closed her eyes and relished the sound of birds chirping.

If she could have described Heaven, this would have been it. The sweet sound of life all around, the comforting warmth of the man next to her, the knowledge that she'd made it through the pitch black night to the sweet morning after. . . .

Okay, so maybe it wasn't exactly Heaven. She decided that a few minutes later when the phone rang for the fifth time.

"I'm coming," she murmured as she climbed from the bed. She should have turned the answering machine off when she'd come in last night, but it had been a long, tiring flight from the Bahamas.

"Don't worry about answering this," Alice's voice called over the machine when Callie was just a few steps shy of picking up.

"Now she tells me."

"I know you're technically still on your honeymoon until tomorrow morning, but I thought I would fill you in on everything that's happened while you were gone. We got that new shipment of angel salt-and-pepper shakers, but they came in damaged. Chipped. I'll have you know, I took care of it. I called and gave the distributor a great big piece of my mind, and he's overnighting a new batch first thing in the morning. It's a good thing too, or I would have driven down there and given him a roundhouse kick right in his gut. Or a sternal punch. Both are very effective if you want to bring someone to their knees really quick. . . ."

Callie couldn't help but smile. Timid, insecure Alice had turned out to be a karate menace. Since the abduction, she'd gone on a major self-defense kick, determined never to become anyone's victim again. She'd been convinced that her abusive husband had pegged a vulnerable label on her, which was why she'd been singled out by the parish killer. She'd been so traumatized during the actual incident, she'd even blocked out the face-off between Alex and the Evil One.

As far as Alice knew, she'd been kidnapped and knocked senseless, only to awaken in the hospital emergency room hours later. An anonymous eyewitness had informed police, who had arrived to rescue both Callie and Alice and found that Alex had killed the parish killer.

It was a nice, neat, normal explanation, preferable to the truth—that there had been supernatural forces at work. Callie thought it best.

". . . five hundred new angel paperweights and one thousand calendars, and that's about it. Oh, and your dad called. He said he didn't want to bother you until you were officially back in the thick of things, so he asked me to tell you that he'll be staying an extra few days in Fort Lauderdale. There's an art exhibit going on, and he's still a few hours short of his diving certification."

Diving, of all things. She still couldn't believe it. Her father had been at death's door just a few short months ago, and now he was taking diving lessons and going to art exhibits and enjoying life.

Thanks to Alex.

Callie stared at the bed where her husband lay, his body a dark contrast to the crisp white sheets. Her heart gave a double thump. He'd not only given her back her own life by defeating the Evil One and Catherine, he'd given her father back his.

By forcing Catherine out of Callie, he'd destroyed both the witch and her curse. Callie and he had returned to the hospital that very night to find her father's condition stabilized. His recovery had been swift—thanks to a new drug, his doctors claimed. Medical science had prevailed once again.

Callie knew better.

". . . see you tomorrow," Alice added, the statement followed by a click as the phone went dead.

Callie drew in a deep breath and walked toward the open French doors. She stared out at the surrounding landscape—the now neatly trimmed hedges and landscaped gardens. Most of the Daimon mansion had been restored to its original splendor, the first floor still in the last stages of remodeling. Oddly enough, the place had still been in the Daimon family, the estate now the property of a distant relative living in another part of the country. The man, a fourth-removed cousin, had practically given the rundown property to Alex, grateful to have someone else worry over the yearly taxes.

But Alex wasn't worried, thanks to a few keen investments made with the reward money he'd earned by bringing in the parish killer. Guidry's death marked the end of the killer's reign of terror, and so police had written him off as the culprit for a few of the deaths. Where DNA evidence indicated otherwise, they'd ruled that the murders had been committed by a string of copycats. While the cases were still open, there were no solid leads. The crimes would go unsolved. Unpunished.

At least that's what everyone would think, but Callie knew differently.

The real killer was dead, back in Hell thanks to

a man who'd sacrificed his life to bring him to justice. Guidry.

The police detective had been right, Alex claimed. This sacrifice Guidry made would remove the Evil One from the world for a while. Killing him while he'd occupied a body had drained him and sent him back to the center of the Earth. Eventually, he would be back to wreak havoc on the world; she had no doubt about that. Once he regained his strength, he would be back in full force.

For vengeance?

Maybe, but the Evil One was a master manipulator who targeted the weak. Alex was too powerful now—his right place as guardian of the Divine Power restored—and too smart to succumb to the Evil One. Callie was, as well. Her love for Alex kept her strong. As long as they stood united, they could prevail against any evil.

While the Evil One might want revenge, he would never have it. Callie and Alex were free. Happy. *Normal.* And they meant to stay that way. Together. Now and forever. Till death did them part.

"What are you thinking?" Alex's deep, mesmerizing voice crossed the room to her, and she turned to see him leaning on one elbow, watching her.

She smiled. "I was just thinking how lucky we are."

"Luck has nothing to do with it. It's fate. It's meant to be. You're my love. My one true love. I've always loved you. I always will love you."

"And I love you."

He grinned before his gaze darkened, and his eyes

took on a smoldering light. He patted the spot next to him. "Care to prove it?"

"Nothing will stop me ever again." And then she went to him.

Her man.

Her husband.

Her one, true love.

Midnight Kisses

Kimberly Raye

Get Ready for . . . The Time of Your Life!

Smooth, sensual, fantastic skin that begs to be tasted—Josephine Farrington just re-invented it. The new plastic is great for making lifelike toys, but she has a better idea: making a man. Tired of the pushy jerks that court her, Josie can now design the bronze-skinned, hard-muscled exterior of a robo-hunk that can fulfill all her deepest fantasies. And she knows just the man to build the body.

Matthew Taylor never had trouble erecting anything, and the handsome scientist knows that Josie's robot is something he can create. But the beautiful biochemist deserves better than the cold devotion of a machine; she needs the fiery embrace of a real man. In an instant, Matt knows his course: by day he vows to build her model of masculine perfection—by night he swears to be it.

___52361-2 $5.99 US/$6.99 CAN